ENCHANTER'S CHILD
BOOK TWO

Midnight Train

ENCHANTER'S CHILD
BOOK TWO

Midnight
Train

ANGIE SAGE

 KATHERINE TEGEN BOOKS
An Imprint of HarperCollins Publishers

Katherine Tegen Books is an imprint of HarperCollins Publishers.

Enchanter's Child, Book Two: Midnight Train
Text copyright © 2021 by Angie Sage
Illustrations copyright © 2021 by Justin Hernandez
All rights reserved. Printed in the United States of America.
No part of this book may be used or reproduced in any manner whatsoever without
written permission except in the case of brief quotations embodied in critical
articles and reviews. For information address HarperCollins Children's Books, a
division of HarperCollins Publishers, 195 Broadway, New York, NY 10007.
www.harpercollinschildrens.com

Library of Congress Control Number: 2020945259
ISBN 978-0-06-287517-4

Typography by Joel Tippie
20 21 22 23 24   PC/LSCH   10 9 8 7 6 5 4 3 2 1
❖
First Edition

For Poppy Strover, with love

Contents

Chapter 1:	Dream Come True	1
Chapter 2:	Oracles New and Old	7
Chapter 3:	Storm Watch	16
Chapter 4:	Min	23
Chapter 5:	Danny and Jay	35
Chapter 6:	Bartlett Is a Banana	40
Chapter 7:	Goodbye, Oracle Rock	49
Chapter 8:	A Dark Hour	52
Chapter 9:	Breathing Beguilers	59
Chapter 10:	Rocadile	63
Chapter 11:	Inside the Star	69
Chapter 12:	Danny	79
Chapter 13:	Under the Silver Star	83
Chapter 14:	Home	92
Chapter 15:	Homesick	98
Chapter 16:	Home Truths	105
Chapter 17:	The King Calls	114
Chapter 18:	Discovered	121
Chapter 19:	Lurking	128
Chapter 20:	Alone	135
Chapter 21:	Revenge	144
Chapter 22:	Near Misses	150

Chapter 23:	The King's Spy	157
Chapter 24:	The House of Ratchet	164
Chapter 25:	Unwanted Guests	175
Chapter 26:	Merle's Mission	186
Chapter 27:	Jackal in the Cove	197
Chapter 28:	Along the Estuary	207
Chapter 29:	Chariots of Fear	216
Chapter 30:	The Beguiler Bell	224
Chapter 31:	Escape	230
Chapter 32:	Wraith Flow	238
Chapter 33:	Exchanges	246
Chapter 34:	First Fire	255
Chapter 35:	An Unexpected Crossing	266
Chapter 36:	Steam Up	274
Chapter 37:	Coal!	287
Chapter 38:	Zerra's Reward	293
Chapter 39:	"By the Hand of an Enchanter's Child"	300
Chapter 40:	Family Reunion	309
Chapter 41:	The Power of Three	321
Chapter 42:	The Midnight Train	329
	Life after the Hauntings	335
	Acknowledgments	341

CHAPTER 1

Dream Come True

MONSTERS. MONSTERS, MONSTERS EVERYWHERE.
Alex RavenStarr was running, but her feet would not
move. Jackal-headed monsters surrounded her, seven feet
tall with white muzzles, pink pointed ears and yellow eyes.
They loomed above her, dribbling and drooling over her
hair, baring their dirty, razor-sharp teeth. Alex inhaled
the smell of rotten meat. "No!" she yelled. "No, no!"

"Alex, shhh!" A beam of light shone into her eyes.

Alex sat up. Befuddled with sleep, she stared at the
tousled-haired boy who was holding up a small lantern,
looking at her with concern. "Hey, Benn," she whispered.

Beyond the pool of lantern light Alex could see nothing

but darkness. *Where was she?* All she could hear was the howl of the wind and the thud of waves crashing upon rocks. And it was cold, *so* cold. Aha. *Now* she remembered. She was in a cave high up on Oracle Rock, hiding from the very monsters that had invaded her dreams.

"Bad dream?" asked Benn.

Alex nodded. "The Jackal."

"Ugh," Benn said with a shudder. Alex too shuddered at the thought of the Jackal—the group of half-human, half-jackal bodyguards that protected King Belamus of Rekadom and ruthlessly did the king's bidding. And right now Alex knew that the king's bidding was to find her and Benn and take them prisoner.

In the dimness at the back of the cave, Alex and Benn burrowed beneath their blankets and listened to the storm howling outside. After some minutes, Benn's regular breathing told Alex that he had fallen asleep, but she was still unable to shake off the terror in her nightmare. She stood up quietly, wrapped her blanket around herself, tiptoed to the narrow mouth of the cave and peered out.

The cave was at the very top of the bell-shaped Oracle Rock, and the dark clouds scudding fast across the sky made Alex feel like a bird gliding on the wind. A sudden squally spatter of rain hit her feet and she retreated a little. Wide awake now, Alex looked down at the foamy seas crashing upon the rocks far below. From across the small stretch of churning water that for now divided Oracle

Rock from the mainland, she saw the towering cliffs upon which the city of Rekadom sat in darkness. Somewhere in that city—deep in a dungeon, Alex supposed—was her newly found father, Hagos RavenStarr.

Alex leaned back against the cold wall of rock, and from a secret pocket inside the broad green sash that she wore around her waist, she drew out a small but surprisingly heavy book covered in battered blue leather. Alex flipped the book open and ran her fingers over a stack of wafer-thin hexagonal cards that were neatly tucked into a pocket inside the front cover. She smiled at the sight of her precious Hex cards. They had been her constant companion ever since her mother and father had thrust her into the unwilling arms of a certain Mirram D'Arbo—who had resentfully looked after Alex ever since—and over the last crazy two weeks they had led to so many discoveries that sometimes she found it hard to take it all in.

Finding comfort in their familiarity, Alex drew out her cards, and as she deftly shuffled them, she counted off the things she had learned about herself.

One: Her mother was named Pearl. She had died in the Rekadom dungeons eight years ago.

Two: Her father was Hagos RavenStarr.

Three: Her father had once been Enchanter to King Belamus.

Four: Which meant she was an Enchanter's child. Which was not a good thing to be right now. Not at all.

It was strange, Alex thought, to be here on Oracle Rock, the actual place where ten years ago the Oracle had told King Belamus that he would "die by the hand of an Enchanter's child." Until then it had been just fine to have an Enchanter for a parent, but just a few words had changed that forever.

Alex shivered and pulled her blanket more tightly around her. Peering a little farther out of the cave, she looked down past the precipitous path that led up to their hiding place. She wanted to see if the sandy causeway that joined Oracle Rock to the mainland at low tide was uncovered yet. The almost-full moon was hidden behind a thick storm cloud and it was hard to tell. Buffeted by the wind, Alex tucked herself back into the shelter of the cave. *What difference does it make?* she told herself. The tide would go down soon enough, and when it did she was pretty sure that the king would send his Jackal across the causeway to get her. It was just a matter of time. Her only chance was if the storm died down enough for her and Benn to escape in his sailboat, Merry. But right now, there was no way little Merry could survive even five minutes in seas this rough.

Suddenly the moon appeared from behind a thick cloud. Alex risked a quick look out again. To her dismay she saw a strip of sand joining Oracle Rock to the beach below the cliffs. It looked like the tide had been down for a while, for the strip was wide and the pale sand shone in the surprisingly bright moonlight, like a stage with a spotlight turned upon it. Alex gasped. Right on cue came the actors. There were five of them: four seven-foot-tall Jackal from her nightmare, their long red coats flapping in the wind, the ghostly silver light of the moon picking out their sharp white ears and pointed muzzles. Almost lost between them was a short figure clad in a long wool bathrobe—Deela Ming, knitter of octopuses, resident of Oracle Rock and holder of the post of Oracle. Alex choked back a sob. Please, not Deela, not lovely Deela Ming, who had given them shelter and shown them nothing but kindness.

"Alex?" came Benn's anxious voice. "What is it?"

"Deela!" said Alex. "The Jackal have got Deela!"

Benn scrambled to join Alex at the mouth of the cave and together they peered out. "Why?" Alex murmured. "Why take Deela?"

Benn frowned. "I guess they couldn't find you but they found Deela. They say that Jackal never leave empty-handed."

Alex felt awful. "I wish they'd taken me," she whispered.

Benn was indignant. "They shouldn't be taking anyone!" He leaned out farther into the wind, trying to get a clearer view. "Is it just Deela?" he asked. "Not Palla too?" Palla Lau was Deela's young assistant, who had hidden Alex and Benn in the cave.

"It's just Deela, I'm sure of it. Palla is much taller. Look."

Brushing a sudden stinging shower of raindrops from their eyes, Alex and Benn watched the weird shapes of the Jackal, loping along on their hind legs, hustling the small figure up the beach on the far side of the causeway. "She must be so scared," Alex whispered as they watched Deela being pushed into the dark archway in the foot of the cliff face. Alex thought she looked like a ghost disappearing into the underworld.

Suddenly there was a clattering of stones on the narrow path beneath the cave. Silently, hearts pounding fast, Alex and Benn crept to the back of the cave, where they dived beneath the blankets and listened to more stones skittering loose.

Something was climbing up the rocks.

And now the *something* was inside the cave, moving stealthily toward their hiding place.

Alex made a decision. She wasn't going to let a Jackal find her crouching and terrified. She wasn't going down without a fight. With a wild whoop and an earsplitting yowl, Alex leaped forward and hurled herself at the intruder.

There was a piercing scream and then all was quiet.

But not for long.

CHAPTER 2

Oracles New and Old

"WHAT DID YOU DO THAT for?" Palla Lau demanded as she staggered to her feet.

"Palla! It's you!" Alex said, laughing with relief.

"I don't see what's so funny. I really don't," Palla said as she brushed the grit from her pants.

"I'm so sorry," Alex said. "But we thought you were the Jackal."

"I am not those disgusting creatures. Why would I be?" Palla said indignantly.

"But we saw them," Benn said quietly. "With Deela."

Palla's indignation suddenly collapsed. She sank to the ground and gave a loud sob. With her hands covering her face, she spoke in hiccupping, muffled bursts. "Deela said they'd come. We were watching. For low tide. We saw them and Deela told me to hide. At first I wouldn't. But she got so cross. She said I must be the Oracle now." Palla gulped. She looked up at Alex and Benn, her tears glistening in the lantern light. "I always wanted to be the Oracle. But not like this."

Silence fell in the cave. Leaving Palla with Benn, Alex got up and once again went to the mouth of the cave. There she sat, feeling the cold wind on her face, watching the clouds racing fast across the indigo sky, the moon appearing and disappearing behind them. She looked up at the cliffs and the high walls of Rekadom and thought about her father, and now Deela, too, imprisoned behind them. And she knew that unless the storm abated before the next low tide, she would be joining them. Feeling thankful that Rekadom had no harbor and so no access to boats, Alex watched until the sea had come in over the causeway, and then she called back to Benn and Palla. "The causeway's covered. We're safe." And then she added under her breath, "For now."

In the gray light of dawn, they headed back along the precipitous path to Deela's cottage, which was perched upon the top of Oracle Rock. There, in Deela's sitting room, Palla knelt beside the fire, gently feeding it one piece of sea coal at a time as if it were a sick animal. Despite the efforts of the fire, a deep chill settled into them as they listened to the unremitting wind and rain outside. But after drinking mugs of Palla's hot spiced milk, Alex and Benn eventually drifted into an uneasy sleep, wrapped in blankets beside the fire.

But Palla could not sleep. She paced the floor of her room below, with one thought whirling around her head. *What is happening to Deela?*

Deela was sitting on a pile of slimy straw in darkness so deep she could see nothing but a few flashes of bright light in her eyes when she forced them open as wide as she could. She could hear a distant *plink plink* of water dropping into something metal, and beneath the overwhelming musty dampness she could smell the rankness of what she guessed was a dead rat. She was in a tiny cell, so narrow that when she put her arms out like the wings of a bird she could rest both palms on the ice-cold surface of the walls. And when she raised her arms up, her knuckles grazed the arched roof. She had given up calling out, asking if anyone was there. She was, she knew, alone.

Some time later—how many hours she could not tell—Deela heard the sharp echo of metal-heeled boots of the dungeon guards in the distance. She sat up and listened hard. The purposeful footsteps were coming ever closer and a flicker of fear shot through her. They were coming for her. She knew it.

Deela took a deep breath. She got to her feet and stood

facing the door, her heart beating in time to the *thud thud thud* of the approaching steps. They came to a halt outside her cell and Deela steadied herself. Whatever was going to happen next, she told herself, there was absolutely nothing she could do about it. All she could do was face it bravely and with dignity.

First came the harsh sound of the key turning the lock, and then came the shock of a shaft of lantern light cutting into the cell. Deela clenched her hands into fists by her side and watched the door swing open. "Hagos!" she gasped.

Flanked by two stolid dungeon guards in chain mail tunics, Hagos RavenStarr stood in his flimsy red cloak like a delicate reed between two rocks. He looked haggard and drawn, and his dark eyes flashed a warning glance at Deela. "Quiet, prisoner!" he said in an oddly high voice. "How dare you insult me?"

Deela felt as winded as if Hagos had punched her. He sounded so hostile.

"This is the new prisoner, Your Majesty," intoned one of the guards.

Your Majesty? Deela thought. *Why are they calling him "Your Majesty"?* Puzzled, she looked at Hagos— and he winked at her. Deela felt a flicker of hope, and her mind began to work again. It seemed that the guards thought Hagos was King Belamus, although how he had made them think that, Deela had no idea. However, she thought it wise to try a shaky curtsey.

One of the guards took out a pair of handcuffs. "No need for that," Hagos said. "I'll take the prisoner." The guard looked disappointed. The king had imprisoned most of the remaining citizens of Rekadom over the previous ten years, and the notorious dungeon fever meant that for some time now there had not been many to handcuff. In fact, Deela was the only prisoner they had right now, and her arrival had been the highlight of a very boring month. But the king always knew best.

Hagos stepped into the cell and Deela felt his bony hand take her arm. She did not resist as he drew her out of the cell and, with the guards almost stepping upon their heels, walked her away from the most desolate place she had ever been. Lit by the guard's lanterns, their long, eerie shadows dancing before them, Hagos guided Deela through the snaking tunnels that looped beneath the city of Rekadom until they came to the foot of a flight of steps flanked by two burning rushlights. Here he turned around to the guards and said, "Leave us."

The guards saluted, clicked their boot heels together and marched away.

"They thought you were the king," Deela whispered. "How did you do that?"

"With some difficulty," Hagos replied. "Let's get out of this awful place."

"We're escaping?"

Hagos sighed. "Er, not exactly. I've struck a deal."

"A deal?"

"With the king. And you're part of it, although he doesn't know that yet. So hurry up. I don't want anyone to see us."

Feeling faint with relief, Deela leaned on Hagos as he guided her up the steps to the sunlight above. She took a long, deep breath of the salty air blowing off the sea, and thoughts of Oracle Rock came back to her. "Your daughter, Alex," she said. "She is safe. Palla hid her. The Jackal took me instead."

Hagos turned to his old friend. "So the king told me. Thank you, Deela." He sighed. "Belamus also told me he has ordered the Jackal to go back at the next low tide and get Alex."

Deela smiled. "Don't worry, your Alex will be long gone by then in her friend's sailboat."

Hagos looked concerned. "In this storm?"

"It will die down soon," Deela said. "Trust me. I've lived on that rock for thirty years. I know the weather by now."

They emerged into an open space known as Star Court. Here in the very center of Rekadom, the three towers—Gold, Iron and Silver—rose up into the stormy sky above. Once Star Court had been a popular meeting place, but now it was deserted. After the great exodus of Enchanters and their families ten years ago, the remaining population in Rekadom had slowly fallen foul of the paranoid king, and the once vibrant city was now little more than a ghost town.

Anxiously, Hagos glanced up at the top of the Gold Tower, where he knew King Belamus lurked with nothing better to do than to gaze out the delicate golden-arched windows onto the emptiness of his domain below. Hagos's trip to the dungeons had taken longer than he had expected and it was now almost eleven o'clock—on the dot of which King Belamus, who stuck to a rigid schedule, would cut a slice of his midmorning chocolate cake and begin rereading a chapter of the book he was supposed to be writing: *My Complete and Unabridged History of Rekadom*. In the old days, when Hagos was both the king's Enchanter and his friend, he would have been sharing the king's chocolate cake and listening to Belamus's latest chapter. He missed the cake, but not the listening.

Hagos hurried Deela across the empty courtyard, past an irritable goat eating a lonely dandelion, then through the shadows of the gloomy Iron Tower, its tiny windows covered with iron shutters, and out into the open again. It felt like it took an age to cross the empty space between the Iron and Silver Towers, but at last they reached the archway that led into the Silver Tower. Hagos propelled the weary Deela inside, and slowly they climbed the long flight of winding steps lit by small lanterns set into niches lined with silver leaf. At the very top was a wide landing with a large blue door decorated with silver stars. Hagos placed his hand upon the lock, then waited until he heard the soft clicks of spring-loaded pins moving into place. Quickly, he pushed the door open—his power to keep a lock open lasted only seconds nowadays. He ushered Deela into a huge, triangular room and hurriedly pushed the door closed.

The rich smell of incense made Deela's head spin, and her feet in their filthy slippers felt as though they were standing on shifting sands. She was wondering why Hagos was ringing bells in her ears when the floor came up and hit her.

"Deela . . . Deela . . ." Someone was calling her at the end of a long tunnel. Deela groaned. *It was all a dream. Hagos hadn't rescued her by pretending to be the king. Of course he hadn't. What a stupid thing to imagine. She was still in her horrible cell.*

"Deela, Deela," came Hagos's voice. "Wake up. There, there. You're all right. Drink this."

Deela sat up slowly. Hagos's anxious face loomed large in front of her, and with a trembling hand she took the offered glass of something red and gulped it down. The liquid burned her throat, but it seemed to clear her head. Deela blinked and the room came into focus—dark and mysterious, hung with thick curtains, lined with books, bottles and jars of all colors and sizes. "So it's real," she murmured. "You did rescue me."

Hagos gave her a rueful half smile. "Not entirely. We are still prisoners."

"But these are your old rooms." Deela gazed around the familiar space where she once used to visit Hagos, his wife and their baby daughter.

"Indeed they are," Hagos agreed. "And I am only in them because I have made a deal with Belamus."

"A deal?" Deela asked blearily.

"I shall explain later. Rest now." Hagos helped Deela to a sofa by a small fire and made her comfortable. And then, as Deela fell asleep, he walked over to a tiny arched window behind his desk and looked up at the stormy sky. Despite Deela's weather prediction, the storm showed no sign of abating. From a drawer in his desk he took out a small spyglass and trained it on the strip of iron-gray ocean just visible beyond the high walls of Rekadom. Anxiously, Hagos scanned the foam-tipped waves, praying that he would not see a small white sailboat with a red sail, not yet, while the storm raged. *Please let her wait until it calms down*, he thought. He looked at his timepiece and saw there were only three more hours until the causeway would once again be clear and the Jackal would return to Oracle Rock. "Just go away will you, storm?" he muttered. "Please. Just go away."

CHAPTER 3
Storm Watch

As Hagos gazed out of his window at the stormy sky, Alex was doing the very same in the tiny sitting room of the cottage. Palla had made them all lemon tea, the fire was burning brightly and the sea coals obligingly spluttered their salty flames, but even so the little room was full of gloom. A row of Deela's multicolored knit octopuses sat on the windowsill looking out; it seemed to Alex they were watching faithfully for Deela's return. The wind set the small panes in the windows rattling like teacups on shaky saucers and howled as though it wanted to be let in, *like Jackal*, thought Alex.

Benn joined her at the window and looked down at

the swirling waters. "I reckon there's about another three hours before the causeway is clear again," he said.

"We will go up to the cave soon," Palla said.

Alex turned around. "Thank you, Palla," she said, "but we're not going to the cave. Benn and I are leaving in Merry."

Palla looked shocked. "But the storm," she protested. "You cannot go out in that."

"It's okay," Benn said, squinting hopefully up at what might possibly be a patch of blue sky. "It's passing now. All we have to do is get down the coast a little way to Netters Cove, and the wind's blowing in exactly the right direction. We'll be fine."

Palla was horrified. "You will not be fine! You do not know the power of the ocean. You have never been shipwrecked."

Alex picked up something in Palla's voice. "Have *you* been shipwrecked?" she asked.

Palla nodded. "Deela rescued me. I was only nine." She rubbed a sudden rush of tears from her eyes. "And in return what did I do? I caused all this trouble for her. And trouble for you, Alex. And for your father."

"It's King Belamus that is causing the trouble, not you," Alex told Palla.

Benn was puzzled. "Why would you even think that you caused the trouble?" he asked Palla.

Palla sighed. "Because I did. After she rescued me,

Deela became ill with a fever. Her throat swelled up and she lost her voice. So when King Belamus came to hear the Oracle—as he often did then—I decided to help out. I became the Oracle."

"But your voice—didn't the king notice the difference?" Benn asked.

Palla shook her head. "The Oracle stands inside the Oracle Bell, which changes your voice completely. It also . . ." She paused. "This is a hard thing for me to say, but it also changes you. Well, it changed me, although I don't think it ever did that with Deela. Deela said that she and Hagos used to get together and decide the best things to tell the king, just to keep him happy. But I could not do that. As soon as I put on the Oracle Robe, I felt like I was a thousand years old and part of something ancient. So when I stood in the Oracle Bell and heard the king's voice asking how he would die, I knew at once what I must say."

"That he would die by the hand of an Enchanter's child," Alex murmured.

Palla looked at Alex. "But it was not I who said that, it was the Oracle. You do understand?"

Alex nodded. "I understand."

"But even so, I still cannot stop thinking about all the terrible things that have happened since then," Palla said. "I remember the day Deela told me about the king throwing all the Enchanters and their children out of Rekadom—except for your father, Alex, whom he arrested. Your poor mother he threw into the dungeons. And you just disappeared. Deela was frantic. But Hagos wouldn't even speak to her." Palla shook her head. "And then we began to hear about the awful entities appearing across the land, hunting down anyone with any Enchantment to them. Those terrible Hauntings . . ."

"Which my father created," Alex pointed out.

"Only because in return the king promised to release your mother from the dungeons."

"Which never happened," said Alex. She got up, went over to Palla and hugged her. "It's okay," she told Palla. "Look." She took the codex from the pocket inside her sash and opened it to show Palla her cards stacked neatly inside the front cover.

Palla's eyes shone. "That truly is an Enchanted book," she murmured. "Look how the edges of those pages sparkle."

"These are the sealed pages," Alex said. She flipped open the book to a block of pages stuck together, edged with a shimmering blue wax. On the front of the block was an empty T-shaped pocket. "That is for the Tau, which has to be there to open the pages," Alex said. "But the king took it away from Poppa yesterday."

Palla sighed. "After all those years that Deela kept the Tau safe for Hagos inside her favorite octopus. It is a very sad end for it, to be back with that wicked king."

Alex pushed away the memory of the day before, when her father had given King Belamus the precious Tau in exchange for her freedom—for that day, at least. She looked at Palla, a determined expression in her eyes. "I'm going to get the Tau back, Palla. And when I do I will put it into its pocket here and unlock the sealed pages. And then I can read the Disenchantment for all the Hauntings. And get rid of them all. Every one of them!" But even as she spoke, Alex could hear how impossible it sounded.

Palla clearly thought so too. "The king will never give you the Tau," she said sadly. "You will have to get rid of him first." She looked Alex in the eye. "And maybe you will. You are, after all, an Enchanter's child."

"No!" Alex was horrified. "That Oracle is not real, Palla, whatever you may think. Don't go making me part of some stupid game."

"It is no game. The Oracle never lies," Palla said.

"It is lying about *me*," she retorted, furious that Palla thought she was the kind of person who could kill someone. "Thank you for helping us, Palla," Alex said stiffly. "We're going now. Aren't we, Benn?"

"Sure." Benn stood up. He understood why Alex was angry, but he felt bad for Palla. "Thanks for everything, Palla," he said.

Palla stood up too. "You are welcome. I wish you a safe voyage."

Alex and Benn headed off down the winding stone

steps that took them through the rock to a small door that emerged halfway down Oracle Rock. The wind was still brisk, but Benn was right, the storm was passing. The clouds were white now and the ocean was dark blue rather than gray, and the waves were long and slow, with flat tops. Benn grinned. "Merry's going to love this!" he said as he headed toward the harbor, longing to see his boat once again.

But when they reached the harbor, they stopped dead. "No!" Benn gasped.

"Oh," Alex said.

Merry was still there, but not on top of the water where a boat should be. About a foot below, held up by her two mooring ropes, Merry's ghostly shape bobbed and swayed.

Alex looked across the harbor to a small rowboat tied up in a more sheltered position on the opposite wall. "We'll have to take Deela's boat."

Benn was indignant. "No way. We can't leave Merry like this. And we can't row all the way to Netters Cove. We need to sail."

"But Merry's *sunk*," Alex said.

"She has not sunk," Benn protested. "She's filled up with water, which is totally different. We just have to get the water out, that's all."

"That's *all*?"

"Yep. We pull her up and bail her out." Benn grinned.

"Good thing we put the oars safely up on the harbor, huh?"

Alex did not reply. She was looking at the drowned boat, rocking slowly beneath the clear green water. It gave her a really bad feeling.

CHAPTER 4
Min

HAGOS HAD A BAD FEELING too. From his window he could see King Belamus crossing Star Court, accompanied by his Jackal, and he knew at once they were heading straight for him.

"Deela!" Hagos raced across the room to the recumbent figure on the sofa. He was greeted by a soft, snuffly snore. "Deela!" None too gently, Hagos shook his friend awake. "Wake up. Belamus is coming. Wake up!"

Deela sat up with a start. She stared at Hagos, trying to remember where she was.

"Deela, the king is on his way here. We must hurry!" Hagos said urgently.

Deela jumped up and looked around wildly. "I must hide!"

"No. The Jackal will sniff you out. Listen, Deela. Remember I said that I made a deal with Belamus?"

Deela nodded.

"I promised to Engender another Hawke—"

"Hagos! You can't make another one of those murderous monsters!" Deela protested.

"I'm not going to," said Hagos.

"But you just said—"

"Deela, just listen, please. This is what I had to offer Belamus in exchange for my life."

"Oh," said Deela. "I see."

"But I promise you, I won't be making another monster for the king. However, I have to pretend I'm doing it."

"Ah," said Deela.

"And," said Hagos, "I also have to explain who you are. So I have a plan. You are a Hawke Meister."

"A what?"

"An expert. On Engendering Hawkes."

Deela looked aghast. "But I couldn't Engender an ant, let alone a Hawke."

"It's okay. You don't have to do anything, you just have to look like you could."

"But 'Meister.' That's a man, isn't it? I'm not a man, Hagos."

Hagos sighed. "I know that, Deela. But soon enough

the king will discover you are no longer in the dungeons. He's not the cleverest of cookies, so I'm hoping he won't be suspicious of a man turning up here at exactly the same time you have vanished."

"Ah, I see. But if a random weird *woman* arrives in your rooms, he might work it out?"

"Exactly," Hagos laughed. "You may be random, Deela, but you're not weird. You are a good friend. Come now." He took hold of Deela's arm and hurried her over to a tall cupboard, where he threw open the doors to reveal an array of somewhat dusty but stunningly beautiful robes and cloaks in shimmering silks. "Choose something impressive," he said. "Quickly. Belamus will be here in a minute."

Deela stared at the rainbow of colors before her. "Oh. These were Pearl's. I can't wear them, Hagos. It doesn't feel right."

"Pearl wouldn't mind. Please, Deela, hurry. Any minute now the king will be—"

An imperious banging upon the door silenced Hagos. As he ran to open it, Deela grabbed a shiny blue cloak embroidered with silver moons, threw it on and pulled its hood up so that it dropped down over her face. The cloak's hem trailed on the ground, for Pearl was a good head taller than Deela. Hurriedly Deela grabbed a low footstool from beside the fire and stood on it so that the cloak swept gracefully to the floor.

The door crashed open, sending Hagos leaping backward, and the king blew in like a thunderstorm. Behind him came his bodyguard, the Jackal. The white-headed creatures, in their long red coats emblazoned with gold buttons, loped into the room on their hind legs, but once inside they dropped onto all fours and began sniffing around. From the safety of her footstool, Deela gathered her cloak around her and kept her eyes on the king. He was resplendent in an array of vivid silks, the buttons of his long yellow waistcoat straining over his fat stomach and his stick-thin legs lost inside wrinkled blue silk stockings. Deela thought he looked like a lemon on toothpicks.

"Your Eminence," Hagos said, performing an oddly complicated bow that put Deela in mind of a chicken trying to lay an egg.

"Yes, yes," King Belamus said tetchily. "Now, Raven-Starr. Don't think you've gotten away with anything. I know you're a double-crossing toad. Who is this?" he asked, pointing at Deela.

Deela saw Hagos's shocked expression at her sudden increase in height and risked a wink.

Hagos recovered fast. "This, your graciousness, is the renowned Hawke Meister," he replied. "He is, as I am sure you know, the world's foremost Engenderer of Hawkes. We are honored that he has deigned to grace us with his presence."

King Belamus looked suspiciously at Deela. "I did not give permission for this . . . this person. What is his name?"

Hagos threw Deela a warning glance. "Forgive his silence, Sire," he told the king. "The Hawke Meister speaks only the language of the Hawke."

"Then *you* speak, RavenStarr! What is his name?"

Deela saw a blind panic flash over Hagos's face. There was a terrible silence, and Deela knew she must break it. "Min!" she said, and then stopped, horrified at the high squeak that had emerged.

"Min," said the king. "He has a peculiar voice, this Min."

Hagos thought fast. "It is the language of the Hawke, Your Majesty. High and sharp, like the call of a bird."

Belamus stared at Hagos. "Very poetic, RavenStarr. But I want results. I want the biggest, keenest-eyed Hawke possible. I want the very best hunter and killer of all the remaining Enchanters that blight my kingdom." Belamus stopped and glared at Hagos with narrowed eyes not unlike those of his much-desired Hawke. "And their *children.*"

Hagos flinched. Was the king telling him that he knew Alex was his daughter? *No,* he told himself, *that is not possible. All the king knows is that there are children on Oracle Rock, and for some reason he thinks they are*

Enchanters' children. But the king sees Enchanters and their children lurking in every shadow. It means nothing, Hagos told himself.

King Belamus was now at the door. "The Jackal will escort you and the Min person to the mews to choose the Hawke egg." Keeping the two largest Jackal for himself, the king turned upon his pointy little heels and strode out the door. Deela waited until the king was out of the room, then she jumped down from the footstool and, along with Hagos, was hustled out by the remaining Jackal.

Ten minutes later, at the top of the ladder in the Rekadom falconry mews, Deela was peering into a high shelf where a small, neat nest held a clutch of four mottled eggs. A dull gloom suffused the air, broken only by a blade of sunlight glancing in through one of the narrow windows just beneath the eaves. Tiny feathers floated in the sunbeam and made Deela's nose twitch. In her hand she held a tiny gold box in which she must place an egg, but Deela was dithering. She had no idea which one to pick.

At the foot of the ladder were Hagos and a stocky, red-faced man in a leather jerkin with a very angry mother hawk tucked firmly under his arm. The red-faced man was Ratchet, the chief falconer, and he was gazing up at the blue-cloaked figure at the top of the ladder with an awestruck expression. Ratchet had never seen a Hawke Meister before. He had never heard of one either, but he was not about to admit that to anyone, least of all to his new trainee Flyer, who was lurking in the shadows, watching with some interest.

The trainee Flyer was a girl of about thirteen. She wore a padded jacket and trousers and a calculating expression in her dark eyes. In addition to being the new trainee Flyer for the Rekadom Hawke, she was—although Hagos did not know it—foster sister to Alex, and her name was Zerra D'Arbo.

It was with some wariness that Zerra watched Hagos, for the previous day on Oracle Rock she had caused his capture by King Belamus. That day Zerra had also shot the Rekadom Hawke dead with her Lightning Lance. She had blamed its demise on Alex, whom she had betrayed to the king as an Enchanter's Child. Zerra was unsure how much Hagos had seen and had decided to keep to the shadows. The last thing she wanted was for Ratchet to know she had killed his precious Hawke. Arms folded, with a scowl on her face, she leaned against the wall and listened intently, ready to interrupt if she had to. There was no way a stupid Enchanter was going to mess up her new job.

Zerra need not have worried; the previous day's events were a painful blur in Hagos's memory. But the trainee Flyer's glowering stare unsettled him, and he called anxiously up to Deela, "Hawke Meister. Have you chosen?"

Deela decided to pick the egg nearest to her. She carefully

placed it into the golden box and then, with some trepidation, she made her way down the ladder. As she stepped onto the somewhat slippery cobbles, Hagos bowed low to her. "My lord Hawke Meister," he intoned. "I offer my grateful thanks for choosing our next Hawke."

Deela had trouble suppressing a giggle as she handed Hagos the golden box with the egg. But as she caught sight of Zerra lurking in the shadows staring at her, the giggle dropped into a pit in her stomach. There was that awful Flyer girl who Alex had said was her foster sister. The one who not only had betrayed both Hagos and Alex to the king but had also, Alex had later told her, shot at her with the Lightning Lance. Resisting the urge to stomp over to the girl and tell her exactly what she thought of her, Deela pulled the cloak's hood forward so that it flopped down over her face and turned away from the girl's piercing glare. She wished Hagos would get a move on before the girl recognized her. Deela was sure that she would have no qualms about betraying her either.

But Hagos was in no hurry. If the Jackal were busy guarding him, then they could not be hunting down Alex. "The Hawke Meister," he was telling Ratchet, unnecessarily slowly, Deela thought, "in his supreme wisdom, has found the perfect egg from which we will Engender the most magnificent Hawke. We will leave you now, Chief Falconer. We must not let the egg grow cold." Ratchet gave a small bow and started back up the ladder to replace the mother bird upon her nest.

Hagos and Deela emerged into the sunlight and Hagos took a few deep breaths of fresh air—washed by the rains of the previous night, it smelled clean and sharp. A glance at the sky, with its white clouds, told him that the storm was abating. Hagos felt his spirits rise. With any luck Alex would be far away from Oracle Rock when the Jackal went over at low tide. And the longer he kept the Jackal with him, the better chance Alex had to escape.

Hagos walked deliberately slowly as the Jackal escorted them across Mews Court and up the wide steps to the golden archway that led into the king's private walkway. Waiting for them was King Belamus with two Jackal, their yellow eyes glinting in the shadows. "So, RavenStarr," the king said. "You have the egg?"

"The Hawke Meister has chosen, Sire," said Hagos.

King Belamus looked at Deela suspiciously and dropped his voice to a loud whisper, which he addressed to Hagos. "He looks much shorter than he did in your room."

Hagos thought fast. "Indeed, Sire. The energy the Hawke Meister used to choose the egg has much depleted him. This is the beginning of the Engendering of the most magnificent Hawke ever known."

King Belamus seemed mollified. "I hope that it will be so, for your sake, RavenStarr. Indeed I do. Now, go!"

Hagos hovered uncertainly, unwilling to lose sight of the Jackal. "Perhaps the Jackal should escort the egg,

Sire. And keep guard over it."

Belamus chuckled. "I never thought you had a liking for my Jackal, Hagos. Very well, I will allow them to accompany the egg back to your rooms and I will allow you one outside your door. But I need the rest for a little expedition I have planned for them to Oracle Rock at low tide. There is at least one Enchanter's brat there, very possibly two. Although not for much longer." The king gave a tinny little laugh.

Like a cracked bell, Deela thought.

Hagos dragged his feet all the way up to his star-covered front door. There, he took as long as he dared to open the lock while the four Jackal watched. When the Jackals' patience began to fray, Hagos reluctantly pushed open the door and he and Deela went inside. Hagos closed the door and through the spy hole he watched the Jackal hurry away, leaving one outside on guard. Hagos flipped the spy hole cover down and turned to Deela with a sigh. "They've gone to get Boo-boo," he said.

"Alex," Deela corrected him. "Your daughter's name is Alex now, Hagos. She has a grown-up name and a grown-up attitude. She won't let those creatures get her."

Hagos walked over to the window and waited until he saw the Jackal racing across Mews Court on all fours, their red coats dragging upon the ground as they went. He watched a burly woman and man—Rekadom gate guards—accompany the Jackal to the foot of the high city wall. There they unlocked a small red door in the wall and then stood back respectfully while one by one, the Jackal walked through into the darkness beyond. Hagos sighed. He knew very well where they were going—he'd come up that way the day before. They were headed down an immensely long flight of steps through the cliffs to the beach and then across the causeway to Oracle Rock. Hagos watched the guards close the door behind the Jackal and stand at attention on either of side of it, waiting for their return.

Hagos didn't want to think about who the Jackal might be returning with. He turned his attention to the sea in the hope of seeing a little white sailboat with a red sail. But he saw nothing.

After a while Hagos saw Ratchet walk out of the mews and look up at the sky. A small speck was visible—some kind of bird, though what Hagos had no idea—and it was clearly heading for Ratchet. The sight of Ratchet put Hagos in mind of Ratchet's old Flyer, Danny Dark.

Hagos smiled wistfully. He owed a lot to Danny. It was Danny who had gotten him out of his exile in Seven Snake Forest. Okay, Danny had been hunting him down on the Hawke, but as Flyer, that had been Danny's job, and Hagos didn't blame him for that. It was Danny who had oh so carefully walked Hagos safely through a lethal Haunting of Air-Weavers, it was Danny who had first seen Alex, and Danny who had led him to find her. Hagos sighed. But like Alex, Danny was lost to him now. In fact, he wondered if Danny was even alive. He had done the best he could, but the Enchantment he had used to bring Danny back from being drowned at the bottom of the river was a tricky one. It didn't always work—and given the feeble state of his Enchanting powers right now, it probably hadn't.

Hagos stared gloomily out the window. *You won't see Danny again*, he told himself. *And probably not Boo-boo either.*

CHAPTER 5

Danny and Jay

A TALL, SKINNY BOY WITH long, tangled red hair sat up and blinked blearily at the young man who was standing beside his bed holding a plate. "Uh?" said the boy.

"Eggs. Scrambled. And toast. I promised that weird Enchanter that I'd wake you in forty-eight hours. Which is what I'm doing," the young man told him.

The red-haired boy gazed around, trying to work out where he was. He seemed to be in a cave with sleeping platforms. Lit by a lantern, most of it was in shadow, but he could see that the roof was low and dirty with soot. It smelled of soot too. "Where am I?" he asked.

"In the bunkroom. Now are you going to eat these eggs

or what?" The young man pushed the plate of eggs and toast into the boy's hands.

"Who are you?" the boy asked.

"Jay. And you're Danny."

"Danny. Yeah. Okay. Jay. Hey, I remember now. You pushed me into the river."

"You pushed me first," said Jay. "Now eat." And he turned and walked out of the bunkhouse, leaving Danny frowning down at his plate.

Danny felt weird, as if he were waking up from a long and very complicated dream. Tentatively, he lifted the toast with the egg balanced on top to his mouth and took a bite. Suddenly Danny realized he was very hungry indeed. In four gulps the buttery toast and egg was gone and Danny could smell coffee. Somewhat shakily, he got to his feet, wrapped his blanket around his shoulders and wandered out of the bunkroom. He stopped dead in amazement. In front of him, in the middle of a towering cavern lit by lanterns, stood what he could only describe as a monster—a great iron cylindrical *thing* on huge wheels. "What is *that*?" he said.

The young man—Jay, was it? Danny couldn't quite remember—appeared suddenly, walking out from behind the monster and carrying two cups of coffee. "That," Jay answered, "is the Puffer."

Danny shook his head slowly. His mind felt so fuzzy that he wondered if he was dreaming. "Puffer?"

"Yeah." Jay pushed a cup of coffee into Danny's hands and then gently took his elbow and guided him over to a bench at the side of the cavern. "Sit down, drink this, and I'll explain."

And so Danny sat and listened.

"It's a steam locomotive. Kids used to call it the Big Puffer. It ran all around the country, until the king ripped up most of the track—but not all. See?" Jay pointed to the ground and Danny now noticed a pair of shining parallel rails running from the front of the engine and heading off through the wide, brick-lined tunnel that led out of the cavern.

"Where do they go?" asked Danny.

"Over the river and as far as the salt oaks for sure. After that, I dunno. They used to go to Rekadom. But not now."

"Rekadom?" Danny frowned. Rekadom . . . the name sounded familiar, but he couldn't think why.

Jay looked at Danny, concerned. When Danny had fallen in the river, Jay had jumped in after him, but couldn't find him. It had taken Hagos RavenStarr, the weird Enchanter who Danny was with, to fish him out. But by then Danny had been under the water for far too long. Jay had watched Hagos perform some strange kind of Enchantment on Danny, and the Enchanter had told Jay that Danny would be fine after two days' sleep. Jay wasn't so sure; Danny seemed very forgetful. He answered

Danny's question carefully. "Rekadom is where the king lives. And the Hawke. Remember?" Jay prompted. "You were the Flyer?"

"Flyer?" Danny murmured. The word made him feel uncomfortable—there was something lurking behind it that he did not want to meet.

"Yeah. You flew on this massive bird of prey and killed people with a Lightning Lance." Even as he said this Jay felt it was a little hard-hitting. But he wanted to shock Danny into reacting. It worked.

"I did not kill people!" Danny protested. Images of two children on a cliff face cowering from him, closely followed by the rather comical sight of a scrawny man in underpants running away through a forest, flashed before him as he began to remember. Turning to Jay, he said, "I didn't kill them. I couldn't do it. I'm not a Flyer anymore." He sat cradling his cooling coffee, staring into his cup. Then he looked up and asked, "Where's Mr. Raven-Starr?"

Jay felt relieved—it seemed that Danny's memory was coming back. "He disappeared," Jay said. "Off the end of the jetty."

Danny looked horrified. "You mean he jumped in the river?"

Jay shook his head. "No. Although when he stood on the end of the jetty and raised his hands up like he was going to dive in, I did think that was what he was going to do," he said. "I ran after him, yelling at him not to, but he just disappeared. There was no splash, and I am sure he didn't jump. He just kind of faded away."

Danny's memories of Hagos were returning fast. "Yeah. I've seen him do that. He's a powerful guy. I wonder where he's gone?" Danny sighed. "I'd love to know. The days I spent with him were the best days of my life. Things felt like they really mattered, and in a good way, too. You know what I mean?"

Jay looked at Danny with new interest. "That's how I feel too," he said. He waved his hand at the Puffer. "When I'm working on *him*."

"*Him?*" Danny grinned. "He's, like, *alive?*"

"You bet," Jay said. "Or he will be soon."

Danny gave a low whistle. "I'd like to see that," he said.

"Want to stay and make it happen?" Jay asked.

"I'd love to," Danny said.

"Great." Jay got up and wandered off, leaving Danny on the bench to ponder yet another strange turn in his life. He sat for a while, allowing the memories of the past few days to arrange themselves into something that made sense; then he realized his coffee had grown cold. And that he was very thirsty. He drank it down in one long gulp and leaned back against the cold rock wall of the cavern. Danny smiled. He was alive. And life was good.

CHAPTER 6
Bartlett Is a Banana

BACK IN HIS OFFICE, RATCHET was sitting at his desk, extracting a little scroll of paper from the tiny metal tube that had been delivered to him by a windswept pigeon. He read the neat, precise words on it and scowled. His deputy, Bartlett, was on her way back from her travels along the North Coast, where she had been flying a new pair of peregrines and collecting mice for the winter food stores. Ratchet had not been expecting Bartlett back for at least another week, and he was not happy. Bartlett wanted his job, Ratchet knew it, and she had a way of making him feel always in the wrong. Ratchet poured himself a small cup of what he called his "reviver." As he gulped the fiery liquid down, the door burst open and Ratchet inhaled half the reviver, spilled the rest down his front, and succumbed to a coughing fit. Gasping, he looked up expecting to see Bartlett's sardonic smile at his clumsiness; but instead his trainee Flyer came bounding in.

Zerra watched coolly as her boss's face ran through increasingly dark shades until it was a deep puce—at which point she thumped him hard on the back. Ratchet sprayed reviver across his desk and then subsided into a wheezing heap. When at last he had caught his breath, he managed to gasp out, "*What?*"

"*She* is nothing to do with Hawkes," said Zerra.

"Uh?" wheezed Ratchet.

"The Min person up the ladder who chose the egg."

"The Hawke Meister to you. And it's 'he,' not 'she.'"

"No, it's not. *She* lives on Oracle Rock. I saw her there yesterday wearing big Wellington boots. She's a fake."

Ratchet considered this. "Hmm. I *thought* something wasn't right."

No you didn't, thought Zerra. But she knew better than to say so.

"Good work, Dark," Ratchet said, addressing Zerra in the traditional way. All Flyers took the last name of Dark to show that they were Dark to Enchantment. This talent was an essential requirement of a Flyer, for their job when Flying the Hawke was to guide it to its prey and see through any Enchantments that the victim might use in order to escape. Ratchet sighed. He really must arrange a Dark to Enchantment test for this new Flyer before Bartlett got back. He didn't want Bartlett making trouble. "Speaking of 'Dark,' Dark," he said. "You'll need a certificate."

"What?" asked Zerra, confused.

"A certificate. To show you're Dark to Enchantment— or Beguilement, as they call it here in Rekadom. We need to do a few little tests to prove you can see through Enchantment. Okay?"

This was most definitely not okay. Zerra knew she was not in the least bit Dark to Enchantment. Only a few days ago she had watched Alex do her creepy disappearing act right in front of her, and however hard Zerra had tried— and she really had tried hard—there had been no way she could see her. Zerra thought fast. She had already seen how much Ratchet loved his birds, and how protective he was of all the eggs, so she said, "I can do a silly test any old time, but isn't the Hawke egg more important? Shouldn't we make sure the egg stays safe? Perhaps I can stand guard or something?"

Ratchet looked at his new Flyer approvingly. He liked the way she was so dedicated to the birds. "Good point, Dark." Ratchet stood up, scraping his chair across the slate floor. "But to be allowed into the Inner Star, you'll need a pass. Can't go anywhere in this benighted place without a pass," he grumbled as he headed out of the office. "Come with me, Dark. You'll have to sign it. In triplicate, no doubt. You can write, can't you?"

"Of course I can write," Zerra said indignantly as she hurried out behind Ratchet.

Zerra already knew that Rekadom was divided into two parts. When she had arrived on the Hawke she had seen the dramatic simplicity of its inner walls shaped as a five-pointed star set inside the circle of the outer city walls, each of the points touching the walls and so forming five triangular outer courts, Mews Court being the name of the one where the falconry was. Zerra had not yet been inside the Star—there seemed to be no easy way of getting in—and as she followed Ratchet she was surprised that he headed for what she had thought was an old plank in an alcove just a few yards along from the mews. Ratchet took out what looked like a large corkscrew from his pocket and pushed it into a hole in the middle of the plank. He twisted the corkscrew and then leaned his shoulder against the plank, which swung open. Then he squeezed himself through the narrow entrance and disappeared into the gloom beyond.

Zerra hurried in after Ratchet. He pushed the plank door closed and it shut with a click. "You can get out by pulling this," Ratchet said, looping his fingers around a long brass lever set into an alcove beside the door. "But to get in from Mews Court you'll need the spike. We've only got one for the mews, so you'll have to ask. Nicely. Got that?"

"Yep. Got it." Zerra grinned. She liked Ratchet's plain speaking. There was no hint of the bully she had first detected in him, but Zerra knew that was only because she had been so full of crazy confidence from Flying the Hawke that she had been brave enough to answer him back.

The unprepossessing entrance into the Star had taken them into a narrow passage—or *ginnel*, as it was called in Rekadom—set between the tall buildings that huddled along the edge of the Star wall. They emerged into a dusty street and Zerra was shocked at the boarded-up windows, curled strips of bleached paint peeling from storefronts, signs swinging mournfully in the wind. Weeds grew tall between the paving slabs, and rabbits hopped around nibbling daintily at the greenery. There was not a person in sight, although Zerra had the distinct feeling that they were being watched from some of the grubby windows above.

Ratchet walked at a rapid pace and Zerra had to trot to keep up. "Terrible here now that it's so empty," he confided. "Only the lowlifes and nastiness left." He looked at Zerra. "You'll be all right though. You understand this kind of stuff."

Zerra wasn't quite sure how to take that.

Ratchet stopped outside a boarded-up store with a faded sign proclaiming "The Old Watch Shop" above a scrappy door. He banged a complicated rhythm on the door and waited, tapping his foot impatiently. At last the door creaked open and an anxious-looking woman peered out. "Oh, it's you," she said. And then in a strangely mechanical voice she intoned, "The ocean brings us fair winds today."

"All is for a porpoise," Ratchet replied in similar tones.

"*What?*" the woman asked.

"Purpose! All is for a purpose!" Ratchet corrected himself hurriedly. "Oh, this is ridiculous, Vera. You know perfectly well who I am. Let us in, will you?"

Vera Watchet, last survivor of the King's Spy and Messenger Service, did as Ratchet asked and led them up some disconcertingly wobbly stairs to an attic room. There, Zerra swore loyalty to King Belamus and was, to her delight, not only given a pass for the Inner Star, but also signed up as the King's Spy. "We don't have one anymore," Vera had said. "So you may as well."

As they were about to leave Vera asked Ratchet, "You still a KM?"

"A what?"

Vera gave an impatient tut and said slowly, "Are you still a King's Messenger?"

"*The* King's Messenger," Ratchet corrected her. "Only me left now."

"Well, the MAP has expired."

"The what?"

"Message Authentication Password," said Vera. "You sure you're still a KM?"

"Yes. And my little Merle is still a King's Bird."

"Then you need to give me a new password. Write it down here. At least ten letters. No profanity."

Ratchet took the pen and paper and thought hard; he found passwords difficult. But then something came into his mind and he smiled. Starting from the wrong end of the phrase, he wrote, ANANABASITTELTRAB. He knew it was childish and silly, but right then it made him feel better. And at least it was something he would remember.

Vera took the paper and gave it a cursory glance. "Fine," she said, and she closed the door with a bang.

Zerra and Ratchet found their way down the dingy stairs and then set off along the street. Both were smiling. Ratchet because he was pleased with his new password, and Zerra because once again she felt important. She loved her Spy Pass—the black-and-gold silk cord around her wrist with its silver seal on which was the secret pass sign for the King's Jackal that allowed her access to the King's Gold Tower. Sitting neatly in her training jacket pocket were the tools of her new trade: a small brass spyglass, a plan of Rekadom and a corkscrew key. It felt almost as good as the time she had been appointed Junior Sentinel in her hometown of Luma. She just hoped it would end better than that had.

"King's Spy, eh?" Ratchet said. "Very impressive."

"Piece of cake," said Zerra.

"Don't forget you are a Flyer first," Ratchet told her. "And your priority is to protect the Hawke egg."

"No problem," Zerra said. "Anyway, it's the king's Hawke, right?"

"But it's *my* egg," Ratchet said. "So go and make sure that the Enchanter and that Meister person are not messing with it. And be sure to get out of here by six at the latest, when the Slicers come out."

"Slicers? What are they?"

Ratchet shuddered. "You don't want to know. Get going with you. I'll want a report this evening at Birds-In."

"Burstin'?" asked Zerra.

"*Birds-In.* Once a week we call the birds into the mews for a count. Six o'clock tonight. The Flyer is required to attend."

"Okay. Got that. See you later."

Zerra watched Ratchet hurry away and disappear off down the ginnel. She stood in the deserted street and breathed in the dusty warmth of its old buildings. For a moment she was reminded of what she thought of as her "old life," when she had lived in the hilltop town of Luma with her mother, her big sister, Francina, little brother, Louie, and her stupid foster sister, Alex. Zerra had always enjoyed noticing what people were doing. Francina had called it "sneaking," but Zerra thought it was an important skill. She pushed away the uncomfortable thought that maybe it would have been better if she had not sneaked on her mother and accused her of "Harboring a Beguiler"— Alex, whose Enchanted cards she had discovered when she had sneaked into Alex's room. She decided not to even consider that maybe it would be nicer to still be living with her family in Luma, which was not nearly such a dump as Rekadom. Resolutely, Zerra pushed aside the troubling thought that if she had not sneaked, her mother, Louie and Francina would be still be safe. And that no one—not even Alex—would hate her.

Determined to enjoy her new life and her amazing new job as the King's Spy, Zerra set off. She was going to be good at this. She knew it.

CHAPTER 7

Goodbye, Oracle Rock

WHILE ZERRA PROWLED THE EMPTY streets of Rekadom, Alex and Benn had got the last of the water out of Merry and the little boat was floating again. They were ready to go. Anxiously, Alex glanced at the sea beyond the protective arm of the harbor wall. The waves were what Benn called "lumpy," but they were nowhere near as wild as they had been earlier. Even so, it still looked a little scary.

But Benn was confident. "Merry will be fine," he said. "The wind will blow us straight along the coast to Netters Cove. We can stay the night in the harbor there, and by tomorrow we'll be back home safe in Lemon Valley."

Alex didn't want to spoil Benn's enthusiasm by pointing out that *she* would never be safe in Lemon Valley while the Twilight Hauntings were at large, attacking all Enchanters and their children, but Benn guessed what Alex was thinking. "I know it's not safe for you," he said, "but it will be soon. We'll get the Tau back somehow. And then you can do that Enchanted thing with the codex and your cards and get rid of all the Hauntings."

Alex looked at Benn. "*We* get the Tau back?" she asked.

"You bet. We're in this together. You, me and Merry."

They were ready to go. Benn was already aboard checking the ropes. Alex was about to jump in when she noticed something was missing. "Where are the oars?" she asked Benn.

"Bother," said Benn. "They're still up on the harbor wall."

"I'll get them," Alex said, running up the steps. Benn had tied the oars to a ring in the rock, and the drenching of the rain had shrunk the rope. As Alex fumbled with the knot, she heard a shout from Benn. "Okay, okay!" she yelled.

"Alex! Alex!" came another shout, and this time Alex heard the terror in Benn's voice. She wheeled around in concern—and then she saw them: four white-headed, pointy-nosed, red-coated Jackal racing toward her, their mouths open, their yellow, razor-sharp fangs glistening.

"Alex, run!" came a desperate shout from Benn. But

it was too late. Already the Jackal were surrounding her; one dropped a lasso of rope over her and another pulled it tight against her waist, pinioning her arms to her sides.

As Alex struggled, she saw Benn racing along the harbor wall toward her. "No!" she yelled at him. "Go away! Go!"

But Benn took no notice. In seconds he was at Alex's side, throwing himself at the Jackal. He knocked two down before he too had a lasso thrown over him and pulled viciously tight.

Far above in the sitting room window, from behind her hands, which were covering her face in dismay, Palla watched two small figures being led across the causeway by the four red-coated Jackal. She forced herself to watch until they disappeared into the dark depths of the cliff and she was the last person left on Oracle Rock.

CHAPTER 8

A Dark Hour

ZERRA WAS NOT HAVING MUCH luck. She'd tiptoed
up the stairs to Hagos's rooms, but the Jackal at the top
had growled at her, even though she waved her King's
Spy wristband at it. She'd hung around for ages outside
the Silver Tower waiting for someone to come out so she
could follow them, but no one had. So how was she supposed to spy on the Enchanter and the so-called Hawke
Meister?

Bored, Zerra had decided to check out the rest of the
Inner Star. She had sat on a swing in a deserted playground
covered in weeds, which was no fun because there were
no little kids to take the swings from. She had wandered

into an empty library, where bats roosted in the top shelves and dried bird poo crunched under her feet. She had even pulled out some books to look at, but their pages were swollen with damp and stuck together. The highlight had been finding a scruffy shop that had three limp cabbages, a sack of apples and some moldy-looking boxes of cookies for sale. It also had a jar of orange candy stuck together in lumps. She'd waved her wristband at the shopkeeper—an elderly man who, Zerra figured, was at least one hundred and fifty—and he had looked scared, which was nice. He had pulled out a lump of the candy, hit it with a hammer, put the pieces into a twist of paper and handed it to Zerra. Then he had said quite politely, "Now go away, please." Which is what Zerra had done. The candy had tasted old and coated her teeth with gritty sugar.

Zerra was resolutely chewing a large chunk of candy when she discovered something interesting—a gated flight of steps that led up to the battlements on the Inner Star wall. She opened the gate with her corkscrew key and headed up the steps to a small path that ran along the top of the wall. From her vantage point Zerra could see Mews Court below. To her left was the long roof of the falconry mews, at the end of which the tall wooden Hawke hut—where the giant Hawke had once roosted—rose up. Ahead was the high city wall, where two guards were waiting outside a small red door. Why, Zerra had no idea. But as she watched, the guards suddenly sprang into action. Fumbling with keys, they opened the door and jumped back. A Jackal holding a rope emerged and then, to Zerra's astonishment, came Alex, with the rope around her, closely followed by more Jackal and her "boyfriend," as Zerra thought of Benn—with a niggle of jealousy.

Their task complete, the guards saluted the Jackal, locked the door and marched away. Zerra watched Alex and Benn being hustled across Mews Court. As they drew close, Zerra saw the fear in Alex's eyes, and she felt just a little bit sorry for her—but she quickly pushed that away. It was all Alex's fault, Zerra told herself. If Alex hadn't put their whole family in danger by playing around with her Enchanted cards in Luma, where everyone knew Enchantment was forbidden, then she, Zerra, would still have a home with Ma, Francina and Louie. Zerra realized with a sharp pang that she had absolutely no idea what had happened to her older sister, Francina, and her little brother, Louie. That was not a good feeling.

To get rid of the bad feeling, Zerra leaned out from the battlements and yelled down, "Hey, Alex! They got you—and your little *boyfriend*."

Zerra was pleased to see Alex jump in surprise, but she was less pleased at the expression in Alex's eyes as she looked up at her. This was not the old Alex, always trying to be nice. This was a new, angry Alex, and it made Zerra uncomfortable.

"He is *not* my boyfriend," Alex yelled up. "Just like

you are not my *sister*. You are a liar, a low-down sneak and a nasty little—"

Alex's tirade was cut off in full flow by a Jackal hand— humanlike, but with coarse fur and curved claws—shoved roughly over her mouth.

"Yeah, shut her up!" Zerra yelled down. "Beguiler's brat!" Suddenly aware of a figure in brightly colored silks approaching along the path, Zerra swung around guiltily. The silks reminded Zerra of her mother, and Ma did not like shouting. It was not, of course, her mother. But it was someone just as unsettling—King Belamus. He looked at Zerra with a pained expression and Zerra knew at once that the king did not like shouting either. She clapped her hand to her mouth. "Oops. Sorry," she said.

"What are you doing on my private walkway, Flyer?" the king demanded.

Zerra waved her black and gold wristband at the king. "I'm your Spy," she said airily. And then, noting that did not seem to have gone down too well, she added, "Sire."

King Belamus made a harrumphing sound and turned to look down at the scene some twenty feet below in the court-yard. "Aha," he said, "the Beguiler brats from Oracle Rock. We have them!" He leaned over the battlements and called down, "Jackal! Take them to the dungeons!" All four Jackal jumped to attention, saluted—and let go of the lassos.

Alex seized her chance.

She wrenched free of the Jackal, launched herself at

Benn and sent him staggering backward.

"Stop her!" screamed the king.

The Jackal leaped after her, but Alex wheeled around and threw a well-aimed punch at one and kicked out at the delicate legs of the other. They tumbled down on top of the other two and lay in a tangled heap of sticklike white limbs and swaths of red cloth. As the Jackal struggled to disentangle themselves, King Belamus screamed at them from above. "Idiots! Fools! Get them! Get the brats!"

With the king's screams echoing in her ears, Alex pulled Benn to his feet and, holding tightly on to his hand, she ducked into the shadows beside the falconry mews. She did not notice Ratchet emerging to see what the commotion was, or a group of guards come running—all she saw was the ground at her feet, and all she was thinking of was being one with the earth beneath her, one with all that she touched. Blocking out all around her, Alex felt the warm buzz of Enchantment course through her as her Fade kicked in and she knew she was now invisible. She looked down and saw how both their hands were shimmering with Enchantment. "We're invisible now," she whispered to Benn. "Just don't let go of my hand, okay?"

Not daring to speak, Benn nodded. It felt strange, he thought, being included in an Enchantment. He was not sure if he liked it much. It reminded him of the time his brother, Jay, had thrown him down the waterslide he had rigged up into the river—exciting, but also out of control.

From his walkway on top of the Inner Star, King Belamus was panicking. "Beguilement, Beguilement! They have vanished! Vanished!"

"Let's get out of here," Alex muttered. "Before they shut the city gates."

Uncannily, as if he had heard her, the king screamed out, "Shut the city gates! Shut the city gates!"

Together Alex and Benn set off at a run, heading for the next courtyard, Gate Court, and the gates of Rekadom before they were closed.

On the battlements the king wheeled around to Zerra. "You, girl!" he yelled. "Tell me where they've gone!"

Zerra did not like the way the king called her "girl." It was just plain rude. "How am I supposed to know?" she told him.

King Belamus stared at Zerra, dumbstruck. *No one talked to him like that—no one.* Normally he would have thrown this girl into the dungeons and hurled the key into the Iron Tower. But unfortunately—for nothing would have given him more pleasure right then—she had powers he desperately needed. And so he screamed at Zerra, his high-pitched voice echoing around the empty arena, "You're a *Dark*, you idiot. All Flyers are Dark. So tell me where they are!"

King Belamus's face was red with anger and Zerra saw that his hand was clenching the hilt of the silver dagger he wore on a little gold belt around his waist. She was going to have to say something fast—and it had better be the right thing, too. "I will pursue them, Sire," she said. "And I will bring them to you. I promise."

King Belamus looked down at Zerra through half-closed eyes. "You had better. *Dark*." Then he leaned over the battlements and gave a long hiss, like a snake. It was the creepiest sound Zerra had ever heard. Mesmerized at the weirdness of it, she watched the Jackal—who were stumbling to their feet—throw themselves back to the ground and lie on their stomachs, whining like dogs. "You, curs!" Belamus yelled down at them. "There will be no meat for you tonight. Go! Bar all the ways into the Inner Star. I want every door, gate, flap, hatch and trap, every little sneaky snicket, every guilty ginnel, locked, barred and bolted. Those Beguilers' brats must not enter the Inner Star. I want them trapped out here."

Laughing, the king turned to go and noticed Zerra staring at him, openmouthed. "Why are you still here?" he demanded. "Track those brats down!" The king gave a tight little chuckle. "Bring them back to Mews Court. We will watch the Rocadiles eat well tonight."

"Yes, Sire!" Zerra sped off down the steps, aiming to get out of the king's way as quickly as possible. She decided to go back to the old library and try to find a book to read. There was no way she was going looking for an invisible Alex and her creepy *boyfriend*. No way at all.

CHAPTER 9

Breathing Beguilers

ALEX AND BENN COULD HEAR the gates of Rekadom being closed. They jumped through the star snicket—the point where the star-shaped inner walls touched the circle of the outside walls. It was a narrow gap with a high step in the form of a beautifully carved stone crocodile. Taking care not to let go of one another, they jumped down into Gate Court and raced across the open courtyard. Two guards with long, sharp javelins were slowly pushing the massive wooden gates closed, but they were clearly very heavy and it was slow work. Alex and Benn raced toward the narrowing gap between the gates, but as they drew near, Benn slipped on a loose pebble and sent it flying, skittering onto the foot of one of the guards.

The guards sprang into an attacking stance, with their javelins pointing forward. "Halt! Who goes there?" they yelled in unison.

Alex and Benn froze.

The two guards—an older, stocky woman and a very young man covered in pimples—also froze. Stock-still, they scanned the courtyard, their gaze traveling blindly across Alex and Benn. There was a strained silence and then the pimply guard whispered, "It's nothing, Auntie. Just the wind."

"I told you, don't call me 'Auntie' on duty," the older guard replied. "It's unprofessional."

Her nephew blushed. "Sorry, Auntie," he murmured.

His aunt rolled her eyes and walked slowly forward, the shining razor-sharp tip of her javelin heading straight for Benn. Benn and Alex took a few careful steps back.

Benn glanced at Alex. "Run?" he mouthed.

Alex shook her head. Their only hope was to get out of the city, and the only way out was through that tantalizing gap between the gates. She glanced anxiously up at a large silver bell that hung over the gates on a delicate iron frame. She guessed this must be the famous Beguiler Bell, which rang every time anyone with any Enchantment about them walked beneath it. If that was true, Alex thought, even if they made it through the gates, the guards would come after them. But even so, if they could stay invisible, they still had a good chance of escape. They would have to be careful—the two javelins were dangerously sharp, and the guards were edgy. Very edgy.

"Breathing," said the aunt suddenly. "Someone's here. Breathing."

"Breathing?" whispered the nephew, sounding spooked. Alex noticed his pikestaff was trembling.

"Commence Concealed Beguiler Discovery Procedure!" instructed his aunt. The nephew looked terrified. He hadn't trained to do this yet. He watched his aunt leap forward, high-stepping like a prancing pony, waving her razor-sharp javelin in a complicated dance that the nephew knew was designed to discover any invisible object in their path. Clumsily, he followed her, hopping from side to side like an anxious goat with boots on.

Benn couldn't help it—he had never seen anything so funny. In one disastrous second, he let out a snort of laughter, gasped in shock and clapped his hands over his mouth. He had let go of Alex. Suddenly, he was visible.

The pimply guard screamed. His aunt, with great presence of mind, leaped back and stood, javelin poised, in the gap between the gates. Chaos erupted and yet more guards appeared in the snicket that led through to the next court. They had no choice but to turn and run for the only escape left to them—the star snicket through which they had just come. Together, Alex and Benn leaped over the stone crocodile and raced into a tall, open-fronted shelter next to the mews. There they threw themselves down and burrowed beneath a heap of pungent straw in the farthest corner.

Alex took a deep breath and managed to summon enough energy to once more include Benn in her Fade. It wasn't so easy this time. She was so angry with Benn for messing up their escape she felt like she had to push through a big barrier to make the Enchantment work. But at last it happened; Alex saw a slight blurring of the edges of Benn's hand. She watched it travel up his arm and run across him as though he had walked into water. She had done it. Alex felt suddenly exhausted and slumped back against the rough wooden side of the shed.

"I'm sorry," Benn whispered, squeezing Alex's unresponsive hand. "I am so, so sorry."

Alex did not have the strength to reply.

CHAPTER 10

Rocadile

FROM THE SHELTER OF THEIR hiding place—which Alex guessed had been the roost for the Hawke—they watched the search for them spread across Mews Court. There was an assortment of javelin-bearing gate guards, some wan-looking dungeon guards glad to be out in the fresh air and a group of excitable young stable hands who glanced casually into the old Hawke roost and then moved on.

But then, leaping through the star snicket, came three Jackal. Alex and Benn felt a flicker of fear. This was getting serious. They watched the Jackal crouching on all fours, their red coats swishing along the dusty cobbles, their noses to the ground—heading straight for their hiding place. Very slowly, Alex and Benn slipped farther down beneath the straw and lay still, their hearts hammering. They could hear the snuffling of Jackal breath, the scratching of claws upon the cobbles as the creatures moved ever closer to them. Alex fought back a longing to break cover—to leap out of the foul-smelling straw, punch her way out of the trap and run for it. But she knew there was nowhere to run. And she knew too that as soon as she let go of Benn he would become visible once more and he wouldn't stand a chance. So she lay there cornered, feeling the Jackal drawing ever nearer.

Suddenly a massive sneeze came from the nearest Jackal, so forceful that it threw the creature backward onto the other two. They leaped up, snarling and snapping at what they considered to be an attack, and launched themselves onto the unfortunate sneezer. The sneezer fought back and the fight tumbled out of the shelter and continued across the courtyard, scattering the other searchers as they removed themselves to a safe distance. There was not a person in Rekadom who would dare break up a Jackal fight.

After that, the heat went out of the search. People drifted away and, still snapping and snarling, the three Jackal loped off to search elsewhere. Alex and Benn waited until the courtyard was empty and then tentatively crawled out from the Hawke roost. The shadows were slanting long across the ground now, the sun had dropped down below the city walls, and above them the clouds were clearing. Benn sighed. It would have been a great afternoon for a sail in Merry.

But Alex had another, more worrying thought. "Hey, Benn," she whispered. "I need to look something up. Can you hold my arm instead?"

"Sure." Careful not to lose contact with Alex, Benn moved his hand so he was holding on to Alex's elbow. He watched Alex take the codex from inside the wide green sash she wore around her waist. Carefully, she flipped through its tissue-thin pages, which were covered in tiny, spidery writing, and then she stopped and began reading intently. Even though Benn did not understand what Alex was reading, he understood well enough from the way she suddenly tensed that it was not good. After some minutes, Alex closed the codex and pushed it back into her sash.

"What's wrong?" asked Benn.

"I thought so. There's a Twilight Haunting here in the Outer Star," Alex whispered. "Rocadiles."

"Sheesh," Benn whispered. "We've had it."

"*I've* had it," Alex clarified. "You'll be all right."

"If a Haunting gets you, I will most definitely *not* be all right," Benn told Alex. "Are there any Hauntings inside the Star?"

"None. Which makes sense, if you think about it. My father lived there when he Engendered the Hauntings. So if he'd done any for the Inner Star, they would have gotten him."

"Yeah. That's true. So it's simple, right? All we have to do is get inside the Star before sunset. Easy."

Alex returned Benn's wry smile. "Yeah. Easy."

"Well, why not?" Benn said. "We just have to find a way through. A door that's not locked."

"But you heard what the king yelled—about locking all the doors?" Alex asked.

"I heard. But he yells a lot, doesn't he? And when people yell a lot, they often don't get listened to."

"But he's the king," said Alex.

"And he yells," said Benn. "Come on, let's go find a door that no one's bothered to lock."

Alex allowed Benn to pull her to her feet. She wasn't at all hopeful, but it was better than waiting to discover what a Rocadile was.

Taking care to keep holding hands, they walked slowly along the foot of the high wall that divided Mews Court from the Inner Star, searching for any sign of a way through. They tried three small doors, but not one shifted an inch. They glimpsed one tantalizing window high up, which was open, but there was no way they could get up to it. They reached the very last door—a wide plank in a narrow alcove behind the falconry mews—and they pushed against it hard. It would not move.

"Locked," muttered Benn angrily. He had to stop

himself from kicking it.

"That's it then," Alex said flatly. "We're trapped." A familiar feeling of dread was welling up inside her. Alex knew what this was. Benn's grandmother, Nella, had called it the Twilight Terrors—the feeling of despair at the onset of twilight that came over those with any Enchantment about them. Suddenly overwhelmed, Alex let go of Benn's hand.

The warmth of the Enchantment left Benn and he shivered with the chill of the evening, and the unwelcome knowledge that he was now visible. He looked at the space where he knew Alex was, and he could see nothing. He stretched out his arm and touched her, just to reassure himself she was still there, but she did not respond. Suddenly, from the clock on the roof of the falconry mews came six rapid, tinny chimes, and Benn heard heavy footsteps hurry out of the mews into the courtyard. A shout of "Dark! Dark!" was followed by an angry muttering of "Where is the darned girl?" And then another, even more irritable yell, "Dark! Dark!"

"Maybe we can hide in the mews," Benn whispered. "I'll check it out. Don't move, okay?"

"Okay," a faint reply came from the shadows.

Benn edged along the side of the mews and peered around the corner. A red-faced, square-set man in a leather jerkin was pacing up and down angrily, but behind him was an open door into the falconry mews. If they could get in without being seen, Benn thought, he and Alex could shelter in there for the night. Benn was about to hurry back to Alex when a movement in the star snicket caught his eye. He stared in amazement—the stone crocodile that had formed the step was no longer lying down, it was standing up on four short, stumpy legs—and it was certainly no longer made of stone. It glistened a smooth dark green, its eyes shining red, its fangs a brilliant white. Benn knew at once that this must be a Rocadile. He watched it begin to move, stiffly at first, as though its joints were gritty with stone dust, and then, with its nose raised, sniffing the air, the Rocadile set off in a lumbering trot toward where Benn knew Alex was standing. The red-faced man in the jerkin stopped pacing and watched the creature, seemingly not bothered by it at all. As it lumbered by, he aimed an irritable kick at it and then yelled, yet again, "Dark! Dark! Final warning, Dark!"

Benn raced back to Alex. Her Fade had gone and she looked utterly dispirited. "Rocadile!" he hissed, and in desperation, he threw himself against the door in the wall. It did not shift. Benn stood in front of Alex, hoping to somehow shield her from the oncoming Haunting. She pushed him aside. "No, Benn. Don't be silly."

But Benn would not move, and from behind his shoulder, Alex watched the Rocadile heading toward them on its power-packed stumpy legs. Its jaw hung slightly open, showing its long, curved teeth glistening with spit, and its brilliant red eyes with deep-blue vertical slits were focused on one thing only—Alex RavenStarr, the Enchanter's child.

CHAPTER 11

Inside the Star

Z ERRA WAS WANDERING ALONG THE empty street, picking the last piece of orange candy off her teeth, when she heard the six tinny chimes of the mews clock. Unwilling to get on the wrong side of Ratchet by missing Birds-In, she picked up speed. A nasty-looking metal bug on wheels came trundling toward her from a shop doorway where it had been lurking, but Zerra outran it and, guided by Ratchet's yells, she raced down the ginnel to the door that would take her into Mews Court. Breathless, she reached up and tugged the huge lever in the wall, the door flew open, and Zerra found herself squashed against the wall, like a fly trapped between two clapping hands.

Rocketing through the door came Benn and Alex.

"Hey!" yelled Zerra.

Benn and Alex stopped and stared at Zerra, horrified. And then, in one fluid movement, Alex shoved Zerra out the door, slammed it shut and leaned against it to stop Zerra from pushing it open. A series of rapid hammerings on the door did not disturb the thick plank at all. Stunned at the rapid turnaround in their fortunes, Benn and Alex looked at one another in silence, and Alex began to giggle with relief. Soon they were both leaning against the door howling with hysterical laughter.

"You were so fast!" Benn spluttered. "Whoosh, out she went. Didn't stand a chance."

"Oh, that . . . was . . . fun," Alex said, trying to catch her breath.

Suddenly a spine-chilling scream, full of dread and terror, echoed from the other side of the door. It was followed by a much deeper shout and a dull thud, like something hitting a thick wad of material.

"Sheesh! What was that?" Benn whispered.

Alex felt bad. "Zerra," she said. "I'm sure of it."

Benn caught hold of Alex. "You're not going out to help her, are you?"

Alex shook her head. "We can't do anything. Come on, let's get out of here before they come after us."

* * *

On the far side of the door, Ratchet was gazing down at the battered body of the Rocadile. Behind him cowered Zerra clutching a bloodied arm, her eyes wide with fear. With a satisfying *craaaaack*, Ratchet delivered one last blow to the Rocadile's thick skull and then gently took Zerra by her good arm and led her into the mews, where he closed the door and swung a heavy bar across it.

A tall young woman in a scuffed leather jerkin, dusty trousers and walking boots was unloading cages of mice from a small cart. At the sound of the door being barred she swung around and eyed both Ratchet and Zerra with some disapproval. "What's going on?" she asked Ratchet.

"New Flyer's been bit," Ratchet growled at the young woman. "Dratted Rocadile. Attacking just anyone now. They must have Turned, darn it."

The young woman regarded Zerra suspiciously. "Turned? Really?"

"*Really.* Blasted Hauntings. They're getting old now. They say it will happen to them all in the end. They'll stop caring whether you're a Beguiler or not and Turn on anyone." Ratchet grinned. "Even you, Bartlett."

"I think not," Bartlett said icily as she stacked up another cage of terrified mice with a clang.

Ratchet took no notice. He guided Zerra into his office, sat her down on his chair and put the kettle on the burner. Feeling very spooked, Zerra eyed the kettle fearfully. And then, even more fearfully, she watched Ratchet reach up to the top shelf and take down a large brown bottle labeled Poison. She jumped to her feet, sending the chair rocketing out behind her on its wheels.

Ratchet spun around. "What are you doing?" he demanded. "Sit down."

"No! I won't. You're not poisoning *me*," Zerra declared.

Ratchet sighed. "Don't tempt me," he said, pulling the cork from the bottle. "However, this is iodine. For your injury. Those Rocs have filthy teeth. You don't want the wound getting infected and then to lose your arm, do you?"

"No," Zerra reluctantly agreed, resuming her seat. But she hated iodine. It stung so badly. "So why are you boiling the kettle?" she asked, still suspicious and twitchy.

"I thought," Ratchet said, "that you might want a cup of cocoa. For the shock."

Zerra watched warily as Ratchet upended the iodine bottle onto a clean rag and its yellow stain spread into the fabric.

Advancing somewhat nervously toward Zerra's arm, Ratchet said, "Hold still now. It might sting a bit."

"Aaargh!" Zerra yelled.

"Calm down," Ratchet said. "Now stay still while I put the bandage on." Surprisingly gently, Ratchet wound a clean white bandage around Zerra's forearm and fastened it above her thumb. He surveyed his handiwork with satisfaction. "You'll live," he said.

Zerra sat staring at the bandage, the shock of the Rocadile's attack beginning to sink in. If Ratchet had not come out of the mews with a massive plank in his hand and thumped the creature so hard on its tail that it had let go of her arm, she would not be sitting here right now, that was for sure. Not so long ago she had removed all the stuffing from her little brother's favorite toy, an elephant named Peg. And now she felt just like Peg had looked—a limp rag. She slumped back in her chair and watched Ratchet set the cocoa down in front of her. With her good hand she shakily raised the mug to her lips and sipped the hot, sweet, chocolaty liquid. The taste was so beautiful that it made tears spring into her eyes. No one had ever made her anything as nice as this, Zerra thought. Although sometimes Alex had tried to—stupid Alex, whose fault this all was.

The door to the office burst open and Ratchet, who had just made himself some cocoa too, looked up warily. It was Bartlett.

"Why was she bitten by a *Haunting*?" she demanded.

"Told you. They've Turned," Ratchet said.

"Oh yes? But it didn't bite *you*, did it? Or me."

"Because I hit it with a plank. And you were in here with them mice."

"Hmm. So, what's her name then, this new Dark?"

"Zerra." It was Zerra who spoke. The cocoa had given

her some strength back, and the pain in her arm was subsiding to a bearable throb. "It's rude to talk about people as if they're not here."

Ratchet hurriedly intervened. "My fault. I haven't introduced you. Bartlett, this is Zerra Dark, our trainee Flyer. Zerra, this is my deputy falconer, Bartlett."

"What happened to Danny?" Bartlett asked.

"Little toad absconded. Still haven't gotten the jacket back."

Bartlett looked down at Zerra, her arm with its bandage, now seeping red, resting on the desk. "So, are you a Beguiler?" she asked.

Zerra returned the stare and said nothing. She wasn't going to give Bartlett the satisfaction of an answer.

"Leave the girl be," Ratchet said.

But Bartlett would not let Zerra be. "It doesn't make sense. The Rocadiles never bother anyone. Danny used to throw cookies for them."

Ratchet smiled at the memory. Danny had been fun. "I *told* you, they must have Turned," he said, and pushed the cookie jar across to Zerra. "Take one. For the shock." Zerra shook her head. She felt quite queasy.

"I'll have one, thank you," said Bartlett. "And a cocoa while you're at it."

Zerra watched Ratchet put the kettle back on the burner. All she wanted to do was lie down in the dark somewhere and forget about today. But Bartlett was barring the door, arms folded and still staring at her. "So who *are* your parents, girl?" she demanded.

"None of your business," Zerra muttered.

Ratchet sat down next to Zerra. "It's a fair question, Flyer," he said. He frowned up at Bartlett. "Although it could be put in a more friendly fashion."

Zerra didn't mind telling Ratchet; he'd saved her from the Rocadile. And he'd bandaged her arm. She felt he was on her side. "Okay. So when we lived here in Rekadom, Ma sewed the king's silk waistcoats and Pa ran dice games and lost all our money. Maybe Pa's still here. I dunno." She laughed. "There is no way either of them is an Enchanter."

"Dice games? Not *Jimmy D'Arbo*?" Ratchet asked.

Zerra nodded.

"Well, well. I'd never have guessed it. You don't look a bit like the old trickster. He married that flighty one, what was her name now?"

"Mirram," Zerra said sourly.

Ratchet looked up at Bartlett, who was still blocking the door. "Neither of them were Beguilers, that's for sure. So it looks like the Rocs have indeed Turned." He grinned. "Best not go out tonight, Bartlett, hey?"

"Huh," said Bartlett.

"It happens, you know," Ratchet said, sipping his cocoa. "Those Air-Weavers out on the High Plains Turned a few years back and started going for anyone. We lost a Flyer to them. And they say some of the Xin up by Netters Cove are beginning to Turn, creeping farther down the cliffs. They terrify my old ma, they do. Like I said, the Enchantments are getting old now. Soon enough they'll *all* be after every one of us and we won't be able to go anywhere." Ratchet chuckled. "I wouldn't like to be guarding the city gate tonight."

"You mean *she* wouldn't like to be guarding the gate," Bartlett said, eyeballing Zerra. "Might get the Beguiler Bell ringing."

"Give it a rest, Bartlett," Ratchet said. "What's got your goat?"

"*Her*," Bartlett snarled. "As deputy falconer I should have been involved with choosing the next Flyer. But I come back to find some brat already in the post. We don't even know if she's a Dark, do we?"

"Of course she is!" But Ratchet's protest sounded hollow even to himself. He had no idea if Zerra was Dark to Enchantment. She had arrived on the Hawke out of the blue. The Hawke had accepted her, so he had to accept her too; what choice did he have? Besides, with Danny gone, there were no other Darks in Rekadom that he knew of. They were lucky to have anyone to fly anything right now; the city was a ghost town. Ratchet decided it was time that Zerra was out of the way; maybe then Bartlett would stop being so riled up about her. "Come on now," he said to Zerra. "There'll be no Birds-In tonight.

You need to get some sleep and to rest that arm. Take this willow bark to chew. It will stop the pain. And there's no need to get up for Falcon-Call tomorrow either."

"Thanks," Zerra mumbled. She gulped down the rest of her cocoa, got up from the table and headed out to the long, shadowy space of the mews at the end of which was a ladder leading up to the Flyer's loft, which was perched above the small cabin where the deputy falconer slept. She climbed up awkwardly using only her good arm, flopped down onto the straw mattress and pulled the rough blankets over her.

As she drifted off to sleep, Zerra reflected that Ma had never *ever* made her cocoa. She'd never bandaged her cuts either. Or stuck up for her like Ratchet had done with the horrible Bartlett. So did that make Ratchet nicer than Ma? Maybe. Although that wasn't saying much, was it?

In the office at the far end of the mews, an awkward silence had fallen. Ratchet was peering out the small, open window watching the darkening sky. "He's late," Ratchet murmured anxiously.

Bartlett did not comment. She sat slowly tapping her fingers on the desk, a frown clouding her deep-set, hawk-like eyes. Bartlett was thinking.

"Ah!" Ratchet said happily and thrust his arm out the window. "Here he is. Come to daddy, Merle. Come on now." The window darkened with a flurry of outstretched wings—and then something dark, compact and powerful landed on Ratchet's leather wristband. Gently, he drew his arm back through the window.

Bartlett sniffed. "Bit small, your merlin."

Ratchet ignored the comment. He gently stroked the top of the bird's head with his thumb while the raptor's keen black eyes watched Bartlett suspiciously.

"You should wear a gauntlet," Bartlett said. "Those talons will rake your hand."

Ratchet raised his arm so he was eye to eye with his bird. "Nah. He always lands so neat and tidy, don't you, Merle?"

The little bird of prey put its head to one side as if in agreement.

"We're a team," Ratchet told Bartlett. "I raised him from a chick after his mother got taken by the Hawke. Merle's never cut me once. Not ever. We're off to bed now. Been a long day, what with one thing and another."

Bartlett watched him with a gaze so piercing it reminded Ratchet of a young Hawke. "Danny," said Bartlett. "He's not dead."

"No?" said Ratchet, lowering his arm and letting the merlin settle.

"I'm sure of it. He's kept his Flyer jacket and ratted us out. You should send that merlin of yours out to find him."

Ratchet sighed. "Even Merle couldn't find Danny if he doesn't want to be found. And I don't reckon he does."

CHAPTER 12

Danny

"YOU'LL FIND IT THERE," JAY told Danny. "In the green box." He grinned. "The one labeled Wrenches."

Danny was impressed with Jay's workshop organization. He handed Jay the wrench he'd asked for and watched as he expertly tightened the last nut on the repaired firebox. Danny crouched on the driver's footplate, trying to imagine what it might be like to be on the engine with a fire inside it, the pressure of steam building and the thrill of such a huge iron monster actually moving. "How fast did you say it can go?" he asked Jay.

Jay stood up and wiped the back of his greasy hand over his forehead. "Eighty-five, so they say," he replied.

"Eighty-five what?" Danny asked, feeling stupid.

"Miles an hour."

Danny's eyes opened wide. "In one hour you'd cover *eighty-five miles*?" he asked.

"Yeah. But that's on a safe, straight track. We've not got that. We'll be lucky to get up to twenty, with the state of the track we have."

Danny smiled. "Guess we'll just have to get that track fixed," he said.

Jay returned the smile. "I've checked it over the bridge and all along the embankment past the salt oaks as far as Netters Halt. After that, well, who knows if it's even there?"

Danny helped Jay clean the tools they'd used that day and watched as he carefully put them away above the workbench that was fixed along the cavern wall.

"I'd better get going," Jay said. "I promised Gramma I'd help out this evening with little Louie. And that idiot pokkle creature the kid has. She can't stand the pokkle, but Louie loves it."

Danny thought of the warm farmhouse kitchen where he'd had breakfast only a few days ago. It made the prospect of a solitary night in the damp, cold cavern feel even more dismal. "Anything I can do to help while you're gone?" he asked. "Get something ready for tomorrow?"

Jay regarded Danny thoughtfully. His immersion in the river had given a papery look to his skin, as though it was almost transparent. And the braid that Danny had plaited to keep his long hair out of the machinery looked like the tail of a dead thing. It felt wrong to leave him alone. "Why don't you come to Gramma's too?" he asked. "Get warmed up a bit. You still shiver sometimes, you know."

Danny was very tempted. "Thanks, but . . . well, I guess I should stay here in case Mr. RavenStarr comes back," he said reluctantly.

Jay respected Danny's loyalty. "You could leave him a note. Say you'll be back in the morning. It's cold in here at night. I think he'd want you to take care of yourself, Danny."

Danny thought about it. He was tempted, but he missed Hagos more than he would have expected and hated the thought of the irritating old guy turning up when he wasn't there. "Yeah. But . . . well . . . er, no," he said. "But thanks for the offer. I appreciate it."

"Okay. I'll see you in the morning," Jay said.

Danny watched Jay head off into the wide brick-lined tunnel that led out to the old dock. He imagined him walking through the evening sun along the path through the reeds to his boat, and he was so tempted to run after him. *No*, he told himself sternly. *Suppose Mr. RavenStarr comes back tonight. You have to be here.*

Danny wandered around the cavern for a while, then he climbed up onto the footplate of Big Puffer and imagined what it would be like to drive it. But as the chill seeped out of Big Puffer's thick iron plates, Danny felt the cold creep deep into his bones. He headed into the bunkhouse, took the blankets from all four bunks and burrowed into his bed. He felt as if he would never be warm again.

CHAPTER 13

Under the Silver Star

As Danny was falling asleep, Alex was wide awake in Rekadom, walking with Benn up the southeast point of the Inner Star, exhilarated at their lucky escape. Unsure where to go, they hurried past windows dark like dead eyes, weeds growing up through the cobbles and boarded-up shop fronts. Feeling a little spooked by the emptiness, they moved quietly, and when they passed a shop selling watches where an attic window was lighted, Alex had the distinct impression they were being observed.

The street widened out as it neared the center of the Star: Star Court. At the last building before the empty windswept area, they stopped. The most delicious smell of cooking was drifting out. "Just like Gramma's chicken soup," Benn whispered. "Oh, it smells amazing. I am *so* hungry."

Alex's mouth was watering. "Me too, I'm *starving*," she said. "But how can we possibly get anything to eat here?"

Benn shook his head. He had no idea. They lingered by the doorway, both hoping that maybe someone might open the door and ask them in for supper, but of course no one did.

"We need to find somewhere to sleep," Alex whispered.

"There are so many empty houses," Benn said. "Let's climb into one. And tomorrow we can get out of this horrible place and go home."

"You make it all sound so simple," Alex said.

Benn was irritable with hunger. "Do you have a better idea?"

"No. But . . ." Alex's voice trailed off. As the darkness deepened, she could see a few more lighted windows above them—it seemed that no one lived on the ground floors. Why was that? A prickle of fear ran through her. *Were Rocadiles here too—or something even worse?* "I think we should find somewhere high up to sleep."

"High up?"

"Up some stairs," Alex said. "Just in case."

"In case of what?"

Benn found his question answered in a way he would

have preferred not. From out of the shadows came something that looked at first glance like a tortoise—but a
tortoise faster and shinier than any he had ever seen. As
it headed over to them, he saw a shining glint of steel zip
out from beneath its smooth carapace. Alex grabbed hold
of him and pulled him up onto the doorstep just in time.
The "tortoise" came barging straight for them, ramming
its carapace against the step with a loud clang. There was
a whirring sound, and as it spun around, they saw three
tiny blades whizzing out from beneath it.

"Sheesh!" whispered Benn. "What is *that*?"

"The reason why everyone is upstairs right now," Alex
whispered back.

"It's horrible. Imagine that getting your foot."

"Ankle," Alex corrected. "It's ankle height."

Benn shuddered. "I don't even want to think about it."
He looked down at the frantically spinning automaton.
"It would be funny if it wasn't for the blade. Look how
much it wants to get up the step, but there's no way it
can."

"There's also no way we can stay stuck on this step all
night," Alex said. "We'll fall asleep and then we'll fall off
and then . . ."

Benn shuddered at the thought of what would happen
then. "I hate this place," he said vehemently. "Why anyone lives here I have no idea."

"I suppose they all look after the king," Alex said.

"So why does the king have these horrid things running around the streets trying to stab people's ankles?"

"To keep people inside at night. Like a curfew. I think it's called a slicer. I remember now they were talking about getting them in Luma."

"That's horrible," Benn muttered.

"Luma *is* horrible," Alex agreed. "You know what, I kind of remember this place. It feels familiar."

"You remember *here*?"

"I was born in Rekadom, don't forget. I know I left when I was only about eighteen months old, but being here reminds me of something." She pointed across Star Court to the dark archway at the foot of the silver-topped tower. And then suddenly her hand flew to her mouth. "Oh!" she said. "Look!"

Benn, who had been watching the slicer spinning and bashing itself against the step, jumped. "What?" he said.

Alex looked at Benn, her eyes wide and shining. "We lived through there! I'm sure we did. When I was a baby. I remember Poppa carrying me through that arch. If you look up when you're underneath it you can see a silver star carved on the keystone."

"Wow. That's a fancy place to live," Benn said. He looked up at the tower, its windows dark except for two triangular lighted ones right at the top. "And whoever is at the top now is well away from this nasty thing here."

"We were at the top once," Alex said wistfully. "I

wonder who's there now?" She looked at Benn, a gleam in her eyes. "I've got an idea," she said.

Benn looked wary. "Yeah?"

"Let's get inside the Silver Tower. There are hundreds of steps there. I remember Poppa carrying me up them. We'd be safe from the slicer because we can sleep on one of the landings and no one could see us from outside, either."

Benn looked down at the vicious silver slicer, which was still bumping up against the doorstep. "What about that thing?" he whispered, wondering if it was listening to them.

Alex pointed to a stack of old wooden planks piled up against the shop front opposite. It looked as if someone had decided to do some repairs and then thought better of it. "If we grab a plank each—see those long thin ones— we can fight it off." She grinned. "We used to play a game in Luma where we hit a puck with sticks."

Benn nodded. "Sand hockey. I saw a match once. But the puck didn't have sharp knives whizzing around, did it?"

"It won't matter once we've got a long stick to push it away with," Alex said. Before Benn could object—and before she could think too much about it—Alex leaped off the step and over the metal bug, then she raced across to the pile of wood. The slicer set off, spinning in pursuit, its silver blades flashing in the light of the windows above. Benn saw Alex struggling with the wood, trying to find something that wasn't rotten. He hurtled after the bug and the slicer turned and whizzed toward him. Benn leaped up onto the woodpile, sending the assortment of planks, boards and beams tumbling down and clattering across the cobbles, taking the slicer with them. Alex grabbed two long, sturdy planks from the bottom of the pile and threw one at Benn. "Run!" she said.

They ran.

The slicer followed. Fast.

As they raced across the empty Star Court, Alex and Benn took turns batting the slicer away. Sometimes Alex missed and Benn hit it, sometimes Benn missed and Alex got it. As they neared the safety of the archway of the Silver Tower, Benn took aim as the slicer came spinning toward him and one of the blades stuck into the wood, and Benn found himself joined in a strange dance with the contraption, which he had no idea how to get out of.

"Benn, let go!" Alex yelled.

Realizing that was the answer, Benn did just that. As the slicer and its new attachment whirled toward them, they ran for the silver arch and leaped inside. They stood inside the arch catching their breath and watching the slicer come to a halt as its new arm thudded into the step. "It's clever, isn't it?" Benn said. "But it's not an Enchantment, right?"

Alex nodded. "Right. Enchantments are living things, not machines."

"If it didn't have those horrible blades it would be fun to have one—like a pet. I wonder who made it?" Benn mused.

"Someone with a very nasty attitude," Alex said, gazing up at the underside of the arch. She turned to Benn, smiling. "I knew it. There's a silver star beneath the keystone. I'm home."

Benn grinned. "Want to show me around?"

Alex led the way up the winding stone stairs, lit only by the light of the moon coming in through the little window on each turn. Halfway up they stopped at a wide landing with a bench beneath a small triangular window. Benn threw himself down on the bench while Alex looked out the window at the orchards below.

"Oh!" she murmured.

"What?"

"My mother. I've tried and tried before, but I've never been able to remember her. And now . . . now I can. I can almost feel her . . . holding me. She had rings. Lots of rings. I remember her hands on my tummy. Holding me up so I could see the horses in the orchards."

"What a good memory you have," Benn said.

"I had to be here to remember, I guess." Alex smiled. "Let's go to the top. I'd like to take a look at our old door.

Maybe I'll remember some more."

"But someone lives there now. We saw the lights on," Benn said.

"They won't know we're there, will they?" Alex set her foot on the next flight of stairs. "You don't have to come. I'll just go up and take a quick look."

Benn got up. "No way. We stick together."

They climbed slowly up, passing more deserted landings, until Alex was sure they were nearly there. As she turned the last twist of the stairs, she stopped so suddenly that Benn bumped into her. "Oof!" he gasped.

Alex swung around, her finger to her lips. "Shhh . . ."

But it was too late. Above them they heard the familiar clatter of Jackal claws upon stone. And a moment later came a loud sniffing sound. Alex's hand found Benn's and the prickly sensation of Enchantment began creeping over him. As they pressed themselves back against the wall, they saw the white-headed Jackal, its pointed nose in the air, ears pricked up, its long red coat sweeping the ground as it descended the stairs toward them. Inside their Fade, Alex and Benn threw each other panicked glances.

Slowly and silently they retreated before the oncoming Jackal, which took up all the space on the narrow stairs. For each step the creature took—sniffing as it went, clearly scenting them—Alex and Benn took a step back until they found themselves on the previous landing. Benn mimed a punch at the Jackal and looked inquiringly at Alex. She nodded.

The Jackal stopped on the landing and sniffed rapidly, like a hound locating its quarry. Suddenly, Benn leaped forward with a short and powerful punch to the Jackal's stomach. The Jackal reeled backward and crumpled to the floor, gasping for breath.

Alex went racing back up the stairs, instinctively heading for home. Benn—who was now visible—sprinted after her. The Jackal caught its breath and let out a howl of fury. Then it staggered to its feet and set off after Benn.

At the top landing, Alex saw a strip of light beneath the achingly familiar door. "Help!" Alex yelled out, battering the door with her fists. "Help, help! Let us in. Let us in!"

The door opened.

It was Poppa.

Of course it was.

CHAPTER 14

Home

Hagos saw only a wild-looking boy hurling himself through the door—but he was sure the voice he had heard was his daughter's. Puzzled, he peered out, only to see coming around the twist of the stairs the white, pointed snout of a Jackal. Hagos slammed the door fast and threw both bolts across it. Leaning back against the door, he surveyed the boy—who looked familiar—and before him emerged the fuzzy outline of . . . "Boo-boo!" he yelled, sweeping Alex up into a hug.

"Poppa, I'm *Alex*," she protested happily, half smothered in his old red cloak—which smelled just like it always used to.

"Alex," Hagos said, setting her back on her feet and laughing. "*Alex*. But how did you get here? I can't believe it. Oh, this is wonderful . . . wonderful."

Alex could not stop smiling either. "Oh, Poppa, I was so afraid you were . . ."

"Dead?" supplied Hagos.

Alex nodded, tears pricking her eyelids.

"Not yet, Boo-boo. Alex. Not yet."

"Did the king let you go, Poppa? Are you friends again?"

Before Hagos could answer, a scratching at the door brought a dose of reality. "No, I'm still a prisoner. That's my guard outside. You're not safe here, sweetheart. And neither is . . ." Hagos looked at Benn, wondering if he ought to know his name.

"This is Benn," Alex told him.

"Hello, Benn. Well, neither is Benn, I'm afraid. Deela . . ." Hagos wheeled around, and to their surprise Alex and Benn saw Deela Ming wearing a long silk cloak embroidered with crescent moons. She was smiling at them broadly.

"Deela!" said Alex.

"Shh!" said Hagos and Deela as an insistent scratching came from the other side of the bolted door.

"I'm going to have to open the door," Hagos said anxiously. "It's part of the deal I made to stay out of the dungeons. Jackal must have access at all times. Deela, take Alex and Benn into my room, will you?"

From behind the heavy curtain that divided Hagos's small sleeping area from the rest of the room, Alex, Benn and Deela watched Hagos hurriedly searching through his desk drawers. As he triumphantly pulled out a small metal tube with a screw top, an impatient yipping started up from the landing. They watched Hagos open the door a few inches, his foot stopping it from going any wider. They saw the Jackal's pointy, white nose push through the gap and heard the rapid *sniff-sniff-sniff* of it picking up a scent. They saw its upper limb, sleeved in red, push through the gap between the door and its frame. Its odd humanlike hand was covered in short white hairs, and the stubby, curled fingers ended in sharp, polished black talons that reached down to claw at Hagos's face. He ducked away and quickly emptied the sparkling contents of the metal tube into his open right hand, which he offered up to the Jackal's questing, sniffing snout. The Jackal drew in a deep, luxuriant breath, and a waft of sparkling dust rose up from Hagos's palm. The Jackal looked at Hagos with a doggy expression of gratitude in its eyes, and then flicked out its long, black tongue and proceeded to lick every speck of powder off Hagos's hand. Hagos stood still as stone, allowing the tongue to curl between his fingers, and even when the Jackal leaned forward and delicately sucked the very last grain of powder from the tops of his nails, Hagos did not flinch.

"Yuck," Benn whispered.

"Eurgh," Alex agreed.

"*Shhhh* . . . ," hissed Deela.

With the last speck of powder gone, the Jackal seemed dazed. It gazed up at Hagos, as if begging for more, but he placed his hand upon its nose and gave the creature a firm shove. Unresisting, it fell back, and Hagos slammed the door. Then he rapidly threw the bolts across and ran to a small sink in the corner of the room, where he vigorously scrubbed his hand clean of Jackal drool.

Alex, Benn and Deela emerged from behind the curtain. "You had us all on edge back there," Deela told him. "Whatever was that stuff?"

Hagos turned around with a smile. "Fizz. I *knew* I had some left. I made it years ago, just before Boo-boo—I mean Alex—was born, when Belamus was still my good friend and I was still his trusted Enchanter. I was frightened for the baby. There were stories of Jackal taking newborns in the night and parents being unable to fight them off. So I concocted something they would find even more irresistible than a baby; a bit like catnip for cats. It worked far better than I hoped." Hagos chuckled. "That Jackal will now be sprawled on the landing, dreaming crazy things and foaming at the mouth."

"Wow," said Benn. "That's such cool Beguiler stuff."

Hagos gave Benn a frosty look. "It is *Enchantment*, an ancient and honorable art. Which I practice."

Benn looked mortified. "I'm sorry," he mumbled. "I didn't mean . . ."

"Of course you didn't," Hagos said soothingly. "'Beguiler' is used here in Rekadom to belittle us, to make our art sound underhand. Which it is not."

The fact that her father had used his art to create so many monsters that had brought misery and death to countless innocent people did not seem entirely honorable to Alex, but she said nothing. Hagos, however, was enjoying his new audience. "The Jackal outside is now in no fit state to tell anyone that we have guests here. Indeed, if it meets a fellow Jackal while it is still foaming at the mouth, it won't last long. They turn on their own when they see weakness, you see. That's why there are only five of them left now. When I first came to Rekadom as a boy, Belamus's predecessor had thirty-two Jackal. Total nightmare."

"How many were there to begin with?" Benn wanted to know.

"One hundred and sixty-nine. An Enchanted number."

"Thirteen times thirteen," Alex said.

Hagos beamed at her. "Spot on, Boo-boo. Alex. The Jackal were Engendered about a hundred years ago for a queen. Her Enchanter took some newborn jackal pups and did a very nasty Enchantment on them." Hagos chuckled. "At least the king won't be getting any more of those abominations. The first thing I did when I became

— 96 —

Enchanter here was to feed the Incantation to a Jackal. I hid it in a sausage. They can't resist sausages. Ha ha. But enough of Jackal. Deela and I were about to have supper. I imagine you both wouldn't say no to joining us?"

"No, we wouldn't," Benn said, his stomach already rumbling. "I mean, we most certainly wouldn't say no. Not at all."

"I suspected as much," Hagos said.

Hagos and Deela busied themselves in the tiny kitchen area in an alcove on the far side of the room and Benn threw himself down onto the big cushion in front of the fire with a sigh of contentment and gazed up at the ceiling, which was covered with silvery symbols of Enchantment. Alex drew up a small footstool and warmed herself by the fire. As she stared into the flickering flames, she noticed a strange feeling creeping through her. At first she thought it was relief at being safe—for a while, at least—and then she thought it was the soft warmth of the fire. But as she breathed in the familiar smells of dusty old rugs, ancient Enchantments and a supper of fragrant rice, she realized it was something much deeper.

It was the feeling of coming home.

CHAPTER 15

Homesick

LATER THAT NIGHT, ALEX WAS back in her old bed-room. She just about fitted into her little bed—which she remembered as being vast—and she lay contentedly gaz-ing up at the ceiling, with its painted silver stars on deep blue. The blue paint was dusty and peeling and the shine of the stars was dulled now, but they still gave her the same feeling of happiness.

The room was not large. The tiny window was covered by a long, faded red curtain embroidered with swirls that looked like prancing dragons. There was a little chest of drawers and a bedside cupboard painted in symbols of Enchantment, and an ancient, speckled looking glass that hung over the mantelpiece above a small, deep-set fire. Hagos had lit the fire to keep away the chill, which seeped in at night from the thick walls of the Silver Tower and lay heavy on the floor—where Benn was to sleep.

Benn lay there now, on a pile of cushions, covered with an old feather quilt and a starry blanket. He too was looking up at the silver stars and faded blue paint, but he wasn't feeling quite as at home as Alex was. "Alex," he murmured. "Are you awake?"

"Mmm," Alex murmured in return. "I can't sleep. It's all so strange. Being home again."

Home. Benn wished he were home so much he couldn't think of anything else. "I guess you must have felt like this when you came to my house," he said. "I didn't think about it until now. But it's weird being in someone else's home, isn't it?"

"But it's not the first time. We were in the cottage on Oracle Rock. In Deela's home."

"Yeah. I guess. And that wasn't weird. Well, it was. But not like this."

"I think," Alex said after a while, "that's because on Oracle Rock we were *both* not in our homes."

"Yeah. And here only one of us is. And this time it's me."

"But I miss your home too," Alex said. "I miss Nella and Louie and just the nice feeling of being there." She sat up, drawing her blanket around her; the chill in the walls was already seeping into the room. "Hey, Benn, shall we see what's happening there? At your place? See what Nella is doing? And Jay maybe? And Louie?"

Benn rolled over onto his side and propped himself up on his elbow. "You mean with your cards?"

"Yes. With the cards."

Benn's eyes shone. "I'd love to."

From her bedside cupboard, which was lined in red felt, Alex took the codex. Then she joined Benn on the rug in front of the fire, and in the flickering firelight she opened the little blue book and drew out her cards.

"I love how they fit in there so well," Benn said. "It's so strange that Gramma had that book just waiting for your cards."

"So much is strange right now," Alex said, "that *that* feels kind of normal." She took the seven mother-of-pearl hexagonal cards—whisper-thin and feather-light—from their blue wallet and placed six of them in a circle on the rug.

With a feeling of butterflies in his stomach, Benn watched intently as Alex carefully placed the seventh card into the hexagonal hole in the center. At once the cards seemed to merge into one and a deep shimmer, shifting and swirling like oil on water, spread across them. In movements that Benn remembered so well from the time—not so very long ago—when he had first met Alex in the marketplace of the hilltop town of Luma, he watched Alex's fingers fluttering over the cards, coaxing them into life. The oily sheen began to swirl beneath the movements of her hands; colors appeared and began whirling into a vortex, in the middle of which Benn saw a dark spot begin to grow. He watched Alex leaning forward, staring intently into the darkness, her hands braced against the floor as if stopping herself from falling.

"What can you see?" he whispered.

Alex could see a luminous picture beginning to form. "Nella. In the kitchen," she whispered.

"Is she okay? I wish I could see her," Benn said.

Alex knew that Benn could not see the things in the cards that she could. She also knew how much he would love to be able to. "Put your hand over mine," she said. "Then maybe you can see too."

Benn placed his hand over Alex's and looked into the picture. "There's Gramma!" he gasped. "In the kitchen. And Louie. Look, he's sitting on Gramma's lap. And there's Jay too."

With equal wistfulness, Alex and Benn stared intently at the scene.

"They seem so sad," Benn said. "Even Jay." He looked up at Alex. "It's us making them sad, isn't it? We've disappeared and they don't know where."

Intently they watched the people they loved gathered together in the cozy kitchen, a candle burning on the table. They watched Benn's grandmother take a handkerchief from her pocket and wipe her eyes, they saw Louie's serious little face, and when Louie rubbed his eyes too, Alex's concentration faltered and the image evaporated like mist from the top of a lake.

"It was awful seeing them so sad," Benn said.

Alex nodded. "Louie looked so lonely," she murmured.

"No sign of your foster mother," Benn said. "You'd think she'd be there looking after Louie."

"Oh, Mirram," Alex said dismissively. "She's always getting people to watch Louie." And then she hurriedly added, "But I don't mean Nella is just any person. Nella will be much nicer to Louie than Mirram."

"No sign of the Flyer either," Benn said.

"Or my other stupid foster sister," Alex added as she neatly collected up the cards. "Not that I want to see either of them anyway."

Benn did not reply. An awful thought had occurred to him. "Gramma thinks I've drowned, doesn't she?"

Alex slipped the cards back into their place in the codex and closed the cover. "I suppose she might think that," she said carefully.

"She does think it. I saw it in her eyes," Benn said. He took a deep breath. "I have to go home. For Gramma."

Alex was not surprised. "I know. But how will you get there?"

"In Merry."

"But how will you get back to Merry?"

"I've been thinking about that. You remember when the Jackal were taking us up those steps inside the cliff?"

Alex grimaced. How could she forget?

"There was a fork in the steps about halfway up, and I saw another flight branching off. I am sure they are the ones that go up to Oracle Halt."

"Oracle Halt?" asked Alex.

"The old railway station on the cliff top. It was the last stop before Rekadom. Gramma told me there were steps down from there through the cliff to the beach below."

"But you've got to get out of Rekadom first," Alex said. "And the gate guards saw you."

Benn was not worried. "They won't remember me, I'm just an ordinary kid. And I won't be ringing the Beguiler Bell, will I?"

Alex thought wistfully how nice it would be to be "just an ordinary kid." She put the codex back into the cupboard and closed the door with a quiet click. How easy it would be, she thought, if she could shut away all the Enchantment in her life in a cupboard and forget about it. But she couldn't. It was part of who she was. She knew that now.

"G'night, Alex," Benn said.

"G'night, Benn," said Alex. Silence fell in the little bedroom.

In the big room next door, all was quiet too. Deela and Hagos were sitting contentedly by the fire. Deela was unraveling an old green scarf of Hagos's so that she could knit it into something. She thought she might move on from octopuses to squid. Hagos was doing nothing much. He was gazing into the fire, allowing just the smallest flicker of something he identified as happiness to creep into his heart. Here he was, after all his long years in the wilderness, reconciled with his good friend Deela, and luxuriating in the knowledge—which he could hardly believe—that his little Boo-boo was back home, sleeping safely in her room.

Life, thought Hagos, was good.

CHAPTER 16
Home Truths

THE NEXT MORNING ALEX WOKE up in her bedroom for the first time in ten years. In the little bed she lay very still under the frayed pink velvet cover with appliquéd rabbits and gazed around the strange—and yet oh so familiar—room. Drowsily, she tried to find the elusive word to describe the mysterious feeling that surrounded her like a warm summer's day. Slowly, it came to her: *belonging.* Here it was at long last: a calm, solid baseline for everything. Alex knew that whatever she felt in the future—however scared, unhappy or even just plain bored—there would always be this feeling underpinning everything. She had found her family. She understood where she came from. She belonged. Everything else was extra.

Alex left Benn sleeping and ventured out into the main room. Deela was sitting by the fire knitting something green and Hagos was hunched over the desk beneath the triangular window that looked out over the other two towers. He turned around to Alex and smiled. "Good morning, Boo-boo. I'm just checking the Hawke egg. Would you like to see?" Hagos showed Alex an open box, revealing a nest of six golden boxes of decreasing sizes, like the bottom halves of a Russian doll with the tops removed. In the tiniest, seventh box in the middle, a little brown-and-white egg lay on a bed of soft, blue velvet.

"The egg will hatch here in the smallest box. When the fledgling grows out of that, we'll put it in the next bigger box, and then the next. After seven boxes it will be fully Enchanted, and then it will go back to the mews, and Ratchet—he's the chief falconer—will look after it."

"And then the king won't need you anymore, Poppa," Alex said anxiously.

Hagos nodded. "This is true. But I have a plan. There is something I made for your momma, something that I knew I could get smuggled to her in the dungeons—a little handkerchief with an Enchanted knot. All she had to do was to unknot it and it would take her to wherever she wanted to go."

"Oh, Poppa, what a lovely thing to do." Then Alex's

face clouded. "But it didn't work?"

"Your momma never had the chance to try it," Hagos said. "She . . . she died before I could get it to her."

"Oh." Alex could hardly bear to think about how close her mother had been to being saved.

"So then I was going to use it myself," Hagos continued, "but I couldn't find it. Not anywhere. But I know it is still here somewhere. I just *know* it." He smiled. "Don't worry, there is plenty of time to look for it. We will be fine. Now tell me, can you feel the Enchantment in this little box here?"

Alex was happy to stop thinking sad thoughts. She nodded. "It's very strong," she said.

"I knew you'd feel it. Even as a little one you were so talented."

"Was I?"

Hagos chuckled. "When you were in a bad mood you used to Fade."

"I used to do *Fades*?"

"Yes. You were very precocious. Your mother, who was a little bit Dark to Enchantment, could just about see you, but I couldn't. Not at all. It terrified me. That's why I never let go of your hand when we went out together." Hagos frowned. "But maybe I had a presentiment too, that I should never let go of you."

"Oh, Poppa," Alex said. "You saved me by letting me go. You know that."

"Knowing is not the same as feeling. Feeling it here." Hagos placed his balled fist over his heart and then, to hide his emotion, he busily opened a drawer in his desk and took out a blue enameled box. He flipped open the lid to reveal a stack of thin tissue paper, which he riffled through, then drew out a wafer-thin piece of paper covered with closely written formulas and symbols. "This is the Hawke's new and utterly benign Enchantment," Hagos said. "Would you like to add it to the codex?"

"I'll go and get it," Alex said. "It's in my bedside cupboard."

Hagos smiled. "No need to fetch it. Shall I show you how the codex works long distance?"

"Long distance?" asked Alex.

"Indeed." Hagos gave Alex the little square of tissue paper. "Just put this on your palm and then tell it to 'go home,'" he said.

Feeling a little foolish telling a piece of paper to go home, Alex did just that. She watched the delicate paper dissolve into wisps of mist; she felt a sudden rush of heat to her palm, and it was gone.

Hagos looked thrilled. "That was very well done, and very fast. Now where do you suppose it has gone?"

"In the codex! I'm going to get it," Alex said excitedly. She hurried off to her room and a moment later was back with the little blue book.

"So," said Hagos. "Now let's see inside, shall we?"

Alex laid the codex on the desk and tentatively opened it. The pages naturally fell open at the new Hawke Enchantment.

"Well done, Boo-boo!" Hagos said proudly. "That is not an easy thing to do. Did you see that, Deela?" Hagos called over to her. "Perfect first time."

Deela looked up from her knitting and smiled. It was wonderful, she thought, to see Hagos proudly teaching his daughter the secrets of Enchantment. "Very nice," she said.

Alex was buzzing. "That is so clever," she said.

Hagos nodded. He was pretty pleased with the system himself. "This is how all the Twilight Hauntings got into the codex. You see, by the time I was making them, my rather hopeless assistant, Sol, had already left Rekadom and taken the codex with him. But I always hoped I would see it again one day."

Alex was busy flipping through the pages to find what she wanted. "Poppa," she said, "you see it says here, 'One is One, Two is One, Tau is Three'?"

Hagos looked a little warily at his daughter. "Yes?"

"And then here, 'One to make it. Three to break it'?"

"Yes. Indeed."

Alex thought her father looked awkward, but she pressed on. "That means there are three things you need in order to break the Hauntings, right? And they are my Hex cards, the codex and the Tau. And they all have to be together at the same time."

"Indeed. This is the Triad. For this the cards and the Tau must be in their places in the codex," Hagos said stiffly. He did not like where this was going.

"And then the sealed pages will open to reveal the Disenchantment, won't they?"

"Well, they *would*, yes."

"Which means," said Alex excitedly, "that all we need to do to get rid of all the Hauntings is get the Tau back from the king."

Hagos sighed. He knew he was about to disappoint his daughter, and he really did not want to spoil the moment. "Unfortunately," he said, "I believe the Tau no longer exists."

Alex was aghast. "Why do you say that?"

Hagos drew her to the window. "You see the Iron Tower?"

Alex nodded. Even lit by the morning sun, it was dark and gloomy. With its windows sealed with iron shutters, it looked blind, and its gray granite stones seemed to suck in the sunlight.

"The Tau is in there," Hagos said. "Belamus made me watch him throw it in. Its Enchantment will be destroyed by now. The Wraiths will have consumed it."

"But how did he get it into the Tower? It's all closed up," Alex asked.

"There's a concealed opening above the door, for the

safe disposal of any Enchanted object or entity. In the old days all of us Enchanters used it. It was essential when I was trying to produce the Gray Walker. That was the toughest Haunting I've ever done, because it had no substance at all. All the other Hauntings, even the Xin, were worked around something physical—the Xin were small threads of spun silk, Alex, I can see you were going to ask—but it is the most delicate and difficult Enchantment to keep an entity together that has no substance. And do you know that once you Engender a Wraith there is no getting rid of it? I had *so* many that went wrong and they all had to be housed somewhere safe. The Iron Tower was perfect." Hagos smiled. "I remember one morning I was particularly grateful for it when Sol put his pet spider in an Enchanting box as a joke and the wretched thing would not stop growing. We got it into the Iron Tower in the nick of time."

Alex shuddered. "Is the spider still in there?"

"I sincerely hope so," Hagos said.

"Then surely the Tau is still in there too," Alex said.

Hagos shook his head gloomily. "The Tau has a finely balanced Enchantment. It is one part of a Triad, which makes it very delicate. I do not believe it can survive the rogue Wraiths in the Iron Tower."

"But you don't know that for sure, do you?" Alex persisted.

"I am ninety-nine percent sure," Hagos said.

"But not one hundred percent? Poppa, the Tau is way too important to give up on," Alex persisted. "It's our only chance to get rid of the Hauntings."

Hagos tried to smooth things over. "Now, don't you worry about those Hauntings, Boo-boo. Once I find the handkerchief, we can make a new life somewhere safe, far away from them."

Alex was shocked. "Poppa, no! You can't just run away and leave all that bad Enchantment behind. You made that mess. You *have* to put it right."

Hagos looked a little uncomfortable. "What's done is done. Please don't worry, Boo-boo—"

"Alex!" Alex told him angrily. "I'm *Alex*."

"Alex. Sorry. Look, Alex, it will be okay. We'll be fine."

"And what about everyone else?" Alex demanded. "Will *they* be fine? What about all the people whose lives you've ruined with your horrible Hauntings? What about when all your old Enchantments wear out and the Hauntings Turn and start attacking everyone whether they are Enchanters or not? Don't you even *care*?"

Hagos adopted a soothing tone that only annoyed Alex more. "Of course I care. But there is nothing I can do."

Alex was silent for a while. "Yes there is," she said quietly. She thrust the codex into her father's hand. "You have the codex. My cards are inside. Now you go get the Tau. Complete the Triad."

Hagos shook his head wearily. "Alex. Listen. If I open

the door to the Iron Tower I will let out all the horrors inside—bad Enchantments that will have become even more dangerous over the years. And like I said, I doubt the Tau has even survived. So what would be the point?"

"The point is not to give up." Alex's voice was raised now. "You have to try. You *have* to."

Hagos shook his head miserably.

Alex felt a wave of anger wash over her. "Clean up your mess, Poppa!" she yelled, and stormed back into her bedroom and slammed the door.

Deela looked up from knitting her squid. "She has a point, you know," she said.

"Don't you start," Hagos snapped. He stared gloomily out the window at the implacable mass of the Iron Tower.

The slam of the bedroom door woke Benn with a start. "Hey. What is it?" he asked, blearily sitting up. "What's wrong?"

"Poppa," Alex said. "He's wrong. *All wrong.*"

CHAPTER 17
The King Calls

SOME TEN MINUTES LATER—WHILE Alex was still explaining to Benn her father's complete lack of responsibility—there came an apologetic knock on the bedroom door.

Remembering how Danny had never let an argument fester, Hagos had decided to make the first move. "Alex?" he said.

Feeling a little sheepish about her outburst, Alex opened the door.

Hagos looked relieved. "Would you both like some coffee? Oh, do you drink coffee? Perhaps you're a little young for it. Um . . . now, what else have we got?" He looked questioningly at Deela.

"I have no idea," Deela said. "I've only been here a day." She looked at Alex. "It was only yesterday morning that your dear father rescued me from the dungeons. He is a good man, Alex. Despite his faults."

"What faults?" Hagos asked sharply.

Deela ignored him. "Actually, I think there is some mint tea in a jar thingy above the sink."

"I'll make it," Alex said, glad of something to do. She went over to the tiny kitchen alcove, opened a small cupboard above the sink and took down the tea caddy.

Hagos wandered over. "So long ago since you were here and you were so tiny, and yet you remember Pearl's tea cupboard," he murmured.

Alex looked at the tea caddy. The little figures dancing around it holding hands, the detail rubbed away by years of use, were achingly familiar. She flipped open the lid, the evocative smell of dried mint swam into her head, and she was suddenly back with her mother, clutching her long embroidered skirt, listening to her soft, singsong voice as she talked to "my little Boo-boo."

Alex stood immobile for some seconds and then she turned and threw herself into her father's arms. "Poppa!" she said, tears streaming down her face. "I *do* remember . . . I remember so much. Oh, Poppa."

Relieved she was not angry with him anymore, Hagos hugged his daughter.

While Alex and Benn drank mint tea by the fire, Hagos fussed around at his desk, glancing out the window every now and then. Suddenly he called out, "No! No! Go *away*!"

Deela, Alex and Benn leaped up and Hagos swung around with a look of panic on his face. "It's the king. He's on his way here!"

Deela grabbed what she thought of as her "Min cloak" and threw it on. "Stop panicking, Hagos," she told him.

"Boo-boo, Benn. You must hide! Oh, but where . . . where?" Hagos gazed uselessly around.

Deela was already hurrying Alex and Benn across the room. "There's a cupboard in the wall of your room. They can hide in there."

"It will be fine, Poppa," Alex said as she disappeared through the curtained-off arch into the little room with the trundle bed where Deela now slept.

Deela opened a hidden door in the wainscoting to reveal a dark, cobwebby space. It was not inviting. "I know it's not ideal, but you can both squeeze in," she said. "It won't be for long, and the door's thick enough to put the Jackal off the scent."

The mention of Jackal sent a chill down Alex's spine. She scrambled inside and was surprised to find how deep the cupboard was; it went right back into the thick wall of the tower. Benn followed, and as he curled himself up beside Alex, they heard banging on the front door and a yell of "Open up, Hagos! There's a dead Jackal out here. What's going on?"

Deela hurriedly closed the cupboard door on Alex and Benn; it fastened with a subdued click. Benn gave it a tentative push, but it did not move. It was not a good feeling—they were locked in until someone let them out. He just hoped that someone was Hagos or Deela and not a Jackal.

Deela pulled her hood down over her face and walked out to join Hagos. She was in time to see him open the door to the king, who was glowering outside on the landing, wearing a profusion of clashing silks. "Gracious me," Hagos was saying, "what has happened to the poor creature?"

"Poor creature my foot," said the king. "This is *your* doing, RavenStarr."

"Belamus, I swear to you, I have not set foot outside this door."

"Humph. It is most inconvenient. This means I am down to four Jackal now. Now let me in. I wish to see the Hawke egg. At once!"

Deela saw Hagos glance over his shoulder to check that all was safe, and she gave an imperceptible nod. Hagos threw open the door and the king, followed by his four remaining Jackal, came in. As Hagos escorted the king across to his desk to show him the Enchanting boxes and the Hawke egg, one of the Jackal dropped onto all fours and began sniffing the floor. From beneath the shadows of her hood, Deela watched it anxiously.

Inside the cupboard Alex sat with her knees up by her chin, feeling as if she was being squashed into a jar. Benn wriggled to try to get comfortable and stuck his elbow in her ear. Alex pressed herself even farther back and found she was sitting on a lump. It was a small piece of knotted cloth—smooth, fine cotton, soft to the touch, with scalloped edges—which she wound around her fingers in an effort to calm herself. She hated enclosed spaces.

Alex noticed that Benn's breathing was becoming fast and panicky. The atmosphere was stifling and there seemed to be no air coming in at all. In an effort to quell her own rising panic, Alex tried thinking about the Tau, remembering how protected she had felt when she had held it on Oracle Rock. How she wished she were with the Tau now . . .

Suddenly, Alex felt something shift. Hoping she'd found more space, she leaned back and felt as though she were on the edge of a great precipice. Giddy with the sense of height and breathless with the fear of it, she gasped.

"Alex, are you okay?" Benn whispered.

There was no reply.

Alone in the cupboard, Benn called out in terror, "Alex, Alex!"

But Alex was gone.

Alex was falling into an abyss. Spinning and whirling through a howling gale of shrieks and screams, buffeted by a freezing wind, she curled herself tightly into a ball as she flew through the darkness, her hands over her mouth to keep out the choking dust that bit into her eyes and filled her ears. Tumbling around and down as though on a crazy helter-skelter, Alex heard distant voices chanting, snatches of a sung melody, a piercing shriek of terror, a sudden rush of water, a crack of thunder, a graveside dirge, desolate and low, and the lost and lonely *yip-yip-yip* of an abandoned dog. As she fell, a forest of sticky tendrils brushed against her, snatching at her clothes, and a waft of putrid breath caused her to retch. Tumbling past a myriad of yellow eyes, through the soft hissing of snakes and eerie flashes of blue lightning, Alex at last came to a stop in a sudden softness that enfolded her. She curled up like a little pill bug waiting, and there she stayed, bouncing gently up and down in what felt like a giant sticky hammock.

Still clutching the handkerchief, Alex lay in the bluish gloom, listening to the sounds surrounding her—a cacophony of furtive rustlings, clickings, twangings, tinny bell-like sounds and a heavy, breathy wheezing filled the air. Warily, she uncurled herself a little, and a tremor ran through the hammock. Out of the darkness she saw a cluster of eight tiny points of red light. The lights pulsed slowly, like a heartbeat, and Alex froze with fear.

Alex forced herself to think. Her fingers found the threads of the hammock, which stuck to her like glue. She lifted her hand and the threads came with it. Another tremor ran through the hammock and the eight eyes mirrored the movement. Alex knew she must stay still. She remembered how she had once seen a beautifully delicate moth trapped in a spider's web. Unable to free the creature without injuring it, she had watched as its every struggle had brought the spider a step closer, until suddenly the spider had pounced and the moth was crumpled up like a tiny paper bag.

Alex had worked it out now. The eight eyes belonged to a giant spider, and the hammock was its web. *And she was the moth.*

CHAPTER 18

Discovered

SCRITCH-SCRATCH . . . SCRITCH-SCRATCH.

Benn heard the Jackal rake its claws down the cupboard door, and then came a deep, throaty sniffing. He curled up into a defensive ball and waited.

Now came the reedy tones of the king. "There's someone in the wainscoting. A door! I see a door!" The faint sound of a pointy-toed silk shoe tapping on the door made Benn shrink even further into himself. "Open it!" he heard the king yell. "Open it!"

In reply came the lower, smoother tones of Hagos. "But Your Majesty, it is but an old store cupboard."

"I am being deceived!" the king yelled. "What are you keeping from me?"

"Your Majesty, we keep nothing from you," Hagos was protesting. Benn wished he wouldn't. He just wanted to get it over with. To get out of the hateful cupboard and deal with whatever was coming.

But Hagos would not give up. "Your Majesty," he was saying. "Inside that closet are the Hawke Meister's tools of Engenderment. They need darkness and tranquility. To avoid contamination, they must be kept away from other Engendered creatures—like your Jackal. If you open that door, your Hawke will never attain the magnificence it deserves."

But the king was having none of it. "You take me for an utter fool, RavenStarr!" he yelled.

Like a snail curling into its shell, Benn shrank into himself, wrapping his arms over his head.

Now came the voice of the king, no longer aggrieved but fully in command. "Open that door, RavenStarr. *Open it.*"

"I will not," came Hagos's voice.

"Then I shall kill you," the king said, so slowly and deliberately that the hairs on the back of Benn's neck prickled. "The Hawke Meister I shall let live until the Engenderment is done. But you, RavenStarr, are finished. Unless you open this door *right now.*"

Benn could stand it no longer. He could not bear it if

Alex—wherever she was—lost her father now. He took a deep breath and banged on the door, yelling, "Let me out. It's only me, Benn Markham. There's no one else in here. No one! Let me out!"

There was a fumbling of the latch and the door swung open. Benn fell out onto the rug and landed hard on the pointy toes of the king's blue silk shoes.

The king gave a screech of pain and leaped back. "Beguiler's brat! It is the Beguiler's brat!"

Oblivious to Benn, who was curled up into a ball on the rug and being clawed at by the Jackal, Hagos stared into the darkness of the open cupboard. Slowly, he registered the fact that his daughter was not there. He could not feel her presence. She was gone. The king's hand landed heavily upon his shoulder and, his mind racing, Hagos swung around to face him.

"You are dead, RavenStarr, do you hear?" King Belamus snarled. "Dead!"

Hagos stared at Belamus, taking in the viciousness in the king's eyes. How, Hagos wondered, had this man ever been his friend?

"Conspiring against me, that is all you have ever done!" the king was ranting, the wings of his crown wobbling in indignation. "And now harboring a Beguiler's brat under my nose!"

Suddenly Deela's voice cut through the noise. "Brat? This is no brat!"

The king wheeled around and stared at Deela with narrowed eyes. Haughtily, Deela returned the stare. Belamus turned back to Hagos and said accusingly, "You said, RavenStarr, that this Min spoke only the language of the Hawke."

Hagos thought fast. "Surely, Your Majesty, you did not think it would take such a powerful being as Min any longer than twenty-four hours to imbibe our modest tongue?"

"What?" said Belamus.

Hagos had recently had practice translating his words for Danny, who had a simpler approach to life, and he now made good use of it. "Min learned to speak our language last night. It is not difficult. Is it, Min?"

"It is simple," replied Deela. "And I demand the king keep his white dogs off my young assistant."

"Assistant?" Hagos and Belamus said together.

"My assistant," said Deela firmly.

Belamus narrowed his eyes and stared at Benn, who lay curled up at his feet. "That is the Beguiler's brat I saw last night."

Hagos hurriedly stepped in. "Your Majesty. It is a known ploy of"—he stopped, took a deep breath and forced himself to say the hated words—"Beguiler's brats to personate innocent assistants."

"What?" asked Belamus.

"Beguiler's brats," said Deela. "Everyone knows they

pretend to be other kids." Without waiting for another objection, she pulled Benn to his feet. "Min's assistant has been with Min all the time. He is here in the closet doing his job of guarding Min's tools of Engenderment," she said. "Min suggests to the king that if he desires to possess the most powerful and beautiful Hawke he has ever seen, he calls his white dogs off Min's assistant at once."

The king gave in. He shooed the Jackal away, leaving Deela gently wiping away their sticky spittle from Benn's face and hands.

"Where is Alex?" Hagos whispered to Benn.

Benn shook his head. He wished he knew.

Alex was on the gluey hammock of a giant spider's web, watching two lines of glowing red eyes staring at her. She saw the shadowy outline of the spider slowly rearing up, its two front legs waving in the air, and she threw herself facedown onto the sticky threads. The web gave a great shudder and Alex felt the rough scales of the spider's legs brush against her. Desperately she scrabbled against the threads, pulling them aside. A small gap appeared, through which—to the shock of both Alex and the spider—a beam of brilliant blue light shone upward. The spider reared up and Alex's spirits soared. Some distance below, she could see a tiny, pulsating T shape. *The Tau.*

Hope gave Alex renewed strength. She wrenched the threads apart and dropped through the gap, landing on the spiral steps that wound around the inside wall of the Iron Tower. Battling through the Wraiths, guided by the light of the Tau, she fought her way down, and as she descended the blue light grew ever brighter, until at last she arrived in the middle of such brilliance that she had to shield her eyes.

The Tau lay in front of the huge iron door that led out of the tower. Alex crouched down and tentatively curled her fingers around it. It was cool and smooth to the touch. The blue enamel shone within sinuous bands of silver and gold, and she could feel its power. A quiet voice came into her mind saying, *I am Tau*.

"I am Alex RavenStarr," she whispered in return.

I am with you, you are with me. We are Two with the Power of Three. Please, take me from this place, the voice murmured in her thoughts.

"I will, I will," Alex whispered. She got to her feet, heart pounding with excitement. Now all she had to do was get out. But how?

With me. I am the key, came the answer to her question.

Alex looked at the door, which towered above her, dark and looming like a massive gravestone, flat and featureless. She could see no keyhole. "Where do you go?" she whispered.

Below.

Alex knelt down, and in the blue light she saw in the

bottom corner of the door a tarnished circle of silver.

There, the voice told her.

With the hem of her sleeve, Alex rubbed away the tarnish so that the silver glimmered in the blue light of the Tau. Fingers trembling, Alex pushed the Tau against the silver. She felt a buzz of Enchantment run through her fingertips and then deep within the door she felt the complex barrels in the lock turning, followed by a final *kerrr-plick* as they whirred into place and drew back the bolt. Alex stood up and pushed the door. It did not move. She leaned against it and shoved with all her might. It did not shift. As the Wraiths swirled around her, sensing her despair, Alex felt all hope drain away.

And then she heard the Tau: *This door*, it whispered, *will always open toward you.*

CHAPTER 19

Lurking

ZERRA WAS LURKING. NOT, THOUGHT Zerra, that there was any reason to lurk—Rekadom must be the most boring place in the whole world, where nothing ever happened—but she took her job as King's Spy seriously and hoped that eventually she would find something worth lurking for.

Zerra was at the foot of the Iron Tower, of which she approved. There was something about its rusted iron door with the streaks of red running down the pitted metal and its tiny windows covered with thick iron plates that felt real. And what lay within fascinated Zerra; she could feel its power seeping out, no matter how many rivets secured the windows and how massive the slab of iron was that formed the door.

In the dusty warmth of the afternoon sun, Zerra kicked at the litter that had collected around the unswept edges of the tower and scuffed at the weeds that grew unnibbled by rabbits or goats. In the shadows of the deep-set iron doorway she idly watched a bevy of young rabbits hop carelessly toward the brilliant enticing green of the weeds. She chuckled when, as they reached the shadows of the Iron Tower, they leaped backward, as if hit by an electric shock, and scooted away, their little white bobtails bouncing as they went.

Blending into the darkness of the ice-cold archway, Zerra saw a flurry of activity emerging from the Silver Tower. Four Jackal came bounding out, closely followed by none other than King Belamus. *Bother*, thought Zerra, *him again*. She stepped back into the shadows and watched the king stride past, his winged crown catching the sun, his bright silks flowing behind him, the tinny tap of his metal-heeled shoes striking the cobbles. She wondered what it must be like to have only those creepy Jackal for company. *Who did he talk to? Did he have any friends at all?* Zerra supposed not. She pushed away a sneaking thought that she didn't have any friends either. *She was an important spy, so what did stupid friends matter anyway?*

Zerra was leaning back against the iron door, admiring

her new wristband, when suddenly the door was no longer there, something shoved her in the back, and she went flying off the step and landed on the cobbles. She lay winded for a few moments, her bandaged arm throbbing with the force of the fall. Slowly, she got to her feet and turned to see what had hit her. "Alex!" she gasped.

The door to the Iron Tower clanged shut behind her and Alex stood blinking in the sunlight, watching a smoky wisp of Wraith that had escaped with her curl itself up like a small black snake and slide off into the shadows at the base of the tower. Suddenly something leaped up and threw itself at her.

"Zerra!" Wondering how come Zerra seemed to lurk behind most of the doors in Rekadom, Alex neatly side-stepped her foster sister, who went stumbling into the wall, bounced off and grabbed Alex once more.

With all her strength, Alex pushed Zerra away and sent her sprawling to the ground. Hurriedly, she tucked the Tau into the secret pocket of her sash and set off at a run.

Alex longed to head back to the Silver Tower and return the Tau to its rightful place inside the codex, but she did not dare. King Belamus was probably still up there, and even if he weren't, Zerra would follow her and betray them all to him. Alex knew that before she could safely go home—she loved the new meaning the word "home" had for her—she must lose Zerra.

Taking the only route she knew—the way that she and Benn had come into the Inner Star—Alex raced across Star Court with Zerra in pursuit. Rabbits scuttling out of her way, Alex headed down the deserted street and almost at the end, where it narrowed to a point, she scooted into the ginnel that led to the door into Mews Court. Behind her came the echo of Zerra's footsteps, fast upon the cobbles—but they were not fast enough.

Alex wrenched down the lever in the wall, the little plank door to the Outer Star flew open, and she hurtled through and slammed it shut. Out in Mews Court, Alex ran past the falconry mews and headed across the open courtyard for the Star Snicket. If only she could get through it before Zerra rounded the end of the mews and saw her, she would be okay. She threw herself through the snicket into Gate Court, hid in the shadows and tried to catch her breath so that she could begin a Fade.

From Mews Court, Alex could hear Zerra yelling, "Beguiler! Beguiler!" As she shrank back, Zerra's yells suddenly changed to "Get off me! Let me go!" Intrigued, Alex could not resist peering through the snicket to see what was happening. She was just in time to see the highly satisfying sight of Zerra being marched into the mews by a steely-looking young woman wearing a falconer's leather jerkin. Alex almost laughed out loud with relief—now she could get back to the Silver Tower.

Alex slipped easily into her Fade, then she set off back

into Mews Court, past the falconry mews—which was oddly quiet—to the door to the Inner Star. When she got to the door, Alex pushed it hard, but it did not move. Of course it didn't, she thought. Not only had she slammed it shut, but Zerra obviously had too. She was going to have to find another way back. Deciding to try the court with the orchards that she had seen yesterday, Alex ran back into Gate Court and then walked quietly toward the Rekadom gates, where the two gate guards from the previous day, the aunt and nephew, had just come back on duty. A flock of crows was perched on the elegant iron hoop that spanned the gates and from which hung the large Beguiler Bell. Alex knew that the bell was Enchanted—by her father, of course—and would ring a warning whenever an Enchanter passed beneath it. A new wave of anger came over Alex with her father for all the Enchantments he had created that made her life so difficult. Right then, it felt like a personal betrayal. Doubts began to creep into her mind. If she took the Tau to him now, would he really Disenchant all the wicked things he had created? Or would he just smile in his inscrutable way and do nothing?

A flash of red on the far side of Gate Court took Alex's attention—it was the coat of a Jackal. Keeping to the shadows of the city wall, her gaze fixed upon the Jackal, which was now tinkering with one of the chariots, Alex crept nearer to the city gates. She needed to go past them to get to the next snicket, but as she inched around the tall pillar that formed the side of the gateway, the flock of crows took to the air with loud warning cries. Thinking she must have made a noise to disturb them, she stopped and waited for them to settle. What Alex did not know was that crows were spooked by Enchantment, and it was her Fade, which had a buzz that made the crows' beaks rattle, that was upsetting the birds. Suddenly, two crows dived at her, pulling up at the last moment. Alex ducked, throwing her hands up over her head to protect herself. Then more crows dropped toward her and circled, cawing a warning, sending the flock above into a loud, echoing caw-fest.

The Jackal stopped what it was doing and watched the crows with great interest. The nearest gate guard— the aunt—put her javelin at the ready and began walking slowly toward the crows. Alex felt as visible as if she were glowing bright orange. Suddenly, the Jackal dropped down on all fours and broke into a run, heading straight for her and the crows. Alex made a decision. Knowing that Jackal were not allowed outside the city walls without the king's permission, she dodged around the approaching aunt, raced past the Jackal and took a sharp right at the open gates, leaving the crows to turn their attentions to another unsettling source of Enchantment—the hapless Jackal, which was now rolling on the cobbles covered with a black blanket of pecking birds.

As Alex ran beneath the Beguiler Bell, it gave a loud warning clang, and the nephew jumped forward, javelin outstretched. The young man stared at the flat, open desert beyond. He thought he saw a few disturbances in the dry, sandy soil, and he let loose his javelin toward them. The javelin landed with a soft thud, burying its tip in the ground only a few feet behind Alex, sending her running faster than she thought possible.

Embarrassed at his useless throw, the nephew hurried out to retrieve his javelin, and then he and his aunt obeyed the Beguiler Bell protocol—they pulled the city gates closed and set the bar across.

Locked out of Rekadom, Alex left the city walls behind her and headed toward the cliff top and the freedom of the ocean beyond.

CHAPTER 20

Alone

ZERRA WAS IN RATCHET'S OFFICE, standing opposite Bartlett, who had taken possession of Ratchet's desk and his swivel chair. "I am not a Beguiler's brat," Zerra spoke with a cold, calm fury. "But by grabbing me, you have let a real one escape. I will report you to the king."

This time Zerra's trick of staring people down and speaking very slowly did not work. Bartlett sprang to her feet and grabbed Zerra's collar. "You will do no such thing, you nasty little owl pellet. You may have fooled Ratchet with your lies, but you don't fool me, girl. Beguiler's brat or not, I know one thing for sure. You are no Dark."

Zerra knew she was on tricky ground here. She had twice watched Alex vanish before her eyes and knew very well she was no Dark. But there was no way she was going to let Bartlett know that. "I am the Flyer," Zerra said, making her voice low and threatening. "And you will do well to remember that, Bartlett." And then she turned around and walked out of the office. She did not get far.

"Oh, no, you don't." Bartlett had hold of her collar again.

Zerra wheeled around angrily and, with her good arm, she grabbed at Bartlett's sinewy hand. "Get off me!" she hissed. "You have no right to grab hold of me."

Bartlett smiled. "Oh, but there you are quite wrong. As deputy chief falconer, I have all kinds of rights over the Flyer—particularly a trainee Flyer. If you do not wish for a practical demonstration of a few of them, I suggest that you modify your behavior right now. Understood?"

The steel in Bartlett's voice cut through Zerra's anger. Slowly, she took her hand away from Bartlett's clutching claw. "Good call," said Bartlett.

But Zerra, although quieter, was still fuming. "Where's Ratchet?" she asked.

"That's 'the chief falconer' to you, girl."

Zerra pushed down her irritation. "The chief falconer. Where is he?"

"Nosy little baggage, aren't you? Well, seeing as you are

so concerned for him, you will be pleased to know that the chief falconer is enjoying himself visiting his mother in Netters Cove. He took a horse this morning and will be gone for three days."

Zerra felt oddly bereft. Why hadn't Ratchet told her he was going away? The thought of three days alone with Bartlett was not good.

"So, girl," Bartlett continued. "Let me tell you your schedule while the chief falconer is away. Four a.m. Falcon-Call. Four thirty, commence cleaning duties. The mews is filthy. I want every speck of bird poo removed from between the cobbles. Midday: fifteen-minute break for lunch, which you will take with the birds. Afternoon, continue cleaning. Six thirty, bread and cheese supper with the birds. Seven prompt, bed."

"But I'm a King's Spy now," objected Zerra. "I have to do that too."

"Tell that to the chief falconer," said Bartlett.

"But he's not here," Zerra said plaintively.

"Exactly," said Bartlett. She handed Zerra a tiny brush, a scraper and a bucket. "You can start on the cobbles under the nesting boxes. They're thick with the stuff. I want them shining by supper, otherwise you'll go to bed without. Understood?"

What Zerra understood was that Bartlett would have to go—there was no way she was putting up with this for three whole days. Sulkily holding the poop-cleaning equipment, she stared down at the cobbles. *What*, she wondered, *have those birds been eating?*

Alex reached the cliff top and climbed up onto the old railway platform. She stood beneath the rusting sign that declared it to be Oracle Halt and looked back at Rekadom, with its high walls and the pointy tips of the three towers rising up from the center of the fortified city. She squinted up at the tiny triangular windows at the top of the Silver Tower, wondering if Poppa knew she was gone. Or was Benn still in that creepy cupboard all on his own? Maybe the king had left by now and Benn was out, telling Poppa that she had vanished. Whatever was happening up there, she knew it couldn't be good.

Alex turned around from the city and, shading her eyes, she surveyed the restless gray-blue sea, then she looked to her left, along the cliff tops. All she saw was a seemingly endless flat expanse of gritty soil scattered with small rocks and scrub, ending in a hazy line where the pale, dusty horizon met the pale, dusty sky. This, Alex knew, was the territory of one of her father's more dramatic Hauntings—the Skorpas. The night before he had told her that to create each one he had taken a live scorpion and placed it in an Enchanting chamber buried in the desert sand. Over the next twenty-four hours the scorpion would expand at a rapid rate until it burst out from beneath the sand, the size of a small house—and a whole lot more venomous. The sting on the tail was loaded, Hagos had told her proudly, with enough venom to kill ten horses at once.

Alex knew that the Skorpas lay dormant beneath mounds of sand during the day. She looked up at the sun. It was still high in the sky, but was already on its downward path toward the distant horizon. She *had* to be out of the desert before it set. She remembered that Benn had said that somewhere near Oracle Halt was a flight of steps down through the cliff to the beach below. But where? How she wished Benn were here with her now. What now felt scary would be fun. They could search for the steps together, and she was sure that together they could find them. Alex sighed. The thought of Benn made her feel even more alone.

The thought of Alex was making Benn feel alone too. Where was she? Hagos was staring out of the window miserably. "Can you see Alex?" Benn asked.

Hagos shook his head and moved over so that Benn could look out too. Benn watched from the window, hoping maybe he'd catch sight of Alex's distinctive green headband and sash, although he still didn't understand how she could have gotten out of the cupboard and now be somewhere else entirely.

Deela joined them. "Alex will come back," she said.

"It's just some silly Enchantment gone wrong. She'll be fine, you'll see."

But Benn could tell that Hagos didn't think that. Abruptly, the Enchanter left the window and strode away to his little room, where Benn guessed he'd be staring into the closet in the wainscoting, as though he might find Alex there after all.

Alone by the window, his longing for home overcame Benn. "I have to go home," he told Deela.

Deela looked anxious. "But, Benn, you're safe in here with us. Alex would want you to stay, I know she would." Deela gave a little laugh. "She's probably playing a trick on us all and is still here. Just done a little Fade for a joke."

Benn was indignant. "Alex would never do that!" he said. "She would never watch us all being so upset about her just for fun. *Never.*"

"Indeed she would not," Hagos said, returning from another fruitless search of the cupboard in the wainscoting. "Benn, if you want to go home, I will help you."

"Hagos!" Deela remonstrated. "You don't know what you're saying. There's another Jackal outside the door." She dropped her voice. "You can't kill another one."

"I didn't kill that one," Hagos said irritably. "Another Jackal must have got it when it was weak. Nothing to do with me." He turned to Benn. "I will see you safely out of the city, but after that you will be on your own. Do you still wish to go home?"

"Yes," Benn said. "I do. And thank you. Thank you very much."

"And Deela, before you ask any more questions, I shall get out of here in exactly the same way I did as when I took you from the dungeons," Hagos told her. "I shall be the king."

Benn and Deela watched as Hagos put his hands up to either side of his head, with the palms facing inward and the fingers splayed out so they resembled, Ben thought, the silver wings of the king's crown. They even seemed a little metallic. And there was a strange silvery light around Hagos's head too. Hagos lowered his hands and began to move them slowly down his torso, and as he did so, the silver light traveled with him and his cloak began to shine like silk. Hagos made a sudden downward, sweeping motion, a shimmer ran over him, and in front of Benn stood an oddly insubstantial image of King Belamus the Great. "Come on, boy, don't keep me waiting," Hagos said, in an eerily accurate impression of King Belamus's pompous whine.

Deela hugged Benn tightly. "Safe journey," she said.

Benn nodded. "Thanks."

"Ready, boy?" Hagos said in his king's voice.

Benn grinned. "Ready, Your Majesty."

"Very well. We will go." Hagos took a deep breath and then threw open the door out onto the landing. The

Jackal jumped to attention and then whined uneasily. The master did not smell right.

Hagos fought back the mix of revulsion and fear that being close to a Jackal always gave him. "Stand aside," he growled menacingly.

The Jackal hesitated.

Hagos knew he had to act fast. He raised his voice to a shrill approximation of the king's angry squeal. "Down, cur!" he yelled.

To Hagos's relief, the Jackal dropped to the ground and groveled. It knew the master must be obeyed at all times—even when the master smelled of incense and fear. From under its tiny hooded eyes, the Jackal watched its shimmering master hurry down the steps with his boy prisoner. Then it got to its feet and stood guard at the door as its master had decreed.

Alex was sitting despondently on the edge of the tiny platform of Oracle Halt. She had searched in vain for any steps and all the time the sun was moving across the sky, and the afternoon shadows were growing longer. Deep in her disappointment, Alex felt her Fade leaving her. She gazed out at Oracle Rock, which lay calm and apparently deserted, a bell-shaped island of granite, crisscrossed with paths and steps, topped with the strange little cottage where she and Benn had briefly thought they were safe. Alex gazed at it for some time, hoping maybe to see Palla and call out for help, but there was no movement but for the wheeling of gulls, no sound but their eerie cry and the swash of the waves. Fiercely, Alex wiped away a stray tear that had escaped and wandered down her cheek. *You're on your own now*, she told herself. *Get used to it.*

The sun went behind a large, gray cloud and Alex shivered. She had to be out of the desert by sunset, and the only place she could hope to reach by then was Netters Cove, the small fishing village where a few days ago she had found Benn waiting in Merry. But Netters Cove was so far away she could scarcely make out its distinctive headland—the Thirteenth Titan—on the misty horizon. She must move fast.

Alex set off at a brisk trot along the cliff top, and soon discovered that beneath a thin layer of sandy grit was the old railway track. She was surprised; at school they had been told that the king had torn up the track across the desert. Her spirits rose a little. She remembered Benn telling her that there was an old railway halt at Netters Cove, and she guessed the track would take her there. Following a track where so many others had gone before gave Alex a strange feeling of companionship. As she hurried along, she no longer felt quite so alone.

CHAPTER 21

Revenge

BARTLETT WAS ENJOYING BEING ALONE in the office. She was also enjoying the sound of scraping as the Flyer got down to some real work for a change. She wandered over to the window and was unscrewing the top of the cookie jar—chocolate cookies were her favorite—when a strange sight caught her attention. Frowning, she watched the progress of the king and a somewhat grubby boy. Bartlett wiped the greasy glass to get a better view—something was not right. In fact, quite a few things weren't right. One: the king was without his Jackal bodyguard, and the king never went into the Outer Star without a Jackal in tow. Two: he was oddly shimmery, and it wasn't just his bad-taste silks. Three: the king was with a scruffy urchin, but everyone knew that the king hated kids. Bartlett screwed up her eyes and stared hard.

Happily, Hagos was unaware of Bartlett's suspicious examination of his Enchantment—or Personation, as it was called. If he had known, he would have been very spooked. Because the Personation moved, spoke and projected itself it had a lot of work to do and depended upon people seeing what they expected to see. It did not hold up if—as Bartlett was doing—someone looked at it too critically.

Zerra was poking at a particularly noxious piece of bird poop when Bartlett threw open the office door and strode past, her boots narrowly missing Zerra's left hand. Stonily, Zerra watched her tormentor head out of the mews into the sunlit courtyard beyond. She listened to the sound of her hurried footsteps, and when she was sure Bartlett was not coming back, Zerra got up and took the bucket of bird mess into the office, where she sprinkled a fine shower of dried dirt into the cookie jar on the windowsill and screwed the lid back on. Then she tipped the rest of the contents of the bucket into Bartlett's messenger bag. Quickly, Zerra took her confiscated training Lightning Lance from where it was hanging behind the door and two lightning bolts from the ammunition box. Then she loaded the lance, tucked it into its holster and strapped it on.

Zerra strode through the gloom of the mews, her hurried footsteps sending the nesting birds into a flurry of warning screeches. At the door, she peered out and was pleased to see the courtyard was empty. With a lightness in her step, she headed out into the sunshine. Mews Court was empty, but Zerra could hear Bartlett's bullying tones from Gate Court next door. Intrigued, she headed across to the Star Snicket and slipped into the shadows of the neighboring Gate Court.

In front of the closed city gates, Zerra saw Bartlett flanked by both gate guards. All three had their back to Zerra, but facing them was, to Zerra's surprise, the king. Although Zerra could not hear what Bartlett was actually saying, her tone of voice was unmistakable—Bartlett was haranguing the king. Zerra was impressed. She just *had* to hear more. Gambling on the king being too taken up with Bartlett to notice her, Zerra snuck along by the wall, keeping to the shadows until she reached the shelter of a wide stone buttress, where she stopped and peered out. Now she could see a new member of the group. To Zerra's surprise, it was the boy who had been with Alex when they had so rudely pushed past her into the Inner Star. Zerra smiled—so Alex's little boyfriend was the king's prisoner now, was he? That served him right.

But as the words of the acrimonious conversation drifted over to Zerra, she became even more intrigued. Bartlett was calling the king a Beguiler! Zerra chuckled.

Oh, this was so good. Bartlett was destined for the dungeons, that was for sure. It was a shame she'd not be able to watch Bartlett eat a cookie from the bird-poo jar, but this was even better.

And then, to Zerra's delight, a fight kicked off. Bartlett grabbed hold of the boy's collar and the king roughly pulled her hand away from the boy. Bartlett lunged at the king again but he shoved her away, pushed open the little wicket inside the barred gates and yelled at the boy, "Run! Get yourself home!" in a surprisingly strong voice that didn't sound like the king at all.

With that, the boy was out of the gate and gone.

Zerra found herself envying the boy. He was free now, out of this dump of a city and on his way home. At the thought of home, Zerra felt a twist of unease. The boy was lucky—he had a home to go to. But she didn't. She was stuck here with no friends and no family. All she'd had for company all afternoon had been a load of stupid birds and a bucket of old bird poop. A little niggle of a thought—*and whose fault is that*—threatened to surface, but Zerra was saved by the sight of Bartlett chasing the king back across the courtyard. They passed close by, but neither noticed her. The king was striding angrily on and Bartlett was matching his strides step for step as they headed for the Star Snicket back into Mews Court. Intrigued, Zerra slunk quickly back along the foot of the wall, keeping pace with them. She saw the king take a surprisingly athletic bound onto the Rocadile step, and then turn to face Bartlett, who was now at a height disadvantage. He raised his arms up very dramatically and then . . . *disappeared.*

Bartlett gave a howl of triumph and lunged forward, but her hands met empty air, and to Zerra's delight, she fell forward and toppled facedown over the snicket in a highly undignified manner.

While Bartlett picked herself up and limped off into the mews courtyard, Zerra mulled over what she had seen. Her hand strayed to the twisted black-and-gold strands with their chunky silver seal on her wrist, and she almost laughed out loud with excitement. She could hardly believe her luck. She'd been the King's Spy for only a day and already she had something amazing to report.

But maybe, Zerra thought, *I can do even better.*

If she could catch the boy and bring him back to the king, how good would that be? And maybe he would lead her to Alex and she could catch her too—and bring them *both* to the king. Zerra smiled. What fun it would be to go visit Alex in the dungeons and make her feel really bad. Of course, after a while it would get boring, and then she could just forget about her. And know-it-all Alex would be gone for good, because no one survived the dungeons for long.

Weaving her dreams of revenge and glory, Zerra decided to go after the boy. She headed over to the city gates and waved her King's Spy wristband at the gate guards, who respectfully opened the wicket gate for her to step through.

Head held high, Zerra walked beneath the flock of crows back on their perch beside the Beguiler Bell. The bell rang and behind her the young guard looked out the wicket gate, puzzled.

"Stupid crows rang the bell," Zerra said. "You ought to get that fixed."

The guard shrugged and closed the gate.

Zerra hurried away. When she was clear of the city, she took out her spyglass and surveyed the vast scrubby desert before her. All was still except for a drifting trail of dust and the distant figure of the boy, running. Smiling, Zerra primed her training lance and broke into a run. She was good at this spying job. No, she wasn't just good— she was incredibly, amazingly *brilliant*.

CHAPTER 22
Near Misses

"ALEX!" BENN YELLED OUT. "HEY, Alex!" With a wonderful feeling of joy and relief, he raced toward the figure running from Rekadom. Then he saw a glint of steel and stopped—*why is Alex pointing a Lightning Lance at me?* It took another long second for Benn to understand that despite the figure moving in just the same way Alex did, it wasn't her at all.

It was Zerra.

Benn's joy turned to terror—he had seen for himself the damage the Lightning Lance could do. He turned and ran back toward the edge of the cliff, where he skidded to a halt. He looked down at the sandy strip of beach far below, and at the clear green waters beginning to creep away from the causeway that joined Oracle Rock to the mainland. At the far end of the causeway, the familiar bell shape of Oracle Rock rose up solid against the sky and his heart gave a wistful twist as he glimpsed his little white boat, Merry, rocking gently in the harbor. Oh, how he wished he was on Merry now, sailing away from this awful place.

But you're not, Benn told himself. He spun around to see Zerra rapidly approaching, the sun glinting off her lance as she raised it and pointed it at him.

Benn took a step to one side to get out of the line of fire, and his foot landed on something hollow. He raised his hands and yelled, "Don't shoot! Please! Don't shoot!" all the while moving his foot to explore what was beneath it. It was definitely a covering of some kind. And then his big toe found a metal ring. Benn thought fast. This must be the trapdoor to the steps, he was sure of it. But they were no use to him if Zerra saw him go down them. He didn't even want to think about the damage a bolt from a Lightning Lance would do in a narrow tunnel in the rock. Somehow, he had to get down there without Zerra seeing him.

Benn took a long, deep breath in. And then, injecting a sudden terror into his voice, he screamed out, "Zerra! Behind you! Skorpas!" and threw himself onto the hatch, so he was scrabbling for its handle while covering his head with one hand as if terrified. Zerra stopped, uncertain. Benn gave the handle an exploratory twist and felt it move. Aware that Zerra was still aiming the lance at him, he raised himself up so he was kneeling beside the hatch and, ramping up the drama now, he screamed, "No! No! Run, Zerra, Run!"

Zerra stared at Benn. She had never seen anyone look so scared. The hairs on the back of her neck began to prickle, and as Benn shrieked out for the third time, "Skorpas! Run!" she was suddenly convinced there was indeed something truly terrible behind her. She spun around—and saw that she had fallen for the oldest trick in the book. Zerra wheeled back and screamed out at Benn two of the new swear words she had learned the night she had spent in the Luma House of Orphans. But he wasn't there. He had *disappeared.*

He's a Beguiler's brat. He's done a Fade. What did you expect, you dummy? she told herself angrily as she set off at a run toward where Benn had been. And then she stopped. *This*, she thought, *is a trick. He's trying to get me to go to the cliff edge and then he'll push me off. Well, I'm not that dumb. I'll show him.*

Zerra raised her Lightning Lance, and taking a very careful aim, she fired at the place where she had last seen Benn. The bolt shot off in a loud whoosh, trailing a band of blue light behind it. Zerra waited for contact with an invisible boy, but the bolt traveled on, over the edge of the cliff and out to sea. Angrily, Zerra watched its trajectory as her wasted missile made a graceful arc down toward the water and disappeared into the sea in a fizzle of white foam.

Zerra employed a few more new swear words. "I know you're there, brat!" she yelled out. "You don't fool me!"

But the only reply Zerra got was the swash of the retreating sea far below and the sudden call of a gull, which was—*she just knew it*—mocking her.

Far below Zerra's feet, Benn was deep inside the cliff, stumbling down rough-cut steps in a tunnel in the darkness. He went as fast as he dared, convinced that Zerra must have seen where he'd gone and would be after him. At last he reached the point where the steps joined those going up to Rekadom, where the Jackal had taken him and Alex the day before. Pushing away all thoughts of Alex, Benn leaped down onto the wider steps, and soon he could see daylight coming up from the entrance on the beach below. A minute later Benn was out on the damp sand of the beach, running toward the causeway. There were still six inches of water covering the highest point, but Benn did not care. He ran into the sea and splashed his way across the soft sand. As he reached the middle of the causeway, the water grew deeper, but Benn continued wading until at last he reached the firm ground near Oracle Rock. Dripping with water, he raced up the steps and headed along the path that led to the harbor. He took a while to free the oars from their knots, but then he was down the harbor steps and jumping into Merry, where he sat, getting his breath back, letting the feeling of relief slowly wash over him.

Some minutes later, Benn was rowing Merry out of the harbor. A feeling of sadness came over him as he remembered how he had arrived there with Alex and with such optimism, and now he would probably never see her again. Slowly, he edged Merry out of the protecting harbor, and as they hit the choppy waves beyond and the wind filled Merry's red sail, Benn felt his melancholy lift. Merry set off like a pony let loose in a field, and Benn took her in close to the cliffs so that if Zerra was watching, they would not be so easy to spot.

Zerra was indeed watching, but from the safety of the old railway platform. Still convinced that an invisible boy was waiting for her to get close enough to the cliff so that he could push her over, she was swinging her lance from side to side saying very loudly—so that he would know she was not scared at all, not one little bit—"I can see you! I can see you! I'll shoot! I will!" But she was met with nothing but silence, and she was beginning to feel just a little bit foolish. Trying to look purposeful, Zerra took out her spyglass and swung around, scanning the horizon. She expected to see empty, endless desert, but to her surprise she saw a distant figure heading away along the cliff top. It looked familiar. It looked like . . . "Alex!" Zerra yelled out. "Ha ha! Alex!"

She was not going to mess this one up. No way.

Alex stopped. She thought she heard someone calling her name. She swung around and saw a small figure on the old railway platform and a bright glint of silver.

Zerra dropped down on one knee to steady herself. She squinted through the sight of the Lightning Lance until in the middle of the crosshairs she saw the tiny dot that was Alex. Then, very carefully, she primed the bolt. And fired.

Alex saw a bolt of blue fire erupt and come arcing toward her. She hurled herself behind a hillock of sand and landed facedown. There was a soft *thump* as the bolt buried itself into the mound and began to fizz ominously.

Expecting an explosion any second, Alex scrambled to her feet and raced away. Skidding over the gritty soil, she ran until she had no breath left and then, when she could go no farther and was convinced the blast must come *right now*, she threw herself to the ground and lay with her arms covering her head, waiting. Nothing happened. Tentatively, Alex looked back at the mound. In a second she was on her feet and running again, faster than she had thought possible. But this time it was not from a

Lightning Lance bolt about to explode, it was from the huge yellow scorpion she had just seen rise up from the mound, the silver barb upon its tail arched over its head and pointing straight at her.

Suddenly, Alex heard a muffled *therwumpp* and a shower of grit and sand landed all around her. She risked a glance back over her shoulder and saw the Skorpas lying on its back, legs in the air, on top of its mound. Zerra's bolt had at last exploded—and killed it.

Alex set off with new hope in her heart. Determined to get to Netters Cove before the sun went down, she broke into a steady trot. She could do it. She knew she could.

CHAPTER 23

The King's Spy

OUTSIDE THE GATES OF REKADOM, the Beguiler Bell rang with a resounding *ker-langgg*.

"Let me in!" Zerra yelled, hammering on the wicket. "I am the King's Spy!"

The little door in the gate opened a crack and the young, pimply guard peered nervously out. "Oh," he said. "It's you."

"Yes, stupid, it's me. And the stupid crows are still ringing the stupid bell. Now let me in." Zerra waved her wristband at the guard and he let her in, knowing that there was no way the king would have a spy who was also a Beguiler.

Zerra headed across Gate Court on her important mission—she was going to see the king, and she had a lot to tell him. Wanting to avoid Bartlett, Zerra used her spy plan of the city to work out another way to get to the Gold Tower. Heading for Horse Court, where the horses for the king and the Jackal chariots were kept, she stepped through the snicket into a succession of peaceful apple and cherry orchards, where a few horses and sheep were cropping grass contentedly.

Zerra thought horses were weird and was pleased when she reached the next snicket into Farm Court. Here were vegetable gardens kept by the few townspeople left in the city. It was mostly full of weeds, but along the far wall by the next snicket Zerra saw an elderly couple working on a line of green things—she had no idea what they were. The couple watched Zerra with deep suspicion as she headed toward them, and as it became clear that Zerra was going into the next court, the woman called out, "Can't go no farther, girl! It's King's Court!"

Zerra ignored them. She was feeling nervous now, but there was no way she was going to let a couple of busybodies see that. Without breaking her stride, she approached the Jackal lounging in the snicket and confidently held up her twisted silk wristband to show the King's Spy seal, with its simple pass sign that a Jackal could recognize: ≈.

Zerra savored the looks of astonishment on the old couple's faces as the Jackal bowed and stepped aside. She flipped them a rude sign and disappeared through the snicket.

King's Court was laid out as a formal garden but was somewhat neglected. The lines of low hedging needed a trim, the gravel paths were scattered with weeds, and the lanterns that sat atop randomly placed posts were tarnished and clearly never lit. One elderly gardener resting on her rake watched Zerra suspiciously as she made her way to the wide archway at the foot of the king's Gold Tower, which rose up from the apex of the triangular court.

A Jackal was leaning against the archway, filing its talons. It looked lazily down at Zerra and a low, threatening growl came rolling from its throat. Once again, Zerra showed her pass sign, but this time the Jackal was more thorough. It lifted the wristband—along with Zerra's arm—with its talon and peered at it closely. As its talon traced the zigzag pass sign, Zerra could feel the meaty warmth of Jackal breath upon her skin. After what felt like forever, the Jackal let her arm drop and stepped aside. Relieved, Zerra hurried away up the winding stone stairs, treading softly upon their threadbare strip of red carpet.

At last she reached the top landing, which was strewn with faded old rugs and had a line of delicate gold chairs placed along the curved wall. Yet another red-coated Jackal stood in front of a polished ebony door, upon which was carved a golden winged crown. Zerra took a deep breath to steady her nerves and once again showed her Spy Pass to the Jackal. This one was easier to convince. It gave a curt nod of its huge head and pushed upon the door, which swung silently open. Nervously, Zerra stepped inside—where she stopped, utterly confused.

The place was stuffed full of gold pillars with golden benches running between them. Standing between the pillars was a pack of scruffy kids in dusty jerkins and crazy hair. Zerra was shocked. Who'd have thought the king would have a crowd of brats hanging around? She put her hand up to her own hair to check that it wasn't as bad as these kids' hair, only to have them all copy her exactly. She snatched her hand away and they did the same.

"Hey!" Zerra yelled out. "Stop that. It's not funny." Her voice echoed in the pillared lobby and, mortified, she realized her mistake—*the kids were her reflection*. Horrified, Zerra stared at her multiple reflections in the mirrors set between the pillars. She looked awful. Rumpled old clothes, knees of her trousers stiff with bird poop, her hair tangled, her face streaked with dirt. But what shocked Zerra the most was that she had not recognized herself.

Zerra walked up to the mirrored wall and stared into her own eyes. It seemed that a stranger looked back at her. This was not the old Zerra who had lived in Luma with her family, who had gone to school every day and been just an ordinary, discontented kid. But then, Zerra remembered how she'd loathed coming home every day to her annoying sisters, her kid brother and her dozy mother, who just ignored everything, and particularly Zerra. *No one is going to ignore me now. No one*, Zerra told herself. She stood up tall, and when a concealed door faced with a mirror opened behind her, she turned around and smiled confidently at the king in his silly winged crown. "Sire," she said, remembering to bow her head. "I am your spy and I have come to deliver my first report."

King Belamus looked at the wild-looking kid standing in front of him. The standard of spies was not what it was, that was for sure. But it had been a long time since he'd had any spy at all reporting to him and he probably couldn't be choosy. He sighed. "Very well, Spy," he said. "Deliver your report."

"I have three things to report."

"Three!" The king was a little disconcerted to hear that so much had been happening in Rekadom.

"The first thing is that your Enchanter—I mean, the Beguiler who is your prisoner at the top of the Silver Tower—has been pretending to be you."

"Me?" Belamus squeaked.

"Yes, Sire."

"But you, being Dark, saw through it."

Zerra was pleased about this. This would show Bartlett. "Yes, Sire. I saw him for what he was."

Belamus was furious. "A low-down no-good cheating trickster."

"Exactly, Sire," Zerra said, her confidence growing. This was going better than she'd hoped.

"What was he doing while pretending to be me?" Belamus asked, hoping it wasn't anything embarrassing.

"That's the second thing I have to report, Sire. The Beguiler was helping another Beguiler escape."

Belamus began to tremble. *"Another* Beguiler?"

"A boy, Sire. One of the ones who escaped from your Jackal yesterday. I believe the Beguiler at the top of the tower was harboring him, Sire. And in addition, Sire, the girl Beguiler has also escaped. I gave chase to both outside the city, but they . . ." Zerra searched for a way to tell the king they had got away without it looking like her fault. "They eluded me. By trickery and Beguilement."

Belamus let out a loud groan and sank down onto one of the golden benches. The room was filled with despairing kings, which Zerra found rather amusing. The king looked up at Zerra, almost pleadingly. "Tell me, Spy. As Flyer you caught so many Beguilers on your first mission. Do you think there are many more left out there?"

It occurred to Zerra that if she said there were any more left, she would have to go out looking for them on the new Hawke once it was ready, and she really didn't want anything more to do with birds, large or small. So, after a pause that made her reply sound very considered, she said, "Those two kids are the last ones outside Rekadom, Sire. If you get them, that's the end of it."

Belamus got to his feet, looking as though a weight of worry was lifted from him. "Then we will get them and make an end of it. Well, Spy, is there anything else you wish to tell me?"

Zerra smiled. There certainly was. "The deputy falconer, Bartlett, Sire. She was at the city gate with the Beguiler, helping the boy escape. The guards will confirm it."

Belamus nodded. "Thank you, Spy. Bartlett will be dealt with."

Thinking that the king was going to tell her what a great spy she was, Zerra waited patiently while trying not to look at her reflections, which still spooked her.

At last King Belamus said irritably, "What are you waiting for? Get back to work. I want you out in Star Court every night. Watching. Particularly the Silver Tower."

"But what about the Slicers, Sire?"

"You're young. You can jump, can't you?"

CHAPTER 24

The House of Ratchet

IT WASN'T OFTEN MA RATCHET had her son back home, for which she was grateful. Ma loved her son, of course she did, but he wasn't easy company. And tonight he was being particularly difficult. "Well, this Bartlett sounds like a very sensible young woman to me," Ma Ratchet said after listening to a long diatribe from her son about his assistant. "And if you've made a mistake with this new Flyer and she isn't a Dark, then you should do the decent thing and own up to it. How many times have I told you that?"

"You don't understand, Ma. This girl, the new Flyer, arrived already Flying the Hawke, so naturally at the time

I assumed she was a Dark. And she told the king she'd caught a 'ton of Enchanters' and now he won't hear anything against her. Not to mention the fact she's become his Spy now. So I'm stuck with her. The trouble is, Bartlett thinks she's a Beguiler."

Ma Ratchet stirred the soup. It was fish heads and beans, her son's favorite. "A Beguiler. Well, well. Won't that be a little awkward for you, dear, Harboring a Beguiler?"

Ratchet resisted stamping his foot—but only just. "I am *not* Harboring a Beguiler, Ma. Don't *you* start as well. Once and for all, my new Flyer is *not* a Beguiler. It's a plot. Bartlett is bad-mouthing me because she wants my job. I can't afford to make any mistakes."

"I thought you were just telling me that you hadn't made any mistakes," his mother said mildly.

"Of course I haven't," said Ratchet.

"So I don't see why you're so upset," Ma said.

"I am *not* upset!" Ratchet yelled.

Ma Ratchet sighed. She picked up a small jar of fish eyes and took them out to the little table by the window that looked out over the harbor. They always looked nice sprinkled on the soup, she thought.

Ratchet followed his mother out of the kitchen and went over to his merlin falcon, Merle, who was perching on the back of Ma's best chair, watching with his bright eyes. Ratchet offered Merle the knuckle of his left index finger to bite, which Merle accepted while he watched keenly as his surrogate parent drew a small waxed-paper packet from his pocket and then offered his left wrist to the bird. Merle stepped daintily onto the thick leather band Ratchet wore around his wrist and allowed Ratchet to carry him across to the table.

Ma Ratchet sighed. "Nigel. Does that bird really have to be at the table?"

Ratchet hated being called by his first name. It reminded him of being teased at school. "Don't call me Nigel, Ma," he said petulantly, as he took his place at the little polished table by the window. "Ratchet is what I am now. And yes, he does."

Merle hopped neatly off his perch on Ratchet's wrist and graciously accepted a fish eye from the jar. Ma Ratchet tutted loudly and went to fetch the soup.

When the soup was ladled out and sat steaming in its bowls and Ma Ratchet had taken her seat opposite her son, Ratchet unwound the roll of waxed paper to reveal a rather sad dried mouse. Merle gave a muted caw of excitement, which was drowned out by Ma Ratchet.

"Nigel, no! I am not having a dead mouse at the table. No, no, *no*."

"It won't be there for long," Ratchet told her as he held it out to Merle. A little shudder of anticipation ran through the bird, he leaned forward, and in a second the mouse was gone. "There you are, Ma. All gone," said Ratchet.

"Either that bird leaves the table or I do," his mother told him.

Ratchet decided his mini rebellion had lasted long enough. He got up from the table and took the soporific bird back to his roost on the shelf above the coats. Merle settled contentedly and began the serious business of digesting a whole mouse.

Ratchet and his mother now did the same with their fish head soup. The muted clattering of spoons, the crunching of fish heads and the soft popping sound of fish eyes sucked in through pursed lips were all that could be heard. As he gulped down the last succulent fish head and then licked the back of his spoon, Ratchet wished he didn't feel compelled to act like a sulky teen whenever he came home. He knew it wasn't fair. But he just couldn't help himself. To make amends, he took the soup bowls out and brought in the fruitcake that his mother always made for him.

She accepted the peace offering and made no comment when behind her Merle coughed up a small pellet of fur and bones. "I do wish you'd get a nicer job, Nigel," Ma Ratchet said.

Some three hundred feet above the Ratchets' quietly combative supper, Alex had arrived at an overgrown platform on which was a tumbledown tower with a pointy roof. Upon the tower, in faded letters, were two words: Netters Halt.

Alex could hardly believe she had made it just in time. The sky was gloomy now with heavy clouds, but a chink of brightness showed on the horizon where the setting sun appeared to be touching the ocean. At the foot of the cliff lay the little fishing village of Netters Cove, where she and Benn had spent a night a few days back. Alex knew two good things about the place: it was free of Xin, and its inhabitants seemed friendly. She wasn't sure where she'd sleep, but she'd work that out when she got down there.

Alex left the old railway track and headed along an overgrown path to a gate, beyond which she could see the path dropping down to the cove. She was about to push open the gate when the earsplitting sound of shattering glass sent her hands flying to her ears to block the sound out.

It was the Xin.

Alex hurled herself through the gate, only to find a cascade of pinprick lights blocking her path. She hesitated a moment, but then pushed forward, knowing that she had no choice but to break through and get to the safety of the cove. Alex knew that the Xin were—like all Hauntings except for the Hawke—what her father called "hefted": they had strict boundaries over which they could not stray. Hands over her head, eyes half closed, she pushed her way through the stinging lights, dancing like fireflies, strands of them joining together to form the dreaded Net of Xin. Alex stumbled on, trying to reach the path to

Netters Cove, but the net of dancing lights blocked her way, and then, looping around her like a lasso of broken glass, it edged her along the cliff top. Desperately, Alex tried to pull away, but the Xin only tightened their hold, pulling her ever closer to the edge of the cliff, sending stinging shocks through her skin.

Teetering on the cliff edge, Alex looked down at the deep water below. Its dark-green depths looked calm and inviting, and the thought of sinking down into them and soothing the stings was irresistible. With the plinking, clinking song of the Xin needling into her brain, and the painful pricking of the shards of light pushing her forward, Alex held out her arms like the wings of a bird.

And then, she flew.

A piercing scream rapidly followed by a distant splash echoed outside. Ma Ratchet jumped to her feet. "Oh my days, what was that?"

Ratchet peered out of the window. "Dunno. Some dim-wit fallen in the water, I suppose."

"Go and have a look, Nigel, there's a good boy."

Ratchet sighed and got up. "I'm forty-two years old, Ma," he said as he wandered out of the little cottage on the quay and went to see what was happening.

A small knot of people were gathered on the harbor steps, many of them pointing to the base of the sheer cliffs that rose up on the eastern side of the village. Two men rowing a sleek boat with a young woman standing holding a lantern were heading fast out of the harbor in the direction of the pointing fingers. Ratchet watched with interest—it looked like someone had fallen off the cliff.

The light from the rowboat cut through the rapidly falling darkness, showing a small white sailboat already at the foot of the cliff. It looked empty. But there was someone in the water struggling, and Ratchet could hear faint cries for help. He watched the rowboat draw alongside the white sailboat, saw the young woman give the lantern to the first rower and then, clutching a large cork float, jump overboard to join whoever was in the water. There was silence on the harbor as everyone waited. Her shout of "Haul in!" was greeted with relief. To Ratchet's surprise, there was not one but two people rescued—kids both of them, he thought. No doubt they'd been showing off and jumping off the cliff. Tombstoning, they called it in Netters Cove—and for good reason.

Ratchet stalked off in disgust. He'd come home to escape annoying kids and the trouble they caused, only to have two half-drowned brats mess up his suppertime. He stomped back to Ma Ratchet's and continued eating his fruitcake in silence. All his mother could get out of him about what had happened was "Darned kids." So she left Ratchet and Merle to their digestion and went to see for herself.

There was a huddle of people on the dockside at the top

of the steps. Ma elbowed forward until she had a ringside view. A girl, aged about twelve, she guessed, lay on the cobbles, saturated with water, which was leaking out of her ears, mouth and nose in a rather revolting manner. A boy, taller and a little older but equally soaked, was kneeling beside the girl. Ma thought he was crying, but she couldn't tell because he too looked full of salt water. And then, straddling the girl, with her hands pushing firmly down upon her chest, was their new harbormaster, a young woman called Kirrin. With each chest compression, water gushed from the mouth of the young girl, and every time it did so, people around her gave a gasp. But it would be no good, Ma Ratchet knew very well. She'd seen her husband after he'd drowned, and it had not worked for him.

But Kirrin was not giving up. She rocked forward and back, pushing the water out of the girl's lungs like she was squeezing out a sponge. "Please . . . please . . . ," the boy was murmuring.

Ma Ratchet was getting bored and had just decided to go and finish her cake when the drowned girl suddenly coughed and a fountain of water spurted from her mouth. "Help me sit her up," Kirrin told the boy. He needed no asking. Already his arm was around the girl, gently lifting her forward. Suddenly, the girl gave a great sigh and began to gasp for breath.

A murmur of relief ran through the huddle of people.

"It's all right, Alex," the boy was telling her. "Just breathe. Take it slow."

"Let her cough," Kirrin told him. "Let her get the stuff out of her lungs."

Ma Ratchet felt cheated. Why hadn't her Albert survived too? It wasn't fair.

She was about to go home when Kirrin said to the boy, "I've never seen so much seawater come out. How high did you say she jumped from?"

"She didn't jump, she was pushed," the boy replied.

There was a small gasp from those watching.

"Pushed?" Kirrin sat back on her heels. "But who would do that?"

"Not 'who,'" said the boy. "'What.' The Xin."

An exclamation of horror ran through the watchers and a murmuring of *Xin . . . Xin . . . Xin* began.

Kirrin, who had been rubbing the girl's back, snatched her hands away like she had been burned. She stood up and wiped her hands on her wet trousers as though they were sullied by touching the girl. "Is she . . . a Beguiler child?"

The boy stood up too and met Kirrin's gaze. He seemed angry. "She—I mean Alex—is a human being like you and me. That's all that matters."

"That sounds like a yes to me," Kirrin said. She addressed the villagers gathered around her. "We can't have a Beguiler here. She'll draw the Xin down. She'll have to go."

"Don't be ridiculous!" the boy said heatedly. "Alex can't go anywhere right now."

Kirrin took no notice of him. "The girl has to go," she told the gathering crowd. "Agreed?"

There were mutterings both of agreement and disagreement, but Ma Ratchet had seen enough. Her little cottage backed onto the cliffs and she wanted to be safely inside before the Xin got any closer. She headed back home, slammed the door shut and threw the bolts across.

"What's up, Ma?" Ratchet asked.

"Bloomin' Beguiler kids out there. Kirrin's told them they have to go. Right now." Ma Ratchet peered out of the window. "Wish they'd get a move on. We'll have the Xin down here any minute."

"Now, now, Ma, you know those Xin are hefted to the cliff tops. They don't come down here, do they?"

"Don't you now-now me, Nigel. The last two nights those Xin have been coming nearer. I hear them zinging and pinging and clinking and plinking all night long. Sets your teeth on edge something horrible. We had a meeting about it earlier. We reckon something's been here that's drawn them down."

"Oh?" said Ratchet.

"There were two kids here a few nights back. Turned

up out of nowhere in a little white boat. Maddie next door sold them some food, silly woman. Anyway, we reckon it was them that drew the Xin down."

"White boat?" asked Ratchet, thinking of the little white boat he'd seen at the foot of the cliffs. "Two kids? Well, well. I wonder . . ."

"No 'I wonder' about it, Nigel. Of course they're Beguiler kids. Why else would the Xin have pushed one of them off the cliff, huh?"

Ratchet looked at his mother thoughtfully. "Why else indeed?" he murmured. He got up, scraping his chair back, and strode to the door. From his perch Merle watched him sleepily with one open eye. Ratchet shot back the bolts on the door.

"Nigel! What are you doing?" Ma yelled.

Ratchet turned around. "I'm going to get those Beguiler kids and bring them here."

"You most certainly are not! Nigel, stop it. Stop it right now, I say!" But even Ma Ratchet's sternest tones had no effect. Ratchet flung the door open and strode out of the cottage.

Ma watched him go with a sense of foreboding. Everyone knew no good ever came of mixing with Beguilers. And she just knew that no good would come of this either.

CHAPTER 25

Unwanted Guests

BENN WAS CROUCHING BESIDE ALEX in the middle of a circle of hostile villagers. Alex was still spluttering and spitting out water, which Benn took to be a good sign—the less water inside Alex the better. But she had also started to shiver uncontrollably, which Benn thought was not good at all. She desperately needed to be somewhere warm, not out on a harbor wall with the wind beginning to get up. But it was not looking good. The young woman who had rescued them—Kirrin, he thought her name was—wanted them gone. And it seemed she was in charge.

Kirrin looked down at Benn, her eyes narrowed with

mistrust. "The rowers have gone to fetch your boat. You must leave at once."

Benn stood up and faced Kirrin. "But Alex just nearly drowned. She's freezing cold. Look how she's shaking. She needs to get warm again. And dry. You can't send us out to sea now. She's too cold. She . . . she won't make it." Benn's voiced faltered as the truth of what he was saying sunk in. Alex would not survive a night in an open boat.

But Kirrin was determined. "You're not welcome here. You're bringing the Xin down among us. You are both going right now. Your only choice is whether you get in your boat or we chuck you off the harbor wall."

"But they're just kids. Same age as my grandkids," one old fisherman protested.

Kirrin rounded on the dissenter. "Okay then. You take them in. And if Netters Cove gets infested with Xin tonight we'll all know who to blame, won't we?"

The old fisherman mumbled awkwardly and looked at his boots. But others in the crowd took over. *We'd be as bad as the Xin if we turn them out to sea tonight . . . Brr, it's bitter out there . . . . Wind's getting up now . . . Do we want Netters Cove to be known as the place that sent two defenseless kids out into the night in a leaky old boat?*

Benn wanted to protest that Merry was neither leaky nor old, but he thought better of it.

"You're putting us all at risk," Kirrin said.

"Vote!" said a voice, and a chant was taken up. "Vote! Vote! Vote!"

"Very well," Kirrin said. "As harbormaster I declare an impromptu vote. Those in favor of keeping Netters Cove safe—"

"Shame on you, Master!" a young man called out. "That's a loaded question. We all want our village safe. Just not at the price of the lives of two innocent kids."

"You propose the vote then," Kirrin retorted, annoyed.

All eyes turned to the young man and his face reddened. But he stood his ground. "All those in favor of letting the kids stay tonight, raise your hands." All hands were raised but Kirrin's.

"Those against."

Kirrin raised her hand.

"Sorry, Harbormaster," the young man said. "The kids stay tonight."

"Who with?" asked Kirrin. "So who wants the Xin tapping on their windows tonight?"

Benn looked at the sea of faces, suddenly thoughtful in the lantern light.

A rasping voice, which Benn thought he recognized, came from the back of the crowd. "Ma will take them. She's got a spare room. And shutters on the windows too."

"Nigel Ratchet?" Kirrin sounded surprised. "Is that you?"

"Yeah. It's me. Like I said. Ma will take them in for tonight."

"Very well." Kirrin turned to Benn and Alex. "This gentleman will take you to his mother's cottage. You will leave at first light." With that she turned abruptly on her heel and strode away.

Silently, the group of villagers drifted away, leaving Ratchet with Benn and Alex. Ratchet eyed his guests happily. It was as he'd expected, these were the same two Beguiler kids he had seen arriving in Rekadom with the Jackal. The Beguiler kids who had then made themselves invisible and escaped. He grinned. He'd hit the jackpot with these two. "Come on now," he said to Benn. "Let's get you back to Ma's."

Benn would have been relieved that they weren't being sent out in Merry on a cold and windy night, if he had not recognized their host. This was the man who'd been yelling, "Dark! Dark!" in Rekadom, and Benn was very wary of anyone from Rekadom. But what could he do? Alex was shivering uncontrollably now—she had to get warm. It would be fine, Benn told himself. They just had to get through tonight.

Benn took Alex's arm, and slowly they followed Ratchet across the dockside to the very last cottage of a row set back against the foot of the cliff. Ratchet pushed open the door, calling, "Ma! Got some visitors for you."

Ma Ratchet regarded Benn and Alex with deep

suspicion. "So I see, Nigel. So I see."

Ratchet flinched. He wished his mother wouldn't call him "Nigel" in front of people from Rekadom. "So, Ma," he said very loudly, "can you get them settled out the back? Light the stove. The girl's frozen."

"If you say so, Nigel," Ma Ratchet said coolly. She turned to Benn and Alex. "Follow me."

"Thanks," Benn mumbled.

They followed Ma Ratchet through a small kitchen into a poky storeroom at the back of the house. There were two wide, low shelves, a pile of old crab pots with dried seaweed stuck on them and a small potbellied stove. The back of the storeroom was bare rock with a film of damp on it, and Benn noticed that the only window was a small shuttered opening well out of reach. The place felt cold, damp and oppressive. "Sit yourselves down on a shelf," Ma Ratchet said. "I'll get some blankets and pillows. I suppose you'll want some dry clothes too."

"Thanks," Benn said once again.

Ma Ratchet went out and they heard her yelling, "Nigel! Fetch some logs, will you?"

Shuddering with cold, Alex collapsed on the nearest shelf. Benn sat next to her and put his arm around her, rubbing her shoulders to try to get some warmth into her. She felt cold as ice. "You okay?" he asked.

Teeth chattering so violently that she could not speak, Alex nodded.

Ma Ratchet returned with a pile of musty blankets and old clothes. Wordlessly, Benn helped get the room ready. He piled the logs into the stove and lit them, he helped make up beds on the shelves, and then he allowed himself to be shooed out into the kitchen while Ma Ratchet helped Alex into a long woolly nightdress about ten sizes too big for her. Ma Ratchet put all the wet clothes over a rail by the stove, apart from the green silk sash, which Alex refused to let go.

The kitchen, like the whole house, smelled of old fish, but Benn was too tired to care. He sat on a stool by the cooking range and let the day's events sink in. The terror of seeing Alex fall from the cliff had not left him, but it was overlaid by the joy of finding her when he had thought he never would set eyes on her again. He was lost in his thoughts when the door from the sitting room opened and the Ratchet man from Rekadom walked in. He closed the sitting room door behind him and leaned back against it, as if trying to stop Benn from leaving. "So," he said, making that little word sound like an accusation.

Benn said nothing.

"Your friend got attacked by Xin, did she?"

Benn gulped. This did not feel good.

"You know that Xin only do that to Beguilers," Ratchet said. "They don't touch *normal* people."

That stung. "Alex *is* normal," Benn retorted.

"Oh, *Alex*, is it? And what is her last name, huh?"

Benn knew better than to fall into that trap. "None of your business," he muttered.

"Funny name—Alex Noneofyourbusiness," Ratchet mused. "Ah well. Sleep tight." With that he was out of the kitchen, the door clicking shut behind him.

Ma Ratchet emerged from the storeroom. "Your friend's asleep," she told Benn. "Time you were in bed too. You'll need to be off first thing tomorrow."

Benn nodded. "Yeah. We will."

Ma Ratchet caught herself feeling sorry for Benn. He looked worn-out, she thought. She cut a chunk of bread and spread it thick with butter. "Take that to bed with you. Looks like you could do with something."

Benn smiled with surprise. "Oh! Thanks."

"You're welcome. You heading home tomorrow?"

Benn nodded.

"Got a long way to go?" asked Ma.

"Lemon Valley. All the way up the river to the round-house."

"My, my, that *is* a long way. Sleep well now."

Benn retreated into the storeroom and quietly closed the door behind him so he didn't wake Alex. As he sat on his shelf in the gloom—lit only by a bar of light from the kitchen creeping underneath the door—and ate his buttered bread, he heard the quiet, slow sound of a key being turned in the lock. He waited a few minutes and then very gingerly got up, tiptoed across the room and tried the door. It was as he expected—locked. He walked quietly back to his shelf, which was covered with rough blankets and an old—but thankfully clean—shirt. He hung his wet clothes over the chair in front of the stove beside Alex's, put on the shirt and then, feeling icy cold himself now, he burrowed under the covers and lay still, listening.

Benn could not get rid of an increasing sense of dread. There was no doubt in his mind now, this house was a dangerous place to be—the red-faced man from Rekadom had made that clear enough. Benn heard heavy footsteps cross the kitchen; he dived beneath the covers and pretended to be asleep. He heard the sound of the door being tried and then Ma Ratchet's annoyed voice, "I *told* you I locked it, Nigel."

"Just checking," was the response. "I'm not letting this opportunity slip away, Ma."

"I don't see how bringing Beguiler kids back to Rekadom is going to do you any good at all, Nigel," came Ma's voice. "I thought the king wanted Beguilers *gone* from Rekadom. What good is bringing them back going to do you?"

"I told you, Ma. Bartlett is going around telling people my new Flyer is a Beguiler. It makes me look bad. And it's dangerous too, to be accused of being a Harborer of Beguilers. But if I bring two *real* Beguiler kids back, then that proves I'm no Harborer. And it makes Bartlett look like an idiot. Right?"

"It all sounds very complicated to me, Nigel. Why don't I make you a nice cup of cocoa?"

Benn listened to the domestic sounds of cocoa being made and his mouth watered. How he would love some too.

Suddenly Ma spoke. "They won't want to go, you know."

"What?"

"Those two kids. They won't want to go to Rekadom."

Ratchet chuckled. "They won't have much choice, Ma. I've just sent Merle off to the king. With a request to send the Jackal here to collect them first thing in the morning."

"Jackal! Here?" Ma sounded horrified.

"Yep. They'll take the kids back and solve my Bartlett problems at the same time. Two birds with one stone, eh, Ma? Make that three birds, counting Merle, ha ha. Or maybe even four. Because—listen to this, Ma, this is really clever . . ." Ratchet's voice dropped and Benn slipped out of bed and tiptoed fast over to the door to catch Ratchet's rumbling tones. ". . . I've said in my note to the king that these are the last two Beguilers in the whole land. So when he gets these kids he'll stop bothering with all this crazy stuff with the Hawke, see? And then it won't matter if the Flyer's not a Dark, because we won't need a Flyer anymore, will we? Because we won't need a Hawke. And then I can go back to nice, ordinary birds of prey."

Ma Ratchet did not sound convinced. "But will the

king believe you, Nigel? About them being the last two ever?"

"He'll believe me, Ma. Because I used the secret password," Ratchet said. There was the sound of rustling paper. "See here. I updated the password at the spy place yesterday. That was a bit of luck, wasn't it?"

"Well, I do hope so, Nigel. We could do with a bit of luck, because Beguilers bring bad luck, you know. And thanks to you, we've got two of them under our roof all night."

Ratchet chuckled. "But they'll be gone in the morning, Ma. Off with the Jackal."

"Good riddance," said Ma Ratchet.

Benn had heard enough. Shivering, he tiptoed away from the door and slipped back into bed. He pulled the blankets tightly around him and lay on the hard shelf, staring up at the ceiling. listening to the creaking of the stairs as Ma Ratchet and her son climbed up to their rooms for the night. He waited until the footsteps moving across the floorboards above his head had ceased, and then he got up and moved quietly across to the pile of crab pots. One by one he placed the pots below the tiny, shuttered window. He made a base of five pots and then put three on top of those and then two, then a final one. It was a flimsy pyramid, but it reached almost to the window, and Benn was pleased with his work. He looked down at Alex, sleeping so soundly, and he longed to wake her and get out of their prison right now. But Benn knew she needed to rest and get warm, and Ratchet had said that the Jackal were not coming until the morning. He must be patient. He crept back to his shelf and burrowed down into the blankets. He was asleep before he knew it.

CHAPTER 26
Merle's Mission

HOLDING A SMALL BRASS TUBE in his talons, Merle flew into the night, heading away from the cliff where occasional flickers of light from the Xin zipped through the air. Merle was small for a bird of prey, but his round dark eyes had perfect night vision. The merlin falcon had been hand-reared with more love than Ratchet had shown any human, and considered himself to be a small, winged human being. Merle comprehended most of what Ratchet said to him and was unaware that his peeping replies and subtle head movements were not actually human speech.

And so, as he flew, navigating by the stars above and the smell of the ocean below, the compact and powerful little bird understood his mission perfectly. Merle's tiny bird heart sang with pleasure as he sped through the cold night air, reveling in his freedom and with not a thought to the damp cottage filled with fear that he had left behind.

After two hours of flight, Merle was plummeting down through the darkness, heading for a dimly lit, colored window at the top of the Gold Tower. About twenty feet above its landing ledge he broke the dive. Splaying his wings, leaning backward and dropping his legs down, he kept his talons tightly curled, even though his instincts told him to splay them out as if to grab a prey. Merle was well trained and he understood he must hang on to the precious brass tube. The landing ledge of stone was just beneath him now, and Merle positioned himself above the hollowed-out dip from which an angled runnel led to a small arched gap in the foot of the window. Hovering, he lowered himself to within a few inches above the dip and then opened his talons. The brass tube landed right in the middle of the dip, and Merle watched it slowly roll down the runnel and disappear through the tiny arch at the foot of the window. A few seconds later he heard the loud *ping* of a bell and Merle landed neatly on the ledge. And there he waited patiently for someone to give him the receipt.

Merle had a long wait. King Belamus was fast asleep, and so was his Jackal bodyguard at the foot of his bed. When the bell pinged, the Jackal leaped up and looked warily around, unable in its sleepiness to remember the significance of the ping. But as the brass tube came rattling down a chute into the king's bedroom, made its way across the room and dropped onto the royal pillow, the Jackal loped over to the king and stood beside him, long strands of drool dropping onto the velvet bed cover.

Blearily, the king sat up and looked at the Jackal. "What?" he asked anxiously. "What's happened? Oh my days. There's a Beguiler here, isn't there? Help, Help!" The king sprang out of bed and the brass tube flew onto the floor and landed with a clang of metal on stone. The king caught a glimpse of it as it rolled under his bed. "A bullet!" he screamed.

The Jackal watched his master dive back under the covers and become a quivering lump beneath the bedclothes. As it stood, uncertain what to do, a seed of disrespect for the leader of its pack was planted. The brass tube rolled out from the other side of the bed and the Jackal leaped into action. It bounded across the bed, leapfrogging over the king's quaking posterior, and grabbed the "bullet." It regained its balance and rolled the tube between its finger and thumb. Then it respectfully tapped the lump beneath the bedclothes, which let out a high-pitched scream of "Go away! Go away!"

The Jackal, obedient as ever, backed away and spent the next ten minutes or so waiting in the shadows as far away from the king as it could get without leaving the room. For that was forbidden. At last the lump beneath the bedclothes began to move. Slowly it lengthened out like a coiled snake unwinding itself, and a disheveled head peered out. Warily, King Belamus surveyed his bedroom. He wished it wasn't hung with so many dark tapestries, for a whole army of Beguilers could be hidden behind them. He would get them removed that very morning, he decided. The king sat up and saw the impassive white muzzle of the Jackal watching him. He relaxed a little. The Jackal would have sniffed out any Beguiler, that was for sure. Feeling a little foolish under the impassive eye of the Jackal, the king barked out, "Don't stand there staring like a ninny-cat. Bring me a strawberry cordial."

The Jackal bowed its head, but instead of going to the little service chamber behind one of the tapestries where cordials, chocolate, sugared nuts and cinnamon nibbles were kept for the king's sweet tooth, it advanced toward the king.

For one terrifying moment the king thought the Jackal was going to kill him, for there was a cold, disdainful look in its eyes. The king shrank away and pulled the blankets up to his mouth. "No . . . ," he whispered. "No . . . please don't."

The Jackal stopped beside the king and wondered if the king did not wish to have the message. But the withholding of a message was a capital offense, and so it extended its hand with its long, doglike claws, and as the king shrank away, it dropped the tube onto the thick velvet bedspread, where it rolled into the dip between the king's bony knees. The king stared at the tube for some seconds, wondering if it was going to explode, and then, at last, he realized what it was.

He snatched up the tube, unscrewed its smooth ebony top, and a tightly rolled piece of paper dropped out. Belamus picked it up and held the thin tissue up to the candle. Ratchet's neat, precise writing showed dark against the light.

> *Recipient: King Belamus the Great.*
> *Delivered by: Merlin Falcon. King's Bird.*
> *Sent by: Ratchet. King's Messenger.*
> MAP: *ANANABASITTELTRAB*
> *Message: I have the pleasure to inform Your Most Gracious Majesty that this night I have captured the very last two Beguilers in your kingdom. They await collection from 13 Harbor Row, Netters Cove. Please send Jackal to arrive at dawn.*

The king read the message three times very slowly, scarcely daring to believe its contents. "The last two Beguilers in my kingdom," he murmured. "Which is exactly what the spy said." He thought a little longer and doubts began to creep in. "But suppose this is a trap? Maybe it's a scheme to lure my last Jackal out and ambush them. To leave me defenseless. Suppose a Beguiler has sent this?" He looked down at the message again to check the Authentication Password. If that was up to date, then the message was a genuine one from the King's Messenger, flown by a King's Bird. Belamus took a pencil from his notepad beside the bed and scribbled down the password, folded it in three, dropped wax on the join, stamped it with his seal and handed the note to the Jackal. "Jackal, go check the password. At once!"

The Jackal took the note and hurried away. Five minutes later it was banging on the door of the Old Watch Shop and sending up a blood-chilling howl.

Vera Watchet looked out the window and fear flooded through her; she was certain that she was about to be taken to the dungeons. Why, she had no idea, but she knew that anyone could end up in the dungeons in Rekadom. Indeed, most people already had.

She picked up her emergency go bag—like all those in Rekadom, she had a small bag packed with things she thought she would need in the dungeons—and kissed her cat, Terence, a tearful goodbye. Dreaming that Vera Watchet was an importunate mouse, Terence flicked her away and caught the tip of her nose. Her nose smarting, Vera hurried down the dark stairs and, with a feeling of dread, she opened the door. To her surprise, the Jackal did not grab hold of her and haul her away. It merely thrust a scrappy piece of paper at her. Vera took it and stared at the paper, unsure what to do. But then she saw the king's seal and her hands began to shake. The Jackal was growing impatient. It growled and pushed a claw under the seal. Vera flinched at the hot breath of the Jackal and watched as the Jackal broke the seal and unfolded the paper. With shaking hands, Vera held the message and read:

> *I, Vera Watchet, officer of the King's Spy and Messenger Service, do confirm that the latest and genuine Message Authentication Password is:*
> *ANANABASITTELTRAB*
> *Signed . . . .*

Vera read the code three times just to be sure. The third time, she read it backward just to check, and Ratchet's meaning became suddenly clear. Vera's heart sank. Now she understood why she was being taken away—she had demeaned the sacred office of the King's Spy and Messenger Service by allowing a ridiculous password to be used. "I—I beg you, please forgive me," she stuttered. "I did not realize at the time. The Chief Falconer insisted upon it. Oh!"

A sudden bark from the Jackal cut her short. It grabbed the king's letter back and its talon tapped impatiently on the place awaiting Vera's signature. "Oh. Yes. Of course," she said in a whisper, knowing this was the end of everything for her. The Jackal handed her a pen and in a trembling hand Vera signed her name. She was, she just knew it, signing her life away. The Jackal snatched the paper, folded it up and dropped it into the capacious pocket of its long red coat. Vera fell to her knees, hands over her face, sobbing. "Forgive me . . . I beg you . . . please."

There was no response. After some minutes Vera looked up to find the street empty and the Jackal gone. Uncertain what to do, she waited—she did not want to be accused of evading arrest. But the empty street stayed just as it was, and it was only when the dull glint of a Slicer began to slink its way toward her that Vera dared close the door. And then bolt it. And put the chain across. And then, after slowly climbing the stairs, lock her bedroom door too. And there she stayed for a whole week until she ran out of everything she had to eat, was drinking the water in the flower vase, and Terence had left to live in the house two doors down.

Back at the top of the Gold Tower, the king perused the shaky signature confirming that the code was the real thing. A slow smile lit up the king's beaky features as the consequences of this message sank in. There were only two more Beguilers left in the kingdom. Well, three if you counted the toad RavenStarr, but he'd already gotten him. It was these last two he needed to get his hands on.

Belamus considered what to do. The problem was, he

was running worryingly low on Jackal. There was the one he'd found dead outside RavenStarr's door—which he was sure RavenStarr had something to do with. And then one had been mobbed by crows down in Gate Court and was limping now—the Jackal pack would have that one soon, for sure. That left only three healthy Jackal and the crow-mobbed one. Belamus made a decision. He would keep the crow-pecked Jackal for his own bodyguard, which would keep it safe from the pack for a few more days, but the rest would have to go. RavenStarr would lose his Jackal guard, but he'd take a chance on that.

Belamus leaped off the bed, grabbed his winged crown and jammed it onto his head. Then he stood up as tall as he could and addressed his Jackal. "Bring me the crow-mobbed Jackal for my bodyguard."

The Jackal hissed its disapproval. The post as the king's personal bodyguard was for the Top Dog only. Not for the weakest in the pack.

Buoyed up by his decisiveness, Belamus was standing for no nonsense. "Do not disobey me, cur. Bring it!"

The Jackal slunk sulkily away and ten minutes later was back with a cowed, shivering and ear-bitten Jackal. At the sight of the king it threw itself onto the floor and groveled. Belamus shoved it aside with his velvet slipper and addressed the other Jackal. "You are to lead a mission. Take the rest of the pack. You will need to get the one guarding the Beguiler. Take a javelin each and two chariots with cages. Go to Netters Cove. Number Thirteen Harbor Row. House of Ratchet. Bring back to the dungeons the two Beguiler brats that you will find there—a boy and a girl. You understand what you are collecting? It is not the Ratchets. It is the *boy* and the *girl*," Belamus told the Jackal.

The Jackal bowed its head to show it understood.

"You will not fail!"

The Jackal, mollified by its new and important mission, bowed low. Then it loped out of the room, its red coat swishing across the carpet as it went.

King Belamus went to the multicolored window and from a small box beneath the ledge he took out a receipt—a silver stick with a winged crown pressed into the end of it. He pushed it under the gap and felt the bird on the other side take hold of it. Belamus chuckled. He had forgotten what fun it was to send messages. It reminded him of the days when he and his old friend Hagos would send messages many times a day. Hurriedly, Belamus pushed that thought away. That would never happen again—because very soon there would be no Hagos to send them to.

Hagos could not sleep. Unable to stop thinking about Alex, he had been watching the old message window, with its colored glass panes lit by a lantern within. He watched the merlin take off from the message ledge with some surprise. *Who is the king sending a message to?* he wondered. The only person who still had a messenger merlin was the ghastly Ratchet. Hagos frowned. Something was afoot. He watched the little bird rise up into the starry sky and disappear into the night, then he resumed his distant stare out to sea and his mournful wondering of where Alex could possibly be.

CHAPTER 27

Jackal in the Cove

WHEELS WERE WHIRLING THROUGH THE darkness, racing along the cliff tops. Jackal, with their doglike pelvis, were unable to ride horseback, and so in order to travel the land they used chariots. These were lightweight, fast-moving vehicles made of steel, with two large metal wheels upon which balanced a small carriage drawn by two fast horses. The Jackal sat on a high driver's seat, which was mounted on a curved metal spring that bounced and swayed with the bumpy ride. The two chariots bowling along that night were specially adapted prisoner transport: behind the driver's seat was a bell-like bar structure that formed a secure cage. They made good progress, and just before dawn they arrived at the old railway station, Netters Halt.

Down in Netters Cove, Alex woke with a start. She sat up suddenly, with no idea where she was. A chink of dim light from a little high window showed her a small storeroom with an old potbellied stove where her clothes were hanging and a pile of crab pots below the window and—to her relief—the unmistakable shape of Benn lying on a wide shelf across from her. A little shakily, Alex got up and put on her dry clothes, then she went over to Benn. "Hey, Benn," she whispered, gently rocking his shoulder.

Benn opened his eyes and looked blearily at Alex. "Uh?" he mumbled.

"Where are we?" Alex asked.

Benn was heavy with sleep. Slowly he took in the small room, shadowy and dimly lit, and he remembered. He sat up fast. "Alex—you're okay!"

"Apart from the bucket of water still in my ears, yes. I'm okay. Thanks to you."

Benn looked up at the window anxiously. "It's getting light. I overslept. We've got to get out, fast. The man here—Ratchet—has sent for the Jackal to get us."

"Ratchet!" Alex looked scared. "But he's the Chief Falconer."

"Sheesh," Benn said. "That makes sense now. I saw him in Rekadom."

"We've got to get out of here right now," Alex said.

"I know," Benn said, struggling into his dry clothes. "They locked us in last night. So I—"

"Piled up the crab pots," Alex finished for him, standing on one and testing it.

Above their heads, they heard the creaking of floorboards. Quickly, Alex clambered up the stack of pots to the little shuttered window where the early morning light filtered through. Silently, she slid back the bolts holding the shutter closed, and it swung open with a small squeak. She stopped and listened for any reaction upstairs. All was quiet. Alex peered out and saw a narrow, cobbled street deep in shadow with a line of cottages on the other side, their curtains drawn, quiet before the day began. She breathed in the smell of the sea and freedom and felt her spirits rise. Teetering on the topmost pot, she swung herself out of the little space and dropped lightly down to the street below. Benn followed a moment later and then they were off, running to the harbor, not daring to look behind them.

At the top of the cliff, the Jackal tied their horses up at the Netters Halt stables, where an anxious whinny from Ratchet's horse greeted them. The Jackal set off down the zigzagging path toward the harbor. A net of Xin, emboldened by the morning twilight, danced toward them, but the Jackal had no fear of Enchantments. Using their javelins, they batted the Xin away and allowed themselves a hoarse *huff-huff-huff* sound—the nearest Jackal came to laughing—as the Xin broke apart with a tinkling sound of breaking glass and tumbled away down the cliffs. Panting with excitement, the lead Jackal lifted the catch on the gate guarding the path down to Netters Cove.

Alex and Benn reached the harbor steps where Merry was tied up, and a voice brought them skidding to a halt. "Don't come back, you hear?" It was Kirrin, the harbormaster, who was sorting through a pile of nets.

"We're headed home. You bet we won't come back to this dump. Ever," Benn told her.

"Good. We don't want trouble here."

Neither Benn nor Alex deigned to answer. They hurtled down the steps to the ever-patient Merry and Benn jumped in.

Alex followed Benn into Merry, feeling as though she was meeting an old friend. She helped Benn raise the sail, and then as he took the tiller, she untied the mooring ropes and stowed them neatly. Then she took the oars and rowed quietly out of the flat, calm waters of the harbor, leaving Benn on the tiller ready to take control of the sail when they found the wind. As they were rounding the protective arm of the harbor wall, Alex saw three red-coated figures with large white heads loping down the cliff path. "Jackal," she said to Benn. "Coming down the cliff."

Benn turned around to look and whistled through his

teeth. "Sheesh. That was close." He grinned. "Looks like Kirrin's got trouble whether she wants it or not."

Alex returned his smile. "Not half as much trouble as those Ratchets are going to have when the Jackal find we've gone."

Benn laughed. "Serves them right," he said. "Here we go!" The wind filled Merry's red sail and they set off at a fast pace, cutting through the waves, every second taking them farther away from a fate that neither dared to imagine.

Back at 13 Harbor Row, fate was knocking on the door. Ratchet had been waiting, clutching his message confirmation stick, while Merle dozed inscrutably on the hat shelf. At the knock he leaped to his feet and pulled the door open with a flourish. Three white-headed Jackal stared at him with unblinking yellow eyes. Even though this was exactly what he expected to see, Ratchet's mouth went as dry as an old towel. He swallowed with some difficulty. "Ah," he managed to say. "Come in."

Ratchet stood aside and the creatures of King Belamus loped in. Ma Ratchet watched from the top of the stairs with an expression of horror. She had always been pleased that her Nigel had not become a fisherman, but had a very important job in the king's strange city. Now she was not so sure.

The Jackal stood in the middle of the main room of the cottage, so tall that the tips of their ears brushed the low beams of the ceiling. With their hot breath on the back of his neck, Ratchet hurried through the little kitchen to the locked door of the storeroom. His hands were shaking as he turned the key and pushed open the door.

Ratchet stood in the doorway, confused. The little storeroom was usually so dark, but it was flooded with light from the open shutter. *Why*, thought Ratchet, *is there a pile of crab pots beneath the window?* With a feeling of dread, he rushed into the storeroom and swept the array of blankets off the two low shelves. He swung around to face the Jackal, whose tongues were flicking across their muzzles in the expectation of a capture.

Ratchet was consumed with panic. He did the only thing he could think of. "Ma!" he yelled. "Ma! Help!"

Ma Ratchet came thudding down the stairs to find the door of the storeroom blocked by a swath of long, red coats. Her first thought was what lovely wool the coats were made from and how she would like one for herself. Her second thought disappeared into a sea of terror. Something very bad was happening. "Nigel?" she called out tentatively. "Nigel, are you in there?"

A terrified croak answered her. "Ma. Those kids. They've gone."

Ma Ratchet was confused. "Gone? How?"

"Out the window. Ma, hurry. Go see where they are. For Hawke's sake. Find them, Ma!"

Ma Ratchet turned and ran. Out of the door, into the

early morning sun and long shadows, she hurtled in her slippers and nightdress along the quay until she found Kirrin. "Those kids," she said, breathless, "from last night. Where are they?"

Kirrin stood up and wiped her hand on her trousers. "Don't worry, Ma," she said. "They won't trouble us again."

Ma Ratchet was not to be fobbed off. "But where *are* they?"

"Gone home." Kirrin pointed out to sea. "Took their boat about ten minutes ago. Good riddance."

"You idiot!" Ma Ratchet screamed. "You let them go!"

Kirrin bristled. "Mind your language, Mrs. Ratchet. You insult the office of harbormaster."

But Ma Ratchet stood her ground. She used to babysit Kirrin and was not going to be intimidated by someone who used to stuff her diapers down the back of the sofa. "With a pack of Jackal in my kitchen, I'll insult whatever office I like, thank you very much."

"Jackal?" Kirrin stopped her work and stared across the harbor to the street where Harbor Row began. "So why are the Jackal here, Ma? It's your son, isn't it? He's brought them from Rekadom with him. Well, *he* can get out of Netters Cove too."

"You carry on like this, Kirrin, and there won't be anyone left in the cove," Ma observed, and with that she ran back to Harbor Row.

She stopped for a moment outside the front door and took a deep breath to calm her fear of what she might find when she went inside. Then she pushed open the door and walked in. She found her son lying on the floor, bound and gagged, blue in the face with his efforts to breathe. The Jackal stared down at him impassively. Ma Ratchet forced herself to stay calm. It was, she told herself, no more than she had expected. Everyone knew that when the Jackal went out on a mission they never returned empty-handed. They always got *someone*.

Ma took another deep breath and said, very loudly, "Jackal. I know where the Beguiler brats have gone!"

Three long, white muzzles swung around to face her. Three impassive sets of yellow eyes looked down at Ma. The Jackal nearest her planted its hands on its narrow dog hips and tilted its head inquiringly. Ma breathed an inward sigh of relief—they were listening to her.

"The two Beguiler kids you're after—the boy and the girl. They've gone home. To the roundhouse in Lemon Valley. I know it. It's Nella Lau's place. You can get there across the Titans and over the old railway bridge. Wait, I've got a map." Ma ran to her desk and scrabbled through the papers until she found her old map from the days she would take the train to Luma. "Here, take this. The roundhouse is on there. Opposite Reed Cutters Halt. They've gone by boat, so you'll easily catch them. Now please, *please* let the Chief Falconer go."

The lead Jackal nodded its head and gave a sudden bark. Closely followed by the other two it strode out, stooping to get through the low front door, and headed into the early morning sunshine. Ma flew to her son, dropped to her knees and began unwinding the gag as fast as she could.

Ratchet took a deep, shuddering breath and struggled to sit up, gasping as though he wanted to breathe in every scrap of air in the whole world. Ma sat beside him, patting his back and feeling weak with horror at what had just happened.

After some minutes, Ratchet said, hoarsely, "Ma. Thank you. But they'll be back when they discover it's not true."

"Oh, but it is true." Ma got up and went into the kitchen to put the kettle on.

Ratchet joined Ma in the kitchen and slumped down at the table. "But how do you know?" he asked, his voice rasping.

"I asked the boy and that's what he said. If someone knows where *I* live, then I want to know where *they* live. It's only fair."

Ratchet was impressed. "Perfectly fair," he agreed.

His mother sat down at the table and took his hand. "Now, Nigel. We'll have a quiet day today. And you must promise me you won't go back to that nasty job of yours. Stay here. Go fishing. Enjoy life."

Ratchet shook his head. "Can't leave my birds, Ma. Not with Bartlett waiting to take over. Can't leave them with her."

Ma sighed and got up to rescue the whistling kettle. Rekadom used to be such a lovely city, she thought. Sparkling with Enchantment, full of people, vibrant with noise and laughter. She remembered how much she had enjoyed catching the train at Netters Halt to visit her son, and how proud she'd been of him when he had become Chief Falconer. But that was in the days before it all went wrong with that awful Oracle. That was before he'd had to look after that monstrous killer Hawke and the weird kids who Flew it. As she poured the hot water into a pot of dried chamomile, Ma reflected that maybe, with these last two Beguiler kids caught, all would be good once again. It was strange, she thought. They'd just seemed like normal kids. Quite nice ones too. It was a shame they'd soon be caught by the Jackal, she wouldn't wish that on anyone. But what could she do? It was her precious Nigel or them.

No contest.

CHAPTER 28
Along the Estuary

"ARGH!" ALEX YELLED AS YET another wave threw a shower of cold water in her face. She picked up the bailer and scooped out the seawater that was swashing around in the bottom of Merry. Benn was sitting on the edge of the boat, holding on to the tiller with both hands, fighting to keep Merry on course as the wind and the tide combined to push them out to sea. Merry was almost flying across the top of the waves, traveling past the tall Titans, rapidly leaving the smallest one behind. The brisk breeze that had been blowing when they had set off no more than a few hours earlier had increased so that now the tops of the waves were flecked with foam and Alex—when she was not bailing—was next to Benn leaning out to balance the relentless pull of the little red sail.

The relentless progress of the Jackal chariots continued. Following the old railway line, with the desert on their left and the foothills of the Thirteen Titans on their right, they headed south toward the dusky outline of the Border Mountains. By midafternoon they had reached the top of a gentle incline and saw the distant glint of sunlight upon the waters of the estuary beyond. Here the track forked and they stopped to consult Ma Ratchet's map. To their right the track continued past a low-lying wood of twisted oak trees, to their left it headed out along an embankment above the marshes, following the line of the river.

The lead Jackal pointed its manicured claw at the right fork and traced the route across the railway bridge to the far side of the estuary. Then it stabbed at the dot indicating the Roundhouse Groves so hard that the sharpened claw went right through the paper. "Hruh!" it half growled, half spoke. *"Hruuuh!"*

The horses set off at a brisk trot, heading past the dark and twisted salt oaks, toward the bridge over the churning waters of the estuary.

Merry was being steadily pushed away from the estuary, out to sea, twisting and turning in the swirl of waters that was tumbling out with a fast ebb tide, bringing with it branches and debris from the storm of the previous day.

"We're not going to make it!" Alex was yelling.

Benn said nothing. He had a horrible feeling that Alex was right. Choppy waves were breaking over Merry's prow and every time the little boat plowed her delicate nose into a wave trough, she lost ground, and when she came up she skittered away, heading ever farther away from the estuary. For the first time ever in Merry, Benn felt scared.

Alex had been scared too, but no longer. In her hand she held the Tau tightly, her fingers folded around the smooth, warm enamel. Into her mind came the voice she had heard the previous night when she had plunged into the deep-green water and a blue bubble of light had surrounded her and pulled her up to the surface: *I am with you. You are with me. We are Two with the power of Three.*

Alex stood up and with her free hand, she took hold of Merry's mast.

"Sit down!" Benn yelled.

But Alex took no notice. Just as she had stared up at the surface of the sea the night before, willing herself to be there, she now focused on the dark choppy waters of the increasingly distant estuary and willed the same thing. Beneath her, Alex felt something in Merry shift. Slowly, slowly, Merry began to push against the outgoing flood tide, making way steadily as she danced through the waves, and the estuary began to draw closer.

"We're doing it! We're doing it!" Benn yelled happily. "Did you feel how she suddenly turned the right way?"

"I did! I did!" Alex yelled back.

As they neared the estuary, Merry hit a counterflow of water flowing from the side of the river. The boat gave a little twist, the wind filled the sail, and they shot forward. Alex felt the Tau relax and she knew the Enchantment was done—Merry was on her own now. Skillfully, Benn steered Merry into the eddy so that it swirled them into the safety of the estuary and sent them heading straight for the reed beds. Merry plunged her nose deep into the reeds and refused to move any farther.

Alex burst out laughing with relief.

"I don't see what's so funny," Benn said grumpily. "We're stuck in the reeds now."

"Who cares? We're safe!"

"Yeah," Benn said, thinking that it was an undignified end to the voyage for Merry. "Let's take the sail down. Not much use in the reeds."

As Benn and Alex were lowering the sail, which showed above the reeds like a red flag, the two Jackal chariots were heading across the railway bridge that spanned the river about a mile up from the estuary. The chariots clattered over the railroad ties, setting the teeth of the Jackal rattling in their long snouts. When they reached

the middle of the bridge, the lead Jackal stopped its chariot and sniffed the air. Sensing something interesting, it
scanned the river with its keen eyes, looking particularly
at the lush green of the reed beds near the mouth of the
estuary. Something, it was sure, was moving in them. But
the horses were restless, spooked by being on a bridge
over fast-flowing water, and the chariots swayed to and
fro, making it hard to fix on anything. The Jackal took
in a deep breath, but any trace of a scent was drowned in
the smell of horse fear, and its acute hearing was clouded
by the rattle of harnesses and the panicky snorting of the
horses. Irritably, the Jackal gave up and the chariots with
their cages continued over the bridge.

On the far side of the bridge the Jackal took the left turn
along the riverbank, going upstream, and followed the
track for some miles until they reached a fork. There they
slowly compared the letters on a wooden sign with those
on the map: "Lau. Roundhouse Groves. 2 miles." After a
disagreement over the map and much bad-tempered snarling, the Jackal set off to the Roundhouse Groves, clouds
of dust rising up as they rattled along toward their destination.

Merry too was heading toward her destination. Using the
oars as poles, Alex and Benn were steering her along a
narrow channel cut through the reeds. Ahead they could
now see a disused dock built from huge blocks of stone.

Standing on the edge was a tall, skinny boy with long red hair tied into a single braid. He was turned away from them, shading his eyes, staring out to sea across the tops of the reeds. On the back of his leather jacket, Alex and Benn saw the outstretched silver wings and the glinting gold beak of the Hawke, something that had shocked them both when they had last seen it—but no longer. All had changed now that the Hawke was gone and Hagos had told them about Danny.

"Hey!" Benn yelled. "Hey, Danny!"

Danny swung around fast. At first he seemed not to understand what he was looking at. He stood and stared, his hands over his mouth as if he were seeing, Alex thought, a ghost. Because suddenly Alex understood that Danny thought that Benn was dead.

"Hey, Danny, it's okay," Alex said. "This really is Benn. And I'm Alex. Alex RavenStarr."

Danny stared at Alex, hardly recognizing the girl he had last glimpsed in the back of a cart, deep in a Fade. "*You're* Boo-boo?" he asked.

"Alex," Alex sighed. "I'm *Alex*."

In three long strides Danny was beside them, taking the rope from Benn and looping it around a post. He helped them climb out of Merry, and as they stood a little unsteadily on the dockside, Danny threw his arms around them as though they were old friends. "I don't believe it. Where have you *been*?" he asked, but before they had time to answer, he said excitedly, "No, don't tell me. Wait until we find Jay. He is going to be so, so happy."

They went with Danny into the mouth of a large brick-lined tunnel that led into the side of the hill. The tunnel was high and wide, with a distinct sooty smell, and running along its floor was the same metal track that Alex had uncovered on her journey along the cliff to Netters Halt. The light was dim, but at the end of the tunnel—which was not long—they could see the bright glow of lantern light in a huge cavern beyond.

Benn knew what to expect at the end of the tunnel, but Alex had no idea. As they approached the light she was stunned to see the "monster" she had glimpsed in her cards the very first time she had met Benn in the market-place in Luma. A steam locomotive sat upon its turntable looking out at the world beyond, as if, Alex thought, longing to be free. This, she knew, was the Big Puffer—the engine that, when she was little more than a baby, had taken her away from Rekadom, away from her parents, and deposited her with Mirram and her two foster sisters at the foot of the hill up to Luma. She stopped and gazed up at its huge round "face," glimmering in the light of a lantern placed on the ground in front of it, as if at a shrine to a monster god.

"Impressive, eh?" asked Danny proudly, and he headed off to the back of the engine, calling out, "Jay! Hey!"

There was a muffled reply of "Hey!" from the back of

Big Puffer. Danny crouched down. "Jay," he said. "Come out from under there, will you?"

There was some muffled grunting and Jay suddenly shot out from beneath the engine on a trolley. He sat up, wiping the dust from his eyes. "What's up?" he asked. Alex pushed the suddenly shy Benn forward. "Go on," she whispered. "Go to Jay."

But Benn hung back. He felt weird; his eyes prickled and something lay heavy in his chest.

Jay got up from the trolley, wiped his greasy hands on his overalls and looked at Danny sourly. "We've got work to do. Stop messing around."

"Jay," Danny said, beckoning Benn forward. "There's someone here for you."

Jay threw his wrench down to the ground angrily. "I told you, no rubberneckers. No one is coming in here poking their pointy beaks at the Puffer. *No one!*"

"Hey, take it easy," Danny said. He went to Jay and put his arm around his shoulders. "Jay, Benn is here."

Jay stared at Danny. "What?"

Alex gave Benn an impatient shove in the back and Benn appeared in the pool of lantern light. "Hi, Jay," Benn said, suddenly awkward.

Jay stared at the little brother he'd thought was dead. "Benn? It's you?"

Benn found himself unable to speak. He nodded abruptly and then threw himself at Jay, who caught him, staggered and tripped backward over the trolley, whereupon they both landed on it and went hurtling across the cavern.

Danny and Alex burst out laughing.

CHAPTER 29

Chariots of Fear

FRANCINA D'ARBO, SISTER TO ZERRA and Louie, foster sister to Alex, was upstairs in the roundhouse. Francina—who had turned up there a few days back looking for Louie—was dreamily drawing pictures of a boy in a Hawke Flyer's jacket. Francina was also sulking. She did not understand why her mother—*who was not even here*—would not let her go visit Danny down at Lemon Dock. Even Nella, who usually talked to Francina like she was a real grown-up, had said no. *Why is everyone being so boring?* Francina asked herself as she sketched in the boy's long braid and wished she had the right shade of red to color it with. *I so wish I could get out of this stupid dump.*

Downstairs in the kitchen, Nella was sitting with Francina's little brother, Louie, as he finished yet another lemon-and-honey pancake. "I wonder where the pokkle is?" Louie was saying. "It didn't come back in last night. I hope it's all right."

Nella, who was no fan of the pokkle after it had bitten her ankle, smiled at Louie. He reminded her so much of Benn at his age when he had first come to live with her after his mother had died and his father found him "too much." Nella thought that Louie's mother, Mirram, seemed remarkably uninterested in her little son—in all her children, in fact—and Nella was already hoping that Louie might stay for a while. She sat down companionably with Louie and sipped her orange tea. "I'm sure the pokkle will be back soon," she told him.

"I hope so," Louie said. "I miss the pokkle when it's not here." He ran his finger around the plate to scoop up the last of the honey. "And I miss Alex too."

"As much as the pokkle?" Nella asked, with a smile in her voice.

Louie considered this as he took a gulp of orange juice. "More than the pokkle," he said. "Much more."

"I miss Alex too," said Nella. "And I miss Benn, my grandson."

Louie nodded. He was learning fast about missing people.

Nella had reached over to take Louie's hand, which

was sticky from the honey, when a loud banging on the door made them both jump. "I suppose Jay has forgotten his key again," Nella said, getting up and hurrying over to the door.

Louie watched anxiously. In his experience, loud banging on the door meant bad people were on the other side of it.

"Don't worry, sweetheart," Nella told him as she drew back the bolt at the top. "You're safe here."

And then she screamed.

"I did not scream!" Alex protested, laughing, as Benn regaled Jay with their difficulties getting Merry into the estuary. They were sitting on the footplate of the Big Puffer—which Jay insisted on abbreviating to "the Puffer"—contentedly drinking Jay's hot spiced orange tea. Jay, however, was restless. "Drink up, you two," he said. "We need to get to Gramma's. Preferably before it gets dark. I don't like the river at night."

Benn threw Alex an anxious glance—he knew what happened once darkness fell. The Gray Walker—a Night Wraith and Hagos's most vicious Twilight Haunting—would hunt Alex down just as it had done before.

Alex understood his glance. "It's okay, Benn," she said. "It's like I told you. Poppa says this cavern is not part of its Haunting ground. It can't cross this threshold." Alex pointed to the huge doors that rolled across the cavern entrance. "We'll close those and I'll be perfectly safe."

"But there's a chimney thing in the cavern roof, isn't there?" Benn said. "Won't stuff come down there?"

Alex had asked Hagos a lot of questions about the Gray Walker, and she knew the answer to that. "The sky chimney comes out way up in the Border Hills. And the Gray Walker is hefted to Lemon Valley."

"Hefted?" asked Jay.

"It means something stays in a particular area. Like the Skorpas stay in the desert and the Xin stay on the cliffs."

"Weird," said Jay. "But good too. So you can stay here, Alex, and I'll take Benn back home." He stood up. "Come on, Benn. We need to go."

Benn shook his head. "No, Jay. Not tonight. I'm not leaving Alex alone with the Hauntings."

Jay was exasperated. "She's not alone, Danny's here. And anyway, like she said, the Hauntings don't even come in here."

With dismay Alex listened to herself being discussed. She understood that nothing had changed; her presence was still causing trouble. "I'll be fine," she said. "You get going now, tell Nella and Louie hello from me."

"Thanks, Alex," Jay said. "We'll do that. Come on, Benn."

"Jay, you're not listening to me," Benn told his brother. "I already said I'm not leaving Alex. I know what the Twilight Hauntings are like. Danny doesn't. Give Gramma my love and tell her we'll be along in Merry in the morning."

"Have it your own way then," Jay said, annoyed. "You always do."

"Me?" Benn spluttered angrily. "*Me?* Get real, Jay. *You're* the one who does exactly what he wants to. Who takes the lemons up the hill to Luma for Gramma twice a week, huh? Not you, is it? Who weeds the groves, picks the lemons, helps Gramma do the digging? *Me*, that's who. So that you, Jay, can do exactly what you want, when you want. Now you can listen to me. For once I'm doing what *I* want. And Gramma will understand, I know she will."

Jay was silent, regarding Benn coolly. His little brother had suddenly grown up. Slowly, he nodded. "Yeah," he said. "Okay. So there's nothing I can say to change your mind?"

"No," said Benn.

"No!" Louie was screaming from under the table. "No, no, no! Go away! Go awaaaaay!" Cowering behind a forest of chair legs, Louie could see Nella sprawled facedown by the door where she'd tried to slam it closed against the horror of the Jackal-headed creatures that had barged their way in. And now they were down on all fours like wolves—Louie was terrified of wolves—their white snouts snuffling, long fangs bared and their claws grabbing at him. Louie closed his eyes and tried to pretend he really was a superhero, just as Alex used to tell him. But that did not stop him from feeling the Jackal dragging him out from under the table, lifting him up by his arms and legs and carrying him outside. All the time Louie kept his eyes squeezed shut, but when he was pushed down into something that wobbled and heard the clang of metal all around him, Louie opened his eyes to find he was in a cage on wheels drawn by two horses. And next to it was another empty cage just the same.

Too shocked to move, Louie watched the Jackal go back into the roundhouse. Louie scrunched himself up into a ball and covered his face with his arms. He was having a nightmare. He would wake up soon. He would be back home with Alex and everything would be all right.

But the nightmare continued. Louie heard Francina screaming. The screams got louder and louder until he knew she was very close to him. He heard the clang of metal again and then a long wail of *"Nooooooo!"* Louie knew that Francina was now in the same nightmare as he was—and that maybe he wasn't going to wake up at home with Alex ever again.

Alex, Benn and Danny watched Jay head down the tunnel, his figure silhouetted against the arch of light at the end.

"I'm sorry," Alex said.

"What for?" Benn asked.

"For the argument between you and Jay."

"It's not your fault," Benn said. "Just like these Hauntings are not your fault either. And anyway, I've been wanting to tell him that for ages."

"Sometimes," said Danny, "you just have to tell it like it is." He smiled at Alex. "I did the same with your dad a few days ago. I hope you get to meet him one day, Alex. He's a good man."

Alex smiled. "Thanks, Danny. He said the same about you."

Danny looked puzzled. "How? You mean . . . he found you?"

Alex nodded. "And then I found him," she said. "It's a long story."

"So tell me," Danny said, grinning. "We've got all night."

Jay was down at the jetty on the river, staring out across the empty waters and muttering a fine selection of rude words, while just a few miles away two Jackal chariots were bumping their way along the riverbank. Inside them, both Francina and Louie lay in their tiny prisons, curled up into balls. Louie had thought that nothing could ever be any worse—and then it was. Something bit his foot. He kicked out and heard scrabbling beside him. Louie did not dare open his eyes. He could feel something moving, inching up toward his head. "Go away . . . ," he whispered. "Please go away."

"Go way!" came an answering squawk.

"Pokkle?" Louie whispered. He peered through his fingers, hardly daring to hope. "Pokkle!" he gasped. "Oh, pokkle . . ." Louie reached out and pulled the feathery creature toward him. It was a dull gray color, so Louie knew it was feeling sad, and it looked somewhat bedraggled too, because it had been clinging onto the back of the chariot ever since it left the roundhouse. The pokkle rarely felt pleased about anything, but something about Louie's squashy hug made it feel almost happy. A pale pink glow spread slowly over its feathers and it set about licking the salt from Louie's tearstained face.

Benn and Danny were about to pull the doors across the tunnel when they saw Jay walking toward them. He reached the cavern and gave Benn a rueful smile. "My boat's gone. Guess I didn't tie it up right."

"It was crazy when we got here," Benn said. "The tide was so fast. Everything was being swept out. I've never seen it so bad. I'd say take Merry but I'm guessing the water's gone and she's stuck on the mud now?"

Jake nodded. "Stranded. But thanks for the offer, Benn."

Benn smiled, pleased to have patched things up with Jay. "Just think how happy Gramma will be when we all turn up together," he said.

Jay nodded. "Yeah. But I really wanted to get back to her tonight," he said. "I dunno why. But I did."

CHAPTER 30
The Beguiler Bell

TWO JACKAL CHARIOTS HAD DRAWN up outside the city gates beneath the Beguiler Bell and were waiting for the bell to ring. The bell, however, remained obstinately silent. The lead Jackal looked up at it anxiously. The mission was accomplished; they had the boy and girl Beguiler brats, therefore the bell must ring. As the guards pulled open the gates, the lead Jackal sprang into the air and punched the bell, sending it frantically clanging, echoing across the whole of Rekadom.

At the top of the Gold and Silver Towers, the raucous ringing of the Beguiler Bell sent the two disparate occupants hurrying to their windows. King Belamus, through his spyglass, watched the chariots rattling into the lantern-lit Gate Court. He laughed in relief at the sight of their two small, terrified passengers. Here were the last Beguilers in the kingdom. Apart from the annoying Beguiler next door, of course.

The annoying Beguiler next door did not have such a good view. He was peering anxiously out the tiny window in his study—the only one to overlook Gate Court—but his view of the gate was almost entirely obscured by the high walls. All he could see were the ominous tops of two chariot cages. "Boo-boo?" he whispered. "Is that you in there?"

Bartlett was sitting up late in the office. She had just made a cup of orange tea and taken a cookie from the jar when she heard the Beguiler Bell ring. She jumped with surprise—what was a Beguiler doing coming into the city at night? Surely someone ought to stop them? Bartlett hurried out through the nighttime rustlings of the darkened mews, with its wakeful birds, and unbarred the door. Mindful of the Rocadiles—two of which were dozing by the wall—she walked quickly across to the snicket and peered through. There, by lantern light, she saw that all was in order. It was not some lone Beguiler come to terrorize them, it was four of the king's Jackal and two prison chariots, presumably carrying a consignment of Beguilers. With the Jackal fussing with the horses, their long coats swishing and the Gate Court lanterns casting confusing shadows, Bartlett could not see who was in the cages. She watched with interest as a horse was taken off each chariot and led away by a stable girl, leaving the remaining horses to pull the chariots in single file to the door to the dungeons. Bartlett smiled. All was as it should be.

As her chariot bumped over the cobbles, Francina could not take her eyes off the huge iron door ahead, studded with nails. It was identical to the door in Luma that led to the prisons—the notorious Vaults—beneath the city. The door opened to reveal a dimly lit tunnel with green slime upon the walls dipping down into the darkness beyond. As the chariots clattered into the tunnel, Francina turned around to comfort Louie in his cage, but he was curled up into a ball like a hedgehog, and Francina was glad he could not see where they were going.

The horses trod carefully down the slippery incline, taking the chariots ever deeper into the warren of passages below Rekadom. The rattling of the iron wheels and the clop of the horses' hooves echoed harshly off the stones and made Francina's head hurt. Eventually they drew to a clattering halt at a barred gate, which was opened with much clinking of keys. The horses clip-clopped through and the chariots drew up in a circular space lit by a few dim lanterns. Four guards appeared from the darkness, rubbing their hands in the chill. Silently, they lifted first the bars from the chariots, then the prisoners, and set them both upon the ground.

"We'll take over now," they told the Jackal.

The Jackal watched impassively as the stunned Louie and Francina were ushered away into a dark corridor. The Jackal waited until they heard the clang of a distant cell door, and then they took the horses back up the incline and out into the night. They had another job to do before the night was over.

Down in the dungeons, the guards were back in their guardroom.

"At least we got some prisoners now," one of them said.

"Just a couple of kids," said another. "Hardly worth bothering about. They won't last long."

"Yeah. They say they're the last Beguilers in the kingdom. So when they're gone, that's it for us."

"Don't forget the smarty-pants Enchanter up in the Silver Tower," said the fourth.

Another laughed. "He won't last long now. Sausages, anyone?"

There was a general agreement that sausages were a good idea.

Bartlett hurried back to the familiarity of the office and sat down at the desk once more. She wondered if one of the prisoners—they had looked quite small—might be the absconded trainee Flyer. She was sure she was a Beguiler child. Bartlett made a note to go and check out the dungeons the next day and took a sip of her orange tea and a bite from her cookie. She frowned. The cookie tasted very odd—the chocolate crumbles were strangely bitter. She took a second bite and chewed slowly. Her teeth hit something soft. It tasted vile. She gagged and spit the mouthful across the desk, where it landed with a splat. Bartlett took a gulp of tea to wash away the taste. *What was wrong with these cookies?*

Bartlett was inspecting the contents of the cookie jar when she heard the key turning the lock of the door into the mews. *Bother*, thought Bartlett. *It's Ratchet. What's he doing back so soon?* She picked up the cookie jar—thinking she'd offer one to Ratchet and enjoy seeing the expression on his face—and opened the office door. She screamed and dropped the jar on the foot of the nearest Jackal—the one with the handcuffs.

Dumbstruck, Bartlett stared at the Jackal. One of them thrust a piece of paper at her with the king's seal. With trembling hands, Bartlett took it and read:

> *Concerning Deputy Falconer Bartlett.*
> *King's Charge: Communing with a Known Beguiler While Engaged in the Act of Treasonous Personation and Facilitating Escape of Another Known Beguiler.*
> *King's Verdict: Guilty.*
> *King's Sentence: Life imprisonment.*

Bartlett had to read it twice before she understood it. "But that's not true!" she protested. "I tried to stop him! Who told the king these lies?" But even as she asked the question, Bartlett knew the answer. "It was that little toad, that filthy owl pellet of a trainee Flyer, wasn't it?" she yelled.

The Jackal did not answer. In seconds the handcuffs were on and Bartlett was being marched out of the mews and off to the dungeons. She ended up in the cell next to Francina and Louie, where the smell of rancid sausages being fried in old fat mingled with the lingering aftertaste of the cookie and made her feel quite sick.

The sausages, however, smelled very fine indeed to the Jackal. And so, just as the guards were about to dig in, they found that their supper was no longer their own.

And the Jackal found they were remarkably hungry. Especially for sausages.

CHAPTER 31

Escape

HAGOS COULD NOT GET THE sound of the Beguiler Bell out of his mind. It had been so strong, so definite, so much like his daughter. He just knew it must be ringing for her. Hagos felt frantic—he had to get to her. *He had to.* But first he must get past the Jackal outside the door.

Hagos squared his shoulders. It would have to be a fight. Not wanting to wake Deela, who was sleeping in his little room, Hagos tiptoed over to the fire and picked up the poker. Pushing aside the thought of the Jackal's razor-sharp fangs, he crept over to the big arched door that led out onto the stairs and flipped up the spy-hole cover to check exactly where the Jackal was.

The landing was empty.

Thinking that the Jackal had fallen asleep on duty and was lying across the threshold, Hagos opened the door just half an inch and, poker at the ready, he peered out. There was no Jackal. Not in the shadows, not sitting on the stairs, not even—he glanced anxiously up at the ceiling—lurking on the rafters. A small flicker of hope began to glow in Hagos's heart. He crept out onto the landing and pulled the door closed with a gentle *click*. Then he set off down the steps on his mission to find his daughter.

Zerra was sitting curled up in the archway of the Gold Tower, staring gloomily out at the empty Star Court. She was cold and miserable and she didn't want to be a King's Spy anymore. In fact, right now she would even rather be poking at bird poop. But wait, what was that shadow at the foot of the Iron Tower? Zerra got out her spyglass and almost laughed out loud—it was the Beguiler. At last there was someone to spy on. Reluctant to venture out—for she had already been chased by two Slicers that night—she watched the Beguiler creep into the archway of the Iron Tower. Zerra grinned. This was what being a spy was all about—catching people out when they thought no one was looking. It was, she realized, what she liked doing best in the whole world.

* * *

Hagos was gazing at the rusted slab of the Iron Tower's door. He was sad to see how decrepit it was. It had once been burnished to a beautiful sheen in those heady days when Enchantment was a blessing, not a curse. Hagos was still proud of what he had created. It was his contribution to civic life—a communal place of safety for Enchantments that had gone wrong and had to be kept securely out of the way. "Bad spell jail," as Sol had called it.

Hagos was also proud of the system he had devised for the deposits. A simple one-way valve in a tube at the top of the door—high enough to stop passing children from dropping their teddy bears in—had worked well. And unfortunately it still did. Only a few days previously he had been forced to watch Belamus throw the beautiful Tau into it. Hagos sighed. If only it were so easy to get the Tau out again. But the only way to do that was to open the door, which was highly dangerous, for who knew what lay behind it now? Hagos shuddered as he thought of Sol's rapidly growing spider that he had so thoughtlessly dropped in one sunny afternoon. How big would that be now? Not to mention all those malevolent Night Wraiths. How powerful would they be now?

Hagos tried to push these thoughts aside, but there was something he could not get rid of—the memory of Alex's angry words the night before. They still echoed in his head: "Clean up your mess, Poppa!" He knew she was right, but how could he do that? He would have to have the Tau. Hagos pondered the implacable rusty slab of iron in front of him. *Suppose,* he thought, *the Tau is just on the other side? All I have to do is open the door, grab it and go. How hard can that be?* Once again, Alex's words came back to him: "You have to try. You *have* to."

Hagos took a deep breath. Boo-boo—oops, no, he *must* remember, Alex—was right. He had to try. Especially since she had left him one of the keys to the door.

Hands trembling at the thought of what he was about to do, Hagos took the codex from his pocket, flipped open the front cover and removed the hexagon with the number 7 on it. He balanced the feather-light shape on his palm and looked into its glimmering depths. He was going to do this. *He was going to do it.*

Why doesn't he do *something?* Zerra thought. She felt quite disappointed. She had hoped the Enchanter might do something really bad, but all he was doing was lurking in a doorway staring at his hand. She sighed. It would have to do. He wasn't in his rooms like he should be, and surely that was enough to go tell the king and have a chance to warm up. But was it? The king could be very picky. Zerra decided to give it a few more minutes. Aha . . . the Enchanter was kneeling down and poking at the foot of the door. He was up to something—that was for sure.

Hagos was searching for the silver locking plate at the foot of the door. The silver was badly tarnished and he could see nothing, but his fingers found its smoothness and felt the low-level buzz of Enchantment running through it. He took a deep breath, gathered his courage and pushed the hexagon against the circle of silver. At once he had heard the complex barrels in the lock turning and then their final *kerrr-plick* as they drew back the bolt. He got to his feet and pushed hard on the door. It did not move. He tried again. It still did not move. Suddenly Hagos remembered that—just to make things a little more difficult—the door always opened toward the person trying to go through. He grabbed the tiny handle on the edge of the locking plate and pulled. The door swung open, an ice-cold blast of air came pouring out, and Hagos pushed his way into the Iron Tower.

Buffeted by the stream of freezing Wraith essence trying to escape, Hagos fell to his hands and knees, searching for the Tau. He felt as if he had fallen into a violent, stormy sea. Deafened by the howls of trapped Enchantments and pounded by a vortex of Wraiths funneling down from the top of the tower, he frantically swept his hands across the iron floor, hoping to find the familiar T shape of the Tau, but all his fingers could feel was the rough chill of the iron floor. And already he knew it was useless—there was no blue light to be seen, not even a glimmer. As he had feared, the Tau's Enchantment had not survived its short time in the Iron Tower.

Suddenly, something rough and very solid brushed against him, almost pushing him over. Hagos looked up to see eight little red lights staring down at him. He then saw the eight long, hairy legs attached to the little red lights. Sol's spider! Hagos screamed, leaped up and threw himself back out through the door. As he struggled to close it, the spider wedged a powerful muscular leg into the gap and the door swung farther open. A trio of Night Wraiths took their chance and Hagos was sent flying backward and hit his head upon the archway. Shaken, he staggered to his feet and saw a stream of darkness tumbling by him, while the spider helpfully held the door open.

Zerra watched the stream of darkness pour out from the Iron Tower with glee. Now she had something really exciting to tell the king. She raced up the red-carpeted stairs to the top of the Gold Tower, where, at the golden door emblazed with the winged crown, she punched the crow-pecked Jackal on the nose—Zerra could tell it was weak—and hurtled into the mirrored lobby. There she stopped and caught her breath, spooked for a brief moment by the group of wild-eyed kids who had gathered there until she remembered the creepy mirrors. And then she yelled, "King! King! The Beguiler has opened the Iron Tower!"

* * *

From inside his rooms, Belamus heard Zerra's shouts. Gingerly the king opened the mirrored door just wide enough to note that his useless, crow-pecked Jackal was kneeling on his best rug clutching his snout and his spy was now in his own private space yelling at him.

"The Beguiler!" the spy was shouting. "He's opened the Iron Tower and let bad stuff out. Look!" And then, with no regard for his kingly dignity, the spy grabbed hold of his velvet night cloak and pulled him across to the royal window. And now she was yelling right into his ear, "There! Look down there!"

Dumbfounded, Belamus did as he was told. Far below in Star Court, he saw a tide of darkness flowing across the cobbles, and within it he glimpsed two lines of little red eyes. *Spider eyes*, he thought. And then, realizing how high up he was, *GIANT spider eyes*.

"What are you going to do?" Zerra asked him.

King Belamus looked at her in confusion. "Do?" he asked.

"You're the king. Don't you have to do something?" Zerra asked, genuinely puzzled.

Belamus looked equally puzzled. There was silence and then he said, very quietly, "But I don't know what to do."

Zerra stared at King Belamus, feeling very let down. If she were king, *she'd* know what to do. She was wondering whether to tell him that when there was another loud hammering upon the door. The king looked vaguely at it, as if he had forgotten what a door actually was. Exasperated, Zerra strode across the room and pulled it open.

Hagos almost fell inside. Wild-eyed and shaking, he gasped, "Belamus. Something terrible has happened." Then he noticed Zerra. "How did you get here?" he demanded.

"Same way as you," Zerra retorted. "Except faster, because *I* didn't stop on the way to let all that stuff out of the Iron Tower like you did."

"You did *what*?" Belamus whispered, staring at Hagos.

"I already *told* you what he did!" Zerra said, exasperated.

"It was a mistake," said Hagos. "A terrible mistake."

"Will it come up here?" Belamus asked anxiously.

Hagos shook his head. "I don't think so." He went to the window and looked down. The Wraith mist was still pouring out, but it was keeping close to the ground and spreading outward. "We must open the city gates," Hagos said. "If we let it out, I believe it will disperse."

"Well, go and let it out then," Belamus said.

Hagos gulped. "Yes. Okay. I'll go and do it. Right away."

"My spy will help you," said Belamus.

"Me?" asked Zerra.

"Yes, you!"

Belamus turned to Hagos and looked him in the eye. "You will pay for this, RavenStarr." And as Hagos left the room, he added under his breath, "With your life."

CHAPTER 32
Wraith Flow

HAGOS AND ZERRA STOOD IN the archway of the Gold Tower, unwilling to step out. Star Court was a swirling mass of dark mist, shot through with flashes of blue light. From deep inside the darkness came an eerie mix of shrieks, growls and moans. It gave both Zerra and Hagos severe goose bumps. As if aware of Hagos and Zerra's intrusion, the outer edges of the Wraith flow broke away, and long tendrils—some with little yellow eyes shining deep within—came curling toward them.

"Will it kill us?" Zerra whispered.

"It could," Hagos said. "There are some nasty Wraiths

in there. Sticky things that won't let you go once they touch you."

Zerra looked at Hagos in horror.

"So we need to move slowly and try not to create a disturbance in the air. You might find this useful." Keeping a watchful eye on the tendrils, which were steadily approaching, Hagos drew the codex from his pocket. He flipped it open, took out one of the hexagonal cards and handed it to Zerra.

"This is one of Alex's cards," she said, puzzled.

Hagos looked surprised. "How do you know?"

Zerra shrugged. "I found them one day. Feels like ages ago. When we were home in Luma."

"Home? In Luma? With *Alex*?"

"Yes. Stop looking at me like that. It's weird."

"So you're Mirram D'Arbo's daughter? Her younger one?"

"Yes. So what?"

Hagos sighed and muttered to himself, "You win some, you lose some."

"*What?*" asked Zerra.

"Never mind. Take this card. Hold it in your fist. Like this." Hagos himself took a card and wrapped his fingers around it. "Now you say these words. Just read them from here." Hagos showed the codex to Zerra.

She looked at some tiny writing curled around in a

circle. "What is it?" she asked suspiciously.

"It's an Enchantment. To encircle you. Keep you safe. You can read?"

"Of course I can read," Zerra said scornfully. "But it's no use my saying your Beguiler stuff, because I'm not a stupid Beguiler."

"You're clearly not stupid," Hagos replied snappily. "So just read the words, will you?"

And so Zerra read her first Enchantment. She whispered the words and felt the wafer-thin hexagonal card buzz in her palm. When she was finished she hurriedly handed it back to Hagos. He waved it away. "Keep it with you. It will protect the Enchantment."

Zerra put the card in her pocket. She noticed that the tendrils that had been reaching out to them had curled back into the main flow, which was, Zerra could not help but think, quite cool. She listened to Hagos muttering his own Enchantment and thought how strange it was to be standing beside a real, grown-up Beguiler. It was not what she had expected—he seemed to be taking care of her, which was most odd. Her thoughts were interrupted by Hagos saying in a low voice, "We must open the door into Gate Court so that the Wraiths flow into there. Then we get the gate guards to open the city gates."

"They won't want to do that," Zerra said.

"They will when they see this heading for them,"

Hagos said. "And now we must be brave. We're going to have to walk through this stuff. Take my hand. We're more powerful as one."

Warily—because at school much had been made of the slippery, cold reptilian touch of a Beguiler—Zerra took Hagos's hand. To her surprise it felt warm and dry, and enfolded her smaller hand in a comforting way. Allowing herself to be led by Hagos, Zerra walked with him into the Wraith flow. At once her legs felt icy cold and the miasma rising up from it made her cough. But as she and Hagos waded down the southeast point of the star, a strange sensation overcame Zerra. It was as though the coiled snake of anger that lived inside her was slowly slipping away. She felt almost happy as she and Hagos moved along the darkened street and then took the small ginnel on the left that ran between the houses to Gate Court. At the end was a tall, narrow door identical to the one that led into Mews Court. Hagos pulled the lever in the wall, the door swung open and they tumbled out into Gate Court, right into the middle of the line of Jackal chariots. They left the door hanging open and, pursued by the snaking swirls of Wraiths, they ran toward the city gates.

"Halt!" the gate guard yelled. Then, seeing the writhing mass of darkness that Hagos had brought with him, the guard faltered. "Who goes there?" he whispered.

Hagos decided to own up to who he was. "Hagos

RavenStarr, King's Enchanter. You are commanded by the king to open the city gates."

The guard stared at Hagos, wild-eyed in his red Enchanter's cloak. "But you're the Enchanter!"

"Yes. I just told you. Now open the gates and let this stuff out before it smothers us all!"

But all the guard could manage in reply was a strangled cough—one of the Wraiths was coiling tightly up around his chest and looping around his neck. It was, Hagos recognized with a shock, his failed Constrictor Enchantment, the one that would have turned earthworms into giant boa constrictors. From the depths of his memory, Hagos managed to find the countermand incantation. The Constrictor Wraith weakened and Hagos steadied the choking gate guard. "Get up the steps to the top of the gate tower," he told him. "You'll be safe there." Needing no encouragement, the spluttering man stumbled away.

Hagos felt something jab him in the back. He wheeled around to find another guard—the night captain, no less—confronting him, her javelin pointing at his throat. "What is this?" she demanded.

Hagos was about to reply when the night captain's javelin dropped from her hand. He saw that she was staring up at something behind him with a look of horror. Hagos wheeled around to see eight red eyes set deep in a round head attached to a scaly abdomen balanced on eight long and spectacularly hairy legs—all of which was advancing toward them.

"By the king's command!" Hagos yelled desperately. "Open the gates and let this out!"

The sound of Hagos's voice released the night captain from the hypnotic effect of the spider. She fumbled for the key she wore at her belt and, with the help of Hagos and Zerra, pulled the Rekadom city gates open.

"Get up here," said the night captain, beckoning Hagos and Zerra to follow her through an archway at the foot of one of the stone pillars on either side of the gates. She led them up the narrow steps within the pillar, where they joined the other gate guard on the observation platform on the top. And there the unlikely group of Enchanter, spy, night captain and gate guard watched a giant spider accompanied by its attendant Wraiths stalk out of the city and head off into the desert.

They watched for three long hours while the entire contents of the Iron Tower swirled and whirled, screamed and moaned their way out of Rekadom and into the world beyond the city. With Zerra's spyglass, they took turns watching the Wraith flow as it spread across the desert, every now and then seeing a brilliant flash of yellow light as it made contact with a Skorpas.

Hagos sighed. What new terror had he let loose on the world now?

When the last of the Wraith flow was gone, they climbed

down and helped the night captain close the gates, and then Hagos found the courage to ask about the chariots that had arrived earlier. When the night captain described the prisoners, Hagos knew that neither could be Alex. His spirits sank—where *was* she?

But Zerra laughed. "They sound just like Louie and Francina," she said. "But it can't be."

"Why not? It has to be someone," Hagos remarked snappily.

The night captain locked the gates and turned to Hagos. "Strictly speaking, Mr. RavenStarr," she said, "we should now be taking you to the dungeons for breaking your house arrest. But if you go home now, we won't remember you were here, will we?" The night captain looked at the other guard inquiringly.

"Remember what?" he asked, and winked at Zerra. She smiled back.

As they walked back up the deserted street, toward Star Court, Hagos said, "Zerra. Do you have anywhere to go?"

"Um. No. Well, I could go back to the mews, but Bartlett doesn't like me."

"Come back to my rooms," Hagos said. "You can have Alex's bed." He gave Zerra a quizzical look. "And before I forget, you can give me back her Hex card."

Obediently, Zerra handed back the card, feeling oddly sorry to see it go.

Wearily, yet feeling oddly content, Zerra climbed the long spiral stairs up the Silver Tower. In less than five minutes, as the sun rose over the rooftops, Zerra was fast asleep under Alex's frayed pink velvet cover with the appliquéd rabbits.

CHAPTER 33

Exchanges

THE SUN WAS RISING ABOVE the early morning mist as Benn rowed Merry up the river on the incoming tide. "Watch out for Stinger Eels," he told Jay, who was trailing his fingers in the water.

Jay laughed. "That's just a story, Benn. You shouldn't believe all those fairy tales."

Benn was rapidly remembering how much Jay annoyed him with his big-brother superiority. "It's not a fairy tale, Jay. Stingers are real. Me and Alex got attacked by one when we came downriver."

"Probably just a big fish," Jay told him.

Alex wasn't sure she liked Jay much. Silence fell and

Alex sat in the stern watching the water, listening to the steady *clunk-unk clunk-unk* of the oars as Benn and Jay rowed easily along with the incoming tide. It was a cool morning, with a few wisps of mist hanging around the riverbanks, but the sky above was clear and Alex felt her spirits rise as she looked forward to arriving at the round-house. She longed to see Louie again, and for Nella to know that Benn was safe and well. It was so good to look forward to something happy for once.

Merry progressed along the meandering river with no sign of a Stinger Eel, and before long they were passing by the orange and lemon groves of Nella's farm. They rounded the last bend and Alex gathered up the mooring rope. As Benn and Jay took Merry alongside the jetty, Alex jumped out and tied the little boat up to the post. Benn leaped out after her and then Jay. Their disagreements set aside, Jay put his arm around Benn. "Gramma will be so happy!" he said.

Alex followed the boys along the path and through the archway into the circular courtyard in which the round-house sat like the bull's-eye in the middle of a target. It was an old fort, built for repelling pirates that had once raided the farms along the river, and that morning Alex thought it felt quite forbidding. But when she thought about Louie, who was probably sitting at Nella's table eating his breakfast at that very moment, and also Nella's warm and welcoming kitchen where she had felt so at home, she could hardly wait to be inside.

They crossed the courtyard, with its colored cobbles, and Benn and Alex hung back while Jay pushed open the door and walked in. "Hey, Gramma?" he called out. "Gramma? Oh, no! Gramma!"

Benn and Alex exchanged anxious glances and hurried in after Jay. There they stopped, horrified. The kitchen was trashed. Pots and pans were strewn across the floor, chairs upended, and the table lay on its back with its legs in the air. But the very worst thing of all was Nella. She lay sprawled upon the floor beside the stove, her hair sticky with blood.

"Gramma!" Benn raced over to his grandmother and fell to his knees beside her. Alex hurried after him, a cold feeling in the pit of her stomach.

Jay looked up, relief on his face. "She's alive," he said. "I can feel her pulse."

A faint moan came from Nella. Benn leaned down and whispered, "Gramma, are you okay?"

Jay rocked back on his heels. "That's a stupid question. Of course she's not okay."

"Benn?" Nella pushed herself up on her arms and twisted around so she was sitting up. "Benn? Is it you?" She ran her hand across her face and rubbed her eyes.

"Yes, Gramma. It's me. Oh, Gramma, what happened?"

"Help me up, Benn. There's a good boy. Oh, Benn. My boy. You're alive. But . . . oh dear . . . oh dear . . ."

"Sit down, Gramma," Benn said and then realized there was nowhere to sit.

While Benn and Jay righted the chairs and table, Alex found a blanket and wrapped it around Nella's shoulders, and then two boys helped Nella into her favorite chair by the stove. Now that she was seated, they could all see a big bruise on Nella's forehead. Alex set about making lemon-and-honey tea, just as she remembered Nella doing it.

Nella reached out her hand and placed it over Benn's. "It really is you," she said. "I am so happy to see you. My dearest Benn. But so sad to lose little Louie. And Francina too."

"Lose Louie?" Alex asked, a twist of fear in her stomach.

Nella nodded. "Oh, the poor little boy."

Alex was horrified. "What happened? Oh, please, what has happened to Louie?"

Speaking very slowly, trying to control the trembling of her voice, Nella said, "Yesterday evening, three jackal-headed creatures in red coats came and took Louie and Francina away."

"The King's Jackal," Alex whispered.

Nella looked up at Benn and Alex. "Oh. Of course that's what they were. They had a paper saying they had come to take two 'Beguiler children.' A boy and a girl. I told them there were no Beguilers here. They didn't care. They took their boy and girl anyway."

Alex and Benn exchanged horrified glances. "It was us they were after," Alex said in a low voice, feeling terrible. "We escaped. But I don't understand. How did they know we were coming here?"

Benn groaned. "Because I told Ma Ratchet."

"Who?" Nella asked.

"Ma Ratchet. It was her house we were in the night before last. She was all chatty and friendly, so I was trying to be nice too. She asked where home was. So I told her."

"And yesterday morning we told the harbormaster we were going home," said Alex.

"Well, *I* told the harbormaster," said Benn.

Jay stopped cleaning up and turned around. "Idiot," he told Benn.

"Jay, please. Don't speak in that way." Nella sounded weary.

"Sorry, Gramma," Jay said. "But Benn's done nothing but bring trouble to us. Ever since he . . ."

Alex knew what Jay was going to say. He was staring right at her, angrily. She finished his sentence for him. "Ever since he brought me here," she said. "I know. I've brought trouble to you all. I am so sorry. This is *my* fault."

"It is no one's fault," Nella said, getting the strength in her voice back. "Apart from that wicked, *wicked* king."

Alex finished making the tea. They drank it in silence, listening to Jay angrily clattering pots as he tidied up. At last Nella spoke. "Well, at least Mirram wasn't here."

No one had given a moment's thought to Alex's foster mother until then. "She might have been some help," Benn said gloomily.

"I doubt it," said Alex tartly. "Where is she?"

"Mirram went to Santa Pesca yesterday, and she hasn't come back," Nella said. "I could see she was bored here, so I asked her to go see your father, Benn. To . . . well, to tell him that you . . . that you were lost. At sea." Nella gave Benn a weak smile. "But you're not. Which is so wonderful. But now we must get hold of Mirram and tell her the awful news about Louie and Francina."

Benn and Alex both spoke together. "No," they said.

"No?" asked Nella. "Why?"

"Because there will be nothing to tell. Because we are going to get Louie and Francina back," Alex said. "Aren't we, Benn?"

"You bet," said Benn.

Nella shook her head. "How can you possibly do that?" she asked.

Benn looked at Alex. He had no idea, but he could tell Alex had a plan.

"They can't," Jay said.

"We can," Benn retorted. "You just wait."

Jay laughed. "For how long?"

"Boys, stop it," Nella said wearily. "Benn, whatever your plan is, I would like you and Alex to stay with me today. I just want to enjoy your company. We can talk things over, and Jay, I would like you to stay and talk too. I want you to be nice to your brother and not go rushing off like you usually do."

Jay folded up the dishcloth and came over to hug his grandmother. "I'm not going anywhere, Gramma. I'm staying right here and looking after you."

Benn felt suddenly wrong-footed. Usually he was the reliable one who stayed with his grandmother, but now Jay had niftily moved into his role. Benn wasn't at all sure how he felt about that. But then he remembered how he had longed to be free, to sail Merry where he wanted. *I guess I can't have it both ways*, he told himself.

Benn and Alex spent the day with Nella as she had requested. The time went quickly. While Jay set about mending a broken chair and, despite Nella's protests, adding more bolts to the door, Alex and Benn told Nella all that had happened since they had left. Under Nella's directions—because no one would allow Nella to do anything—Benn made cheese omelets for lunch and Alex perfected the art of making lemon pancakes. But soon the afternoon sun was getting lower in the sky and they reluctantly told Nella that it was time they were going.

Nella was resigned. "You take care on the river now, won't you?" she said.

"We will," Benn said, his face clouding a little as he thought of the Stinger Eel they had been attacked by the last time they had left the roundhouse. He'd taken care not to tell Nella about that.

"Will I see you tomorrow?" Nella asked. Benn glanced at Alex. Infinitesimally, Alex shook her head. But nothing was lost on Nella. "Ah, maybe not," she said. She reached out for both their hands and held them. "Now, you two. I will not ask you what you intend to do because I do not think you will tell me. But I just want to say to you to consider everything very carefully. Make sure that whatever you are planning is actually possible and, if it is, do it with the utmost care and consideration of all outcomes. Do not risk everything for nothing."

Alex nodded. It was good advice. "I think," she said, "that we are risking *some*thing for *every*thing."

Nella nodded. "I suppose there is nothing I can do to help?"

"Help what?" Jay asked, coming back in from the shed with a large screwdriver and two flat iron bars for the door.

Nella sighed, releasing Benn and Alex's hands. "Nothing, Jay, dear. Benn and Alex are off now."

Benn, then Alex, hugged Nella tightly. "Thank you for everything," Alex said. "We will see you very soon."

"I do hope so, dear," Nella murmured. She hugged Benn once again and wordlessly watched them go. Nella leaned back in her chair and closed her eyes, and a few tears ran down her face. Determined not to let Jay see, she rubbed them away and got to her feet. "I'm going to rest a while, Jay."

"Do you need a hand up the stairs, Gramma?" Jay asked.

Nella smiled. "Now don't you go fussing over me, Jay Markham."

Nella climbed the stairs more slowly than she had ever done before, and when she reached her room, she felt exhausted. But even so, she walked over to the little window and looked out. She watched the little white boat moving slowly down the river, with Benn and Alex at the oars, rowing together. She watched until they rounded the bend and she could see them no more, and even then she kept watching. At last she turned and went to her bed, where she lay down and closed her eyes. But she found no rest. All she saw were huge white jackal heads, baring their teeth. And all she heard were the screams of a terrified little boy.

CHAPTER 34

First Fire

THE TIDE WAS RUNNING IN their favor and Alex was surprised how soon they were heading into the narrow cut through the rushes. They poled Merry along, and as they drew near to the old Lemon Dock, they saw Danny sitting outside in the sun, eyes closed, smiling in the late afternoon warmth.

At the sound of the mooring rope hitting the stone, Danny leaped up like a coiled spring. Then, seeing Merry, he grinned and ran over to help. "Hey, guys. Had a good time? You'll never guess what . . ." Danny's voice trailed off as he saw their expressions. "Hey, what's up?"

"The Jackal. They were there last night. They took Louie. And Francina."

"Francina!" Danny dropped the mooring rope. "The Jackal took *Francina*?"

"And Louie," said Alex.

Danny spun around on his heels as if it was all too much to take in. "But why? Why, why, *why*? What has Francina done to them? And what were they even doing out there?"

"Looking for me and Benn," Alex told him.

Danny shook his head. "I don't get it. I just *don't*. Sheesh. She'll be so *scared*." He was crouching down now, tying endless knots in Merry's mooring rope.

"Hey, take it easy, that's enough knots," Benn said, taking the rope from Danny. "She's not going to escape, you know."

Danny misunderstood him. He looked up at Benn, his face anguished. "I know. How can she possibly escape from those dungeons? No one ever does. It's a terrible place. My . . . my mom and dad died there."

Alex and Benn were both shocked—they had never given a thought to Danny's family.

Danny read their expressions correctly. "Yeah," he said bitterly. "I'm not just some evil kid who Flew the Hawke. I'm human too. Just like you. *Sheesh*." He turned and walked away, striding off into the dark mouth of the tunnel, back to his den.

Alex and Benn followed slowly down the tunnel. Alex sniffed the air. "Smells weird," she said.

"Yeah. What's he been doing?" Benn muttered, speeding up. They arrived at the cavern to find the lanterns burning brightly. A bitter, sulfurous smell caught in the backs of their throats, but the strangest thing was a soft swishing sound, as though something big was breathing very slowly. Alex felt goose bumps run down her neck. "Benn, remember in Luma," she whispered, "when I had my cards and you asked me if the monster would always be cold, if its joints would always hurt?"

"And if its heart would always be stilled," Benn finished for her. "How could I forget? If I hadn't asked you that, you wouldn't be here now."

And Louie wouldn't be in a dungeon in Rekadom, Alex thought. She shook the thought away—getting upset was not going to help Louie right now—and looked up at the locomotive, sitting still and dark in the middle of the cavern. Something about it had changed. "Well, that's what it feels like now. Big Puffer's heart is beating. He's breathing."

"Fire," Benn whispered. "He's breathing fire. Just like you said." He reached up and patted the locomotive's nose. "It's warm," he whispered.

They walked along the length of Big Puffer, past its tubular body, past its domed copper water tank, heading for the driver's cab at the back, from which an orange glow was emanating. There they found Danny kneeling on the footplate by an oval opening into the body of the engine. Into this he was feeding small pieces of wood one at a time, as though tempting a fussy baby to eat. Danny looked down at Benn and Alex. "He's hungry," he said.

"That's not fair, Danny," Benn told him. "Jay's worked on the Puffer for years. He was always talking about making the first fire. You should have waited."

"I thought there was no harm in testing it. You have to let the Puffer warm up slowly. Don't want anything to expand too quickly. So I thought I'd just feed him a little tonight. I was going to let the fire go out again, and clean out the firebox. Jay didn't need to know, did he?"

Feeling an unexpected surge of brotherly loyalty, Benn said, "That's not the point, and you know it. Anyway, Jay *will* know. He knows the Puffer inside out."

Danny shrugged. "There you go," he told the Puffer as he fed in another tasty morsel of wood. "Anyway, turns out it's a good thing I did start the fire, huh?"

Benn persisted. "It is *not* a good thing. Jay's going to be really upset when he finds out you made the first fire."

Danny gave a brief laugh. "Not half as upset as he's going to be when he finds the Puffer gone."

"Gone?" asked Benn. "What do you mean, *gone*?"

Danny left the embryo fire, came over and sat down on the footplate. "Gone to get Francina." He looked at Alex. "And Louie. Gone to rescue two helpless kids from those disgusting dungeons beneath Rekadom."

Benn and Alex were speechless. Benn spoke first. "You mean you want to go to Rekadom on the Puffer?"

"Not 'want to.' Going to." Danny slipped down from the footplate, picked up his lantern and headed to the back of the cavern, where the tunnel that led beneath the mountains was shut off by the remains of the passenger carriage—once known as Old Wormy—now used as shuttering. He opened a carriage door and stepped through, disappearing into the blackness beyond.

Alex and Benn exchanged confused glances. "What is he doing?" asked Alex.

Benn shook his head. "No idea."

A few seconds later, Danny stepped back through the door. His hands were clenched into fists and for a brief moment both Benn and Alex thought he was about to punch them. In fact, nothing would have surprised them—Danny's behavior was increasingly strange. But at least he was smiling.

"I know why you looked so shocked when I said I was taking the Puffer," Danny said. "It was because you didn't see any fuel, did you? In fact, you probably thought I'd forgotten all about that, didn't you?"

Benn and Alex shook their heads. The truth was, neither had given any thought whatsoever to fuel. "You mean coal?" Alex asked.

"Indeed I do," Danny said—and, like a magician

producing a small animal out of a disconcerting item of clothing, he opened his fists to show two round nuggets of dusty blackness. "Ta-daa! Coal!"

Benn and Alex stared at the two lumps of coal in Danny's hands. "So you found the coal tender," Benn said.

Danny looked deflated. "You knew it was there?"

"Of course I did. Jay made me help him cover it up to stop water from dripping into it."

Danny went over to the driver's cab, jumped up and reverentially placed the two pieces of coal into the firebox. He spun around, firelight glinting in his eyes. "First coal for ten years." Then he jumped lightly down from the footplate and headed over to the bunkhouse, leaving Benn and Alex dumbstruck.

"He's gone crazy," Benn said in a low voice. "Even if he could get the Puffer going, there's no way it can get all the way to Rekadom. There's no track. Okay, I know it goes over the bridge across the river, and Jay says it goes past the salt oaks, but everyone knows that Belamus tore up the track in the desert."

Alex leaned back against the warm metal of the footplate. "No, he didn't," she said.

"Yes, he did," insisted Benn. "They even came halfway down Lemon Valley tearing up the track. Gramma saw them. They threw the rails into the river. Hey, what's so funny?"

A feeling of hope had been creeping up on Alex, and

she realized she was smiling. "But that was the track up to Seven Snake Forest. There was another railway track from here that went up the coast."

"Yeah, I know. I remember Gramma saying. The train used to stop at little places on the way. Halts, she called them," Benn said. "But in school they said the king got rid of that one too."

"They told us that too," Alex said. "But it's not true. The track is still there. I walked along it all the way to Netters Cove. So if we can get the Puffer to Netters Cove, then we can get it to Rekadom."

Benn looked at Alex in surprise. "Are you serious?"

Alex nodded. "I am. And you know, I think Danny is right. How else are we going to get to Rekadom so quickly? People die in those dungeons, Benn."

Benn nodded somberly. "Yeah. I'm sorry. Your mom."

"And both Danny's parents too," Alex reminded him. "We have to go and get Louie out of there. Fast."

Benn grinned. "Don't forget Francina."

"Ha ha. If only." From the secret pocket inside her sash, Alex took the Tau and held it in her palm. The T-shaped charm threw a brilliant blue, shimmering light over her face.

Benn took a step backward. "It's so bright."

"And powerful," Alex said, closing her fingers over it so the light dimmed, although her hand still had a strange blue glow. "Benn, it's not just Louie I'm going back for, it's this too. I want to get the Tau back to Poppa." She looked at Benn, her eyes shining with excitement. "With this we can get rid of the Hauntings forever. Just think, Benn, we can *all* be safe. Together."

Benn sighed. "I get all that. Really I do. But taking the Puffer without Jay feels so wrong."

"But the Puffer doesn't actually belong to Jay, does it?" Alex said.

"In a way it does. If it wasn't for Jay, it would still be a heap of junk," Benn said. "We can't just steal it."

"We're not stealing. Jay will get it back."

Benn was silent, biting his lip in thought. "I'm going to check on Merry," he muttered. "See you later."

Alex watched Benn head off along the tunnel, his lanky shape dark against the light. She put the Tau back into her sash and went to find Danny.

Danny was sitting in the bunkhouse on one of the sleeping platforms, peering so intently at a thin and very grubby notebook that he did not notice that Alex had appeared in the doorway.

Unwilling to interrupt, Alex waited for him to look up. She tried to match the studious-looking teen with the terrifying Flyer on the Hawke who had aimed his Lightning Lance at her, but she couldn't. There were, of course, physical differences. Danny now wore his long red hair in a braid tied back like a pig's tail. Gone was his Flyer headband, and although he still wore his Flyer

Jacket, it was now ingrained with soot, and the silver Hawke with its beak of gold was no more than a dim shadow. But it wasn't these external changes that made Danny unrecognizable—something in his very essence had shifted. Now he emanated a steady calm, a feeling of purpose. Not only was he no longer the enemy, he now felt like a friend.

Suddenly aware of her presence, Danny looked up. "Hey," he said, smiling. He held up the notebook. "Want to take a look?" he asked.

"Sure," said Alex. She walked over and sat beside him.

"It's the driver's handbook," Danny said. "For the Puffer. It tells you everything you need to know, from a cold start, getting it running at a steady speed, and then to fire down. It's brilliant. And at the back, see . . ." Danny flipped the dog-eared, greasy pages to the back, where there was a selection of simple maps. "It has all the routes. And this, here . . ." Danny's sooty fingers flipped through the pages until he found the map for the track that led up the coast to Rekadom.

"Is where we're going!" Alex finished for him.

Danny looked at Alex, a slow smile dawning. "You're in on this? Really?"

Alex nodded. "I can't bear to think of Louie terrified in those dungeons for one second longer than he has to be."

Danny nodded. And then together both he and Alex said, "Or Francina," and laughed.

"Don't know how we'll get them out though," Alex said.

Danny pushed his hand deep into his pocket and pulled out a large iron key. "Key to the dungeons. Stole it when I was the Flyer. Because I was never, ever going to have anyone I loved stuck in that place ever again."

"Oh, Danny," Alex murmured. Touched that he had taken her into his confidence, Alex decided to do the same. She took the Tau from her sash, and its brilliant blue light burst into the dark little bunkroom.

Danny gasped. "What is *that*?" he murmured.

"It's a kind of amulet. It's called the Tau."

Danny stared at it. "That's the Tau? I thought it would be bigger than that."

"You know about the Tau?" Alex asked.

"Yeah. Mr. RavenStarr—your dad—he went on and on and *on* about it. You have no idea how much. He said it would . . . well, it would make everything right, I think. Though I can't remember how. Something to do with a book and some cards."

"He actually said that?" Alex was amazed. "About making things right?"

"Yeah. He did." Danny chuckled. "Not that I ever understood much of what he said. He had a habit of making simple things complicated, you know?"

Alex nodded. She knew. So in the simplest way she could, she explained to Danny about the Tau, and the codex and the cards, and how they must all three be together in order to end the Hauntings.

Danny listened attentively, and when Alex had finished, he said, "You and Mr. RavenStarr have to do this, you really do. I'll help you any way I can."

"Just get me back to Rekadom," Alex said. "I'll do anything to help us get there. I'll put the coal in, clear the track, whatever you need. I don't mind."

"It's a deal," Danny said, jumping up excitedly. He handed Alex the notebook. "You'd best take a look at this," he said. "And Benn too."

In the excitement Alex had forgotten about Benn and his objections. "Benn thinks taking the Puffer is disloyal to Jay," she said. "I don't think he'll come with us."

"I'll go see him," Danny said.

"He's with Merry," Alex told him. "I think he wanted to talk to her."

"Talk to a boat?" asked Danny.

Alex grinned. "Like you talk to the Puffer."

Danny laughed. "Okay. You got me there."

Alex watched Danny stride away. She wasn't at all sure he would have any luck with Benn.

CHAPTER 35
An Unexpected Crossing

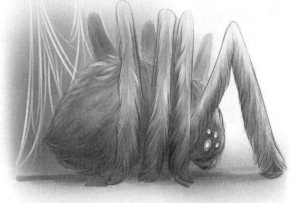

Danny came out of the tunnel to find the tide had retreated from the reed bed, leaving Merry lying on the mud below the dock. Inside her sat Benn, lost in thought.

Danny sat on the crumbling old dock and swung his legs over the side. He looked at Benn below. "Hey down there," he said.

Benn did not reply.

"Benn, will you come to Rekadom with us in the morning?" he asked.

Benn looked up. "Us?"

"Me and Alex."

"Huh," Benn said. "That would be mean to Jay."

"Is that a no?" Danny asked.

"Yes," said Benn.

"Great!" said Danny, leaping up.

Benn looked up at Danny, annoyed. "I meant yes, it's a no. Now go away."

Danny did as requested. He wandered off down the raised path that led through the reed bed to the estuary. He headed for the jetty and walked slowly to the end, where he stood looking out across the mud with a thin channel of deep water winding down the middle. It was a very low tide that evening and the water was still, poised between the ebb and flow. On the far side, Danny could clearly see the pebble beach, beyond which lay a rambling wood of stunted salt oaks. Lost in his thoughts of Francina being terrified in the Rekadom dungeons, it took Danny some minutes to realize that something big was moving through the trees.

What was it?

Using his old skills as a Flyer, Danny focused on the darkness between the trees and caught a glint of red high up in the canopy. He slipped back into Flyer mode, watching so intently that when a giant spider, about twenty feet tall, suddenly broke cover, Danny did not move a muscle—at least not on the outside. On the inside his heart began hammering fast.

Against the darkness of the treetops, the spider's cluster of red eyes shone like beacons. Had Danny not been Dark to Enchantment, he would have also seen the Enchanted dark mist swirling around the lower part of its legs—but the spider was enough for Danny. Fascinated, he watched the creature delicately pick its way down the pebble beach, its fat abdomen swaying to and fro, its eight eyes scanning the surroundings. At the bottom of the beach the retreating tide had left a wide strip of mud, but this did not deter the spider. Lifting up its spindly legs and carefully placing them into the soft mud, it walked forward into the estuary bed. When it reached the narrow but deep channel of water in the middle of the estuary, it stopped and looked straight ahead—at Danny.

Confidently—because there was water between him and the spider, and everyone knew that spiders drowned in sinks when you ran the tap—Danny returned the stare. Until it felt just a little too creepy, and then he turned and jogged back along the jetty and retraced his steps to the path through the reeds, where he was less exposed.

From the cover of the reeds, Danny watched the spider. To his surprise, it suddenly plunged into the channel—but it did not disappear. The muddy brown water completely covered its legs so that its body looked like some kind of bizarre spider boat, slowly but surely making its way across. Danny began to feel just a little concerned. He watched, crossing his fingers for luck, and when, in the middle of the channel, where there were swirls of current, the spider wobbled and seemed to lose its footing, Danny gave a small cheer. But it regained its balance and continued doggedly on until Danny realized he could now see the top of its legs—the spider was climbing up to the mud on this side. It had crossed the estuary.

"Sheesh!" muttered Danny. He turned and ran, racing along the reed path, scooting onto the old dock and skidding to a halt in a hail of loose stones, which rained down onto Merry and Benn below.

Benn looked up, glowering. "Very funny," he said. "Not."

"Get out! Quick!" Danny shouted.

"I told you, Danny. *Go away*," Benn said angrily.

Danny hopped up and down with frustration. He always lost his words when things were going wrong. All he could manage was, "Dumbo! Get out! Now!"

"Get lost," said Benn.

At last Danny found his words. "There's a giant spider. Massive. Twenty feet tall. Hairy legs, red eyes."

Benn laughed. "Ha ha. I'm not that stupid."

"Benn, I'm not kidding. I watched it cross the river. It's so big it just walked it. And now it's over here. Please, Benn. Get out of the boat. Please!"

"Yeah, yeah," said Benn. "Buzz off, Danny."

Danny gave up. He scrambled down the ladder to Merry, grabbed hold of Benn and roughly pulled him to his feet. "Look, you total turnip head, get up that ladder right now!"

Benn felt like a tsunami had hit. Danny pushed him up the ladder, threw him onto the dock and roughly pulled him to his feet. Angrily, Benn shoved Danny off and sent him sprawling backward onto the stones. He was about to drag Danny to his feet and punch him when he caught a glimpse of movement above.

"Look up, you dingbat!" Danny yelled as he scrambled to his feet.

But Benn was already looking up—at a twenty-foot-high spider lurching toward him. He grabbed Danny's hand and, dragging him along, raced into the mouth of the tunnel along the track and hurtled into the dark warmth of the cavern.

"Shut the doors!" Danny yelled.

Together Benn and Danny sent the doors trundling along their runners and slammed them shut with a bang. Asking no questions, Alex helped throw the locking bar across.

"Sheesh!" said Danny. "That was close."

"What was close?" Alex was not sure she wanted to hear the answer.

"Spider," Danny and Benn said in unison. "Huge."

"Twenty feet tall at least," said Danny.

"Horrible hairy legs," said Benn.

"And staring red eyes," added Danny.

Alex regarded Benn and Danny suspiciously. "Is this some kind of joke?" she asked.

"No!" they chorused.

"I thought Danny was joking too," Benn said. "I didn't believe a word and he had to drag me out of Merry." He looked at Danny. "Thanks. I wouldn't have blamed you if you'd just left me to stew."

"We're all in this together, right?" Danny said.

Alex was confused. "But it's not twilight yet, so it can't be a Haunting." She remembered the spider in the Iron Tower. Surely it couldn't be that one, could it?

"Shh!" Benn hissed loudly. "Listen."

On the far side of the heavy doors, they heard a soft scratching noise. Benn shuddered. He really did not like spiders.

"It won't get in," Danny said confidently. "These doors are massive."

"That's what you said about the spider, too," Alex muttered.

They listened to the scratchy, restless sounds of the spider outside in the tunnel. "Do you think it's making a nest?" Benn whispered.

"Spiders don't make nests," Danny said. "Must be a web."

"Spiders do make nests," Alex corrected. "To lay their eggs in."

"Oh, cute," said Danny. "We'll be trapped in here with lots of massive baby spiders running around. Great."

Benn had made a decision. "No we won't," he said.

"Because tomorrow we're taking the Puffer out of here."

Alex and Danny looked at Benn, surprised.

"*We're* taking the Puffer?" asked Danny.

"Yeah," Benn said. "Count me in."

Alex and Benn did what they could to help Danny prepare the engine. They brought small sticks from the kindling pile and then coal, handing them to Danny while he fed them through the open doors of the firebox in the driver's cab. With a long rake, Danny pushed the burning wood as far forward as it would go, and added more. While Danny worked, they brought him bread and cheese they had found in the bunkhouse and brewed lemon-and-honey tea. Once Danny was satisfied that the fire was burning steadily, he beckoned them over to the workbench at the back of the cavern, where his grimy, dog-eared notebook lay open. With a pang of guilt, Benn saw that it was written in Jay's neat and precise handwriting.

Danny was pointing to a list. "This is the greasing procedure," he said. "I need to start that now. But you guys should get some sleep."

"We don't need sleep," Benn protested.

"Yes, you do. It's hard work running an engine. I've done nothing but sleep for days. I'll snatch a couple of hours when I'm done and wake you when we're almost ready to go. Okay?" He went to find the grease gun. There were bearings to be greased.

Alex and Benn reluctantly headed to the bunkhouse but within minutes they were deeply asleep on the hard, narrow beds. Neither had realized how tired they were. And while they slept, Danny worked tirelessly through his checklist, feeding the fire deep in the Puffer's belly, greasing the old stiff joints, balancing the steam, checking the valves and slowly, with the aid of Jay's precious book, bringing the cold tangle of tubes, metal plates, rivets and rust to life.

CHAPTER 36
Steam Up

"WAKE UP! HEY, WAKE UP, you guys!"

Danny looked as though he'd been in an explosion. His face was streaked with black grease and shone with sweat. His hair looked wet and his hands—in which he was clutching two steaming mugs as grease-streaked as he was—were covered in soot. He looked blissfully happy. "I made tea," he said, handing Alex one of the filthy mugs.

"Did the kettle blow up?" she asked.

Danny laughed. "It's way better than that."

Benn's voice came sleepily from the bunk. "What's that smell?"

"Well, thanks a bunch, buddy," Danny said, going over

to the lump in the covers on the bottom bunk. "*I* bring you tea and *you* tell me I smell."

Alex heard the laughter in Danny's voice—he was bubbling with excitement. She breathed in the air, humid and heavy with the smell of soot, hot metal and boiling water. It caught the back of her throat and made her cough. "The Puffer's ready, isn't he?" she said.

"The Puffer," Danny said as he almost danced out of the bunkhouse, "is ready and waiting. All we have to do is hook up the tender, open those doors and we're off. We'll knock that spider out of the way before it knows what's hit it."

Over the top of their mugs, Benn and Alex exchanged glances. They'd forgotten about the spider.

Outside the cavern, dawn crept slowly up the valley. In the scattered cottages along the river, home to shepherds, rush cutters and gatherers of marsh berries, early risers peered out their windows, wondering if it was another misty morning. All river dwellers loved the mist. It was a time of quiet softness, like the first snowfall, a lull before the day began. But today when they pulled back the curtains in each cottage there was a gasp of shock, for today the low mist hanging over the water was a deep, sooty black shot through with eerie flashes of blue and yellow light.

Farther up the river in the roundhouse, Nella Lau was moving quietly around the kitchen, waking up the stove with a few small logs and setting the kettle to boil. Usually Nella enjoyed the early morning stillness; it was precious time to herself before she went upstairs to wake Benn and get the day started. But today her sad thoughts, and a thick silence that seemed to have quieted even the birds, oppressed her. The abduction of little Louie and poor Francina had shown Nella how powerless she truly was. It had made real the evil that still lay in Rekadom, something that in her daily life she managed to forget.

But what really worried her that morning was Benn. Ever since he had met Alex—of whom Nella was very fond—Nella had watched Benn grow from being her little grandson who liked nothing more than to help out on the farm to a young man who had his own life now, and—more worryingly—his own plans. Benn was caught up in a whole new world, and there was nothing she could do about it.

Sighing, Nella opened the shutters on the small kitchen window above the sink. It was still dark. Puzzled, she checked the clock, which showed seven thirty. A flicker of worry ran through her—the sun should be up by now. And the birds should be singing. What was going on? Quietly, Nella climbed the stairs up to her room, where she opened the shutters very slowly, suddenly afraid of what lay outside.

She gasped. The roundhouse was an island in a sea of mist. Mist from the river was not unusual; it lay low in the mornings, especially this time of year, and Nella loved it—but not when it was sooty black and riven with weird flashes of light. Nella peered down at the slightly undulating and, in places, patchy, flatness. It was, she reckoned, about two feet deep and as dark as a moonless night. Was there a fire somewhere? Nella wondered. Or was it a Wraith? What would it do if you opened the door—would it come in? Would it choke you? Nella took a wrench from the toolbox she kept under her bed and then she crept quietly upstairs, past Benn's room, where Jay was sleeping. A ladder was set neatly against the wall and Nella pulled it out and set it so that it led up to a small sealed trapdoor. Nella climbed the ladder, undid the large bolts holding the trapdoor closed, pulled away the rubber seal around the door and pushed it open. The attic was quiet and dim, but enough daylight came up from the hatch for Nella to see where she was going. She swung herself up from the ladder and made her way across to a tiny window. She unscrewed its heavy shutter and looked out. Nella gasped. A vast lake of mist, a mixture of blues, blacks and grays, covered the land. The orange and lemon groves rose out of it and in the distance she saw the old railway bridge rising serenely over the blanket of darkness. Beyond the bridge Nella was relieved to see the glimmering of the ocean as it stretched out to join the pale morning sky. She thought of Benn, Alex and Danny in the cavern and wished they were here with her.

Nella decided to keep watch. She went downstairs, filled a basket with a thermos of tea and some lemon cookies, took a blanket and cushions from her room and climbed back up to the attic. Jay was a late riser and Nella was not about to wake him. Who knew, maybe it had come in with the tide and would flow out again? But as Nella settled down in front of the tiny roof light to watch over the strange blanket of shadowy mist with its eerie flashing lights, she somehow doubted it.

Alex and Benn walked into a fug of steam and noise. In the middle of it stood the monumental shape of the locomotive, with steam hissing from its funnel on top of the boiler and from various joints and tubes around the wheels. An orange glow lit up the driver's cab and Alex knew that what she had seen in her cards the first time she had met Benn had now truly come to be. And that amazingly, she was part of it.

Danny set them to work. They helped push the tender—full of coal and astoundingly heavy—along the rails so it met up with the back of the engine. They helped lift the coupling mechanism and jam it into place so that the tender was attached.

"Now we get the pressure up," Danny said. "Which means getting much more coal into that fire, and fast."

Alex and Benn took a shovel each and set to work. The

heat from the fire was scorching, but they kept on shoveling in the coal, while Danny pushed it forward with the fire rake so there was always more space. Before long both Alex and Benn were drenched in sweat, covered in sticky coal dust and consumed by a raging thirst. But caught up in the drama of building up steam, in making a creature come alive, they continued shoveling until Danny at last yelled, "Stop!"

Alex and Benn threw down their shovels and wiped their brows in unison like old hands at the job. Beneath their feet they felt the thrum of energy running through the metal. They were ready to go.

In the roundhouse attic, Nella put down her lemon tea and peered intently out of the little window. Emerging from the top of the hills were what appeared to be wisps of white smoke. She shaded her eyes against the brightness of the sky and stared. It wasn't her imagination, there was definitely smoke. Nella wondered if someone was signaling for help? And then she remembered something Jay had once said. That the cavern where the Puffer was hidden had a vent that emerged high in the Border Hills. And that she would know when the engine was ready to go because she'd see the steam coming out of the hilltops. *Is that steam?* Nella wondered. And then she wondered: *Is that Benn's plan?*

The Puffer was buzzing with pent-up energy.

"We're gonna have to be quick," Danny told Alex and Benn. "Pull the doors open and then we just go for it. We're bigger and nastier than any spider. Okay?"

"Yep," said Alex.

"Okay," said Benn.

"Okay!" Danny yelled above a sudden hiss of steam. "Let's go!"

Alex and Benn ran to the doors. "One, two, three, pull!" they shouted, and each wrenched their door open. Thanks to Danny's greasing of the runners during the night, the doors ran back so fast that the speed sent both Alex and Benn sprawling to the ground. They picked themselves up and glanced nervously outside and saw a mass of gray threads looped across the tunnel. They raced back along the side of the engine, past the great drive wheel, and leaped up into the safety of the driver's cab.

"Hey, spider!" Danny yelled. "We're coming through!"

With a piercing whistle, the locomotive lurched forward. They all felt the pent-up power of the huge machine as Danny eased it slowly along the track and into the tunnel, where they hit the giant web. The Puffer crept steadily forward, its heat sending the strands of steel-strong silk fizzing away into blackened shreds and filling their nostrils with the acrid smell of scorching. And then suddenly, with a great billow of steam, they were out into daylight.

"Sheesh, look at that mist!" Benn yelled above the noise of the Puffer.

Danny took no notice. "Coal!" he yelled at Benn. "More coal!"

While Benn swung around to get the coal, Alex stared down at the strange, undulating darkness that hugged the ground like a quilt. She watched its shifting swirls and saw the needle-sharp flashes of light within, like tiny electric storms. She shivered. It felt just like the stuff inside the Iron Tower. And there was that spider too, just like in the Iron Tower. A niggle of worry began to gnaw at Alex—she had closed the door to the Tower, hadn't she?

Alex's thoughts were interrupted by Benn's anxious tones. "Hey, Danny, slow down!" he was yelling. "You can't see the track! Suppose it's broken? Or there's a rock on it? Slow down!"

Danny looked annoyed. "What are you talking about?" he said.

"That dark mist, what do you think?" Benn yelled.

"What dark mist?" Danny shouted.

Now Alex knew for sure—this was an Enchantment. And where else could it be from but the Iron Tower? "It's okay, Danny!" she called over. "Ignore him!" She turned to Benn. "It's an Enchantment. A massive Wraith or something. Danny can't see it because he's Dark to Enchantment."

"But he saw the spider," Benn objected.

"Because the spider is *real*. Like a Skorpas. Or the Hawke. It's just much bigger, that's all."

"So Danny can still see the track?"

"Yep," said Alex.

An expression of relief crossed Benn's face.

"Coal!" yelled Danny. And Benn happily threw in another shovel of coal.

Some minutes later they rounded the last outcrop of rock before the bridge and Alex saw the spider scuttling away through the dark swirls, like any house spider that has been swept out of a comfortable corner with a broom. She watched it go with a feeling of despair. *What have I done?* she thought. *I've let loose the very worst Enchantments that scared even Poppa—and now they're everywhere. This is a thousand times worse than Poppa's Hauntings.* Her hand strayed to the Tau sitting snug in the secret pocket of her sash and she felt the warmth and reassurance of it as her fingers found its smooth surface. Alex felt a little better—she, Poppa and the Tau could fix this too. She grabbed the shovel from Benn and scooped up more coal—the sooner she could get to Rekadom, the better.

With a deep, resonant *chuffa-chuff . . . chuffa-chuff . . . chuffa-chuff . . .* the Puffer moved along the broad track beside the river. Danny leaned out to watch its huge drive wheel slowly turning as the Puffer crept powerfully forward. "We're rolling!" he yelled, exhilarated. "Coal!"

Alex readily threw in another shovel of coal into the red-hot hole of fire and then leaned out of the cab. The undulating sea of blackness spread out before them like a carpet, and in the distance she could see a huge spider striding away, along the riverbank. Alex shook her head—it was so unreal it felt like a dream. *No, a nightmare*, she thought.

They were now heading up the gentle rise of the embankment, which rose clear of the Wraith mist and led to the bridge over the river.

"Coal! Coal!" Danny yelled.

Benn threw two more shovels in as the gradient increased and the Puffer chuffed its way up the track. Alex watched a cloud of sparks fly out from the firebox and arc into the Wraith mist below.

"Coal!" yelled Danny as they approached the bridge.

Benn threw in another shovel of coal and then, to take his mind off his fear of the bridge cracking under the weight of the locomotive and sending them all tumbling into the river, he looked out up the river. Dark above the Wraith mist, he too saw the spider stalking along the riverbank. And, as they reached the top of the bridge, in the distance on the familiar bend in the river, Benn saw the roundhouse rearing up above the dark lake in which it sat. And it seemed to him that was the very place the spider was heading.

Nella did not see the spider. She had eyes for only one thing—the magnificent sight of the locomotive rising out of the blackness, like a whale breaching the ocean. She watched it moving up the incline to the old railway bridge, steam pouring from its funnel—and then it was on the bridge. Nella held her breath as *oh so slowly* the massive machine crept across the worryingly delicate metal lattice-work of the bridge, its solid dark shape clear against the pale sky, brilliant orange sparks arcing down toward the blackness below. Nella could hardly bear to watch, but watch she did from between her fingers, hands clamped to her face.

When it reached the halfway point across the bridge, Nella heard the haunting sound of the train's whistle traveling across the silence of the strangest morning she had ever known. It brought memories rushing back that Nella had pushed to the dusty corners of her mind—happy times spent traveling to Rekadom, summer trips to Netters Cove to stay with her best friend, who had married a fisherman, and taking the morning train to Luma to go to the cafe at the station and meet up with friends. Nella felt shocked at the realization of how, over the last ten years of King Belamus's wicked Hauntings, she had become so solitary.

But even so, Nella found she was smiling. She was sure the whistle had been Benn saying hello. Pushing away her next thought—that he was really saying goodbye—Nella wiped the mistiness from her eyes and watched with relief as the engine safely reached the far side of the bridge and set off down the long sweep of the curved embankment, its plume of steam trailing behind it as it rode above the misty darkness that covered the reed beds. She watched until she could see it no more, then she closed the shutter and went downstairs to the kitchen.

There she found Jay making tea and breakfast pancakes. Nella took a deep breath. "Jay," she said. "I have something to tell you."

Two minutes later, Jay was furiously pacing the kitchen floor.

"Don't swear please, Jay," Nella was saying.

"I'll swear if I want to, Gramma. My sneaky little brother has stolen my train and I have every right to pigging swear as much as I pigging want to." He threw himself down at the table and put his head in his hands.

Nella put her arms around Jay's shaking shoulders. "Don't cry, Jay dear. Benn will bring your train back. I know he will."

"I'm *not* crying," came Jay's muffled voice.

"No, dear. Of course not. I'll fix us a nice cup of lemon tea, shall I?"

Jay did not answer.

Quietly, Nella moved around the kitchen, tending to the tea. Deciding to sneak a peek outside and see what was happening to the mist, she opened a shutter a few inches. She screamed and slammed it shut. And then she sat down and began to laugh.

"What's so funny?" Jay asked, sulkily.

"Oh, nothing. Just a giant spider in the courtyard."

Jay strode to the window. He pulled open the shutters and slammed them fast. "Sheesh," he said. "I don't see why you're laughing, Gramma. I really don't."

"Oh, Jay," Nella said. "I'm thinking how I used to worry about Sol's little pet spider all those years ago. And now there's a giant one outside and, well, it really doesn't seem to matter all that much. How times have changed."

CHAPTER 37

Coal!

"COAL!" DANNY SHOUTED OVER THE rhythmic rattle of the wheels upon the track. "Coal!"

Benn and Alex were hot and aching from the constant shoveling of the coal—and increasingly annoyed with Danny's peremptory demands for it.

"He might at least say 'please,'" Benn grumbled to Alex as he heaved another shovel into the searingly hot fire.

"Huh," said Alex. "Why does it eat so much coal anyway?"

"Coal!" yelled Danny.

Benn threw down the shovel. "Do it yourself," he told Danny. "I need some water." He grabbed the flask and tipped it up, the water running down his sooty chin, leaving a clean trail behind it. Alex picked up the shovel and threw another load in. She didn't care how hard they were going to have to work—all she wanted to do was to get to Rekadom.

The Wraith mist was thinner now, and as the Puffer chugged slowly along, both Benn and Alex could see the rails of the track ahead, glinting in the sunlight. Alex was surprised how shiny they looked; Jay had done a good job, she thought. She looked over to the left and could see the tops of the salt oak woods, and ahead she saw the gradual rise of the Thirteen Titans, undulating like a huge green ocean with the dirty slick of Wraith mist lapping up against them. The track now swept into a wide bend, taking them around a rocky outcrop, and as they rounded the escarpment Danny yelled out, "Rocks! Rocks on the line!"

There was a shrieking of brakes, and with Danny frantically pulling levers, the Puffer slowly ground to a halt just in time. "Sheesh," he said, wiping his brow. "I nearly locked the brakes. Gotta be more careful next time."

They jumped down from the cab and surveyed the landslide. It wasn't big but, as Danny said, it wasn't small either. They set to work, shifting the rocks and shoveling the loose, gritty soil. It was very slow going, particularly as Alex and Benn found themselves doing most of the work while Danny fretted about steam pressures and escape valves and kept disappearing into the cab "just to check."

It was late in the afternoon, and Ratchet was checking on his horse. The path down to Netters Cove was too steep for horses, so a stable was kept at the old Netters Halt for horse-riding visitors. But as the breathless Ratchet reached the top of the cliff path, he saw that the stable door was smashed and hung open, swinging on its hinges. Muttering a series of rude words under his breath, Ratchet warily approached the stable and peered in. There, on the floor, lay a wad of horsehair and a long streak of blood. Ratchet shuddered to think what creature could have done such a thing. Feeling very spooked, he trod quietly away, noticing now how the ground around the stable was gouged out in deep scuff marks. The horse had clearly put up a good fight.

Ratchet stepped up onto the old railway platform. Shielding his eyes against the sun, he scanned the vista for clues as to what might have happened, but the desert gave nothing away. Ratchet saw no more than a dull brown sweep of gritty scrubland and the towers of Rekadom in the far distance, the low sun glinting off their gold tips. To his right were the rolling hills that led up to the Titans, and it occurred to Ratchet these could hide all manner of horse-devouring creatures. He was about to beat a retreat when he thought he saw a thin white pillar of smoke moving toward him from behind the nearest hill. Suddenly, Ratchet was back to being a teenager once more, waiting with his friends for the Big Puffer to take him to Rekadom for a night out in the Glittering Star Bar. He sighed. How things had changed since that terrible Oracle prediction ten years ago. Suddenly a piercing whistle broke into his thoughts, and from behind the hill came an apparition.

"No . . . ," Ratchet murmured. "No. It can't be. Not the Puffer."

But it was. With much screaming of brakes, the Puffer drew slowly into the Halt and stopped. Two young teens, covered in soot, jumped down from the footplate and then, at the sight of Ratchet, stopped dead. "It's him," one said to the other anxiously.

"So what," said the other. "It's three against one."

"Steady on," said Ratchet. "I dunno who you are but I mean no harm. I'm just amazed to see the old Puffer out again. I never dreamed the day would come. It's wonderful."

The driver, also covered in soot, looked down warily.

"You stopped for water like in the old days?" Ratchet asked. "There's a tank full here. I used to help out when I was a boy. Need a hand?"

"Yeah," the driver said in an oddly gruff tone.

Ratchet strode across the platform to the pointy-topped tower and swung out a wide metal pipe that was tucked neatly against its side. Then, from inside the pipe he pulled down a waxed canvas tube. "Okay then. Unscrew the water top."

Ratchet didn't think much of the two assistants; they seemed to have no idea what to do. The driver had to climb up the copper dome and unscrew the top himself. Ratchet swung the pipe over and the driver maneuvered it in. Ratchet disappeared into the tower and turned the wheel on the stop tap, and water gushed into the tank with a great hiss of steam.

The driver seemed relieved, Ratchet thought. "You done this before?" Ratchet asked.

The driver laughed. "No. It was a bit of luck finding you. Thanks." And then he stopped. "Oh, rats," he muttered.

"Danny? Is that you?" Ratchet said.

"Yeah. It's me. Hello, Mr. Ratchet."

Ratchet tried to figure out how his lost and much lamented Flyer could possibly have transformed into the engine driver of the Puffer—a job Ratchet had craved as a boy—but try as he might, he could not. So he contented himself with a grouchy, "Is that your Flyer jacket? It's in a terrible state."

"Yeah. Sorry about that. Now we must be getting on."

"Where you going?"

"Rekadom, of course. Not much choice. We have to stick to the track, you know."

"Very clever, ha ha. Er. Do you need a hand? I'm a good fireman."

"No thanks," said Danny.

"You'd shovel the coal?" asked Benn.

"All the way to Rekadom?" asked Alex.

"I'd be happy to," Ratchet said.

"No," said Danny. "We're fine."

"*You're* fine," Alex corrected him. "Because all you do is yell, 'Coal!' So now you can yell it at someone else."

Danny quite liked the idea of yelling at Ratchet. "All right. Get yourself up here."

Ratchet jumped up onto the footplate and Alex threw him the shovel.

"Coal!" yelled Danny, and with a slow *chuffa-chuff . . . chuffa-chuff . . . chuffa-chuff*, Big Puffer pulled slowly away from Netters Halt and set off along the track on the top of the cliffs. "Coal!"

CHAPTER 38

Zerra's Reward

"WHERE HAVE YOU *BEEN*?" KING Belamus demanded petulantly. His three Jackal stood before him looking, Belamus thought, decidedly ill. Still queasy from the effects of the guards' sausages they had commandeered the night before, their long red coats stained with grime, their muzzles grubby, ears flopping forward and their lolling tongues letting go long strands of drool, they did not look good. Even multiplied to a small army of Jackal by the mirrored lobby, they were not impressive. Unfortunately, the effect was not helped by multiple views of the body of the crow-pecked Jackal that was curled up in a corner, having most inconsiderately died overnight. It looked like there had been a massacre. Belamus shuddered. This was a bad omen. Maybe he should go ask the Oracle what to do? But one look at his pathetic array of Jackal told him otherwise. He had to act now and finish the Beguilers fast, before he had no Jackal left.

Belamus sprang into action. He sent one Jackal to the dungeons to collect the Beguiler children and take them out of the city to Oracle Halt. He then set off with his remaining two Jackal to the Silver Tower to wreak his revenge on his onetime friend.

Hagos saw King Belamus coming. He sent Zerra to hide in Alex's room and told Deela to hide too. "I will not," Deela told him indignantly. "We are in this together, Hagos."

"Please hide, Deela," Hagos begged. "This is looking bad."

"No," said Deela, and she took Hagos's hand. "Together, okay?"

The door burst open and King Belamus strode in, leaving his two bedraggled Jackal out on the landing. They did not add to his kingly dignity.

"I think," the king said to Hagos, "that we will go and see the pretty lights on the cliffs, eh?"

"Pretty lights?" Hagos said with a careful smile. "Ah, you mean the Xin." *So that's it*, Hagos thought. *He's going to get the Xin to push me off the cliff. Then he can pretend he had nothing to do with it.* But Hagos was determined not to let the king see how afraid he was.

Belamus laughed, enjoying himself now. "I do indeed mean the Xin. Those charming Xin that you created to push Beguilers off cliffs. Fascinating creatures, with which I'm sure you would like to be reacquainted. And your little Min friend here, he will enjoy a cliff walk too, I am sure."

"No!" Hagos protested. "No, he wouldn't."

Belamus was pleased to have at last rattled Hagos. "Well, that's a shame, because he's going anyway," the king said snappily. "Now, are you coming or do I get the Jackal in to fetch you?"

"We're coming," Hagos said hurriedly.

Outside on the landing, the king told the Jackal, "Take them to Oracle Halt. Wait for me there." Hagos and Deela were hustled down the stairs with the king following behind, enjoying the defeated droop of his ex-Enchanter's shoulders.

Zerra crept out from her hiding place under Alex's bed and took stock. It was not lost on her that she had felt safer and more cared for with Hagos in the past twenty-four hours than she had with her own mother for the last thirteen years. The thought of Hagos being thrown off the cliffs by the Xin gave her an empty feeling in the pit of her stomach. She had to do something.

A little reluctantly, Zerra left the security of Hagos's rooms and set off down the stairs. She emerged stealthily from the Silver Tower, crept out into Star Court and then down the street, at the end of which she took the ginnel that led into Gate Court. As she slipped in through the little door behind the line of Jackal chariots, a flurry of activity caught her eye at the entrance to the dungeons, and she ducked down behind the nearest chariot.

Horrified, Zerra saw her little brother and big sister, each with their wrist on a long chain attached to a Jackal, blinking as they emerged into the evening sunlight. Zerra, who made a point of never *ever* crying, found her eyes grow blurry. Roughly she wiped her sleeve across her face and gulped down the lump that had risen in her throat. Louie looked so lost, she thought. His eyes were big with fear, and he was clutching something tightly to him. Francina looked disheveled and terrified. Her blue tunic was streaked with dirt and her leggings were torn at the knees. Louie looked like he'd fallen into a slime pit. Even his hair had strands of muck in it.

Shocked, Zerra watched Louie and Francina, pulled impatiently by the Jackal as though they were bad dogs on a leash, stumbling out through the city gates. Something inside her chest did a painful twist.

Suddenly a quarrel erupted at the gate. The aunt and nephew were back on duty and the nephew was saying, "Look, Auntie—"

"Don't call me Auntie on duty. I'm *ma'am* to you. How many times do I have to tell you?"

"Sorry. Ma'am. But it's not my fault that the stupid Beguiler Bell didn't ring this time," the nephew was saying. "It rang for the old Enchanter just now, didn't it? So you can't blame me. And I oiled it yesterday like you said."

"You must not have done it properly then," his aunt told him. "It's not reliable. We've got two Beguiler kids—two—walking right underneath now and it's silent as the grave."

"Maybe they're not Beguilers," the nephew said sulkily.

A gasp came from his aunt. "Be careful what you say—hey, what are you doing? Put that pole down!"

There was a sudden clang as the nephew jumped up and hit the Beguiler Bell, which obligingly rang. "There," said the nephew. "Happy now?"

Zerra nervously watched the gate guards return to their positions, and then she took a deep breath and walked as confidently as she could toward the city gate. As she approached, the guards stood to attention and saluted. Zerra smiled, pleased at their deference. But suddenly the woman guard barked, "Make way for the King's Majesty! Make way!" Zerra wheeled around to see King Belamus rapidly approaching.

Flustered, Zerra leaped out of the way, hoping the king had not noticed her. But no such luck—the king stopped and regarded her with an unnervingly friendly expression. "Spy," he said. "I wish to thank you for alerting me to the perfidy of the Beguiler in the Silver Tower. As a reward you will accompany me to see not only the end of that devious rat but also the end of the very last two Beguiler children in the land."

Zerra stared at the king. She thought of Francina and Louie being led out of the city in chains, and she just knew that the king was talking about them. And then she thought of Hagos and how kind he had been to her and how he had made her feel—for the first time in her life, ever—that she mattered, and she began to feel quite ill.

Belamus seemed amused at her hesitation. "Come, Spy, do not be shy. You deserve to be in on this at the end."

Miserably, Zerra thought the king was right. She did deserve this. She had caused it all to happen by Naming Alex in Luma, and now she deserved to face the consequences of what she had done.

"Guards." Belamus was now addressing the aunt and nephew. "You will accompany us. We no longer need to guard the gates of Rekadom, for the very last three Beguilers in the land will soon be no more and your king will be free from that pernicious prophecy of the Oracle—that he will die by the hand of an Enchanter's child." He laughed and pointed up to the Beguiler Bell. "And that will never ring again."

Glancing at one another in confusion, the aunt and nephew did as they were commanded and took their places on either side of the king.

"Lead on, Spy," King Belamus told Zerra. "You will escort us to Oracle Halt."

Dutifully, Zerra walked out through the gates, but as she passed beneath the Beguiler Bell, it rang.

The king froze. "What is wrong with this bell?" he demanded. "Why does it ring?"

The nephew looked terrified. "It hasn't been working right today, Your Majesty. I tried to oil it, really, I did. But it doesn't ring when it should. And now it rings when it shouldn't."

Not wishing her nephew to be thrown into a dungeon for bad bell maintenance, the aunt stepped in hurriedly. "It was damaged by that Beguiler fog the night before last, Your Majesty. We have tried our best to repair it, I assure you."

"Huh," grumbled the king. "Well, we won't be needing it anymore anyway. Get a move on, Spy."

Zerra led the way along the well-trodden path around the city walls and then headed across the dusty expanse of scrub toward the old train platform of Oracle Halt. Ahead she could see her brother and sister stumbling along behind the Jackal. Beyond them, waiting on the Oracle Halt platform, were the figures of Hagos and Deela dwarfed by their two Jackal. And beyond them all lay the cliff edge and the wide blue stretch of the ocean, darkening with the ending of the day.

CHAPTER 39

"By the Hand of an Enchanter's Child"

"COAL!" YELLED DANNY.

"Coal, Driver!" Ratchet yelled in reply, reverting to his boyhood role and the old protocols with great enthusiasm as he threw in another shovelful.

Danny grinned. "You're out of a job!" he yelled to Alex and Benn. "I've got a much better one here!"

Alex and Benn were out of the heat and hassle of the driver's cab, standing on the walkway that ran along both sides of the locomotive. It was hot as they chuffed slowly along the cliff-top track, but despite the heat, Alex was shivering. In the short time since she left Luma, Alex had

learned to recognize and control the Twilight Terrors—
the feeling of dread and fear that overtook her every
evening as twilight descended. But tonight it was tinged
with another, deeper fear—a fear that something terrible
was about to happen.

"Hey, look!" Benn called out. "There's a weird bunch
of people at Oracle Halt." He turned to Alex and laughed.
"Looks like they're waiting for a train!"

On the weed-strewn, crumbling platform of Oracle Halt,
the weird bunch of people were waiting not for a train,
but for a king.

Four humans—two children and two adults—chained
to three seven-foot-tall jackal-headed creatures wearing
long red coats were watching the approach of a round
figure on spindly legs. It wore a winged crown, the tips
of the wings catching the last rays of the setting sun, and
was bedecked with multicolored silks that flapped in the
breeze that was blowing in off the ocean. It also wore a
grim smile of satisfaction—King Belamus the Great was
about to defeat the Oracle and its pernicious prophecy
that had dogged his life for the last ten fear-filled years.

On the platform the two children—a small boy clutching a large feathered lizard to his chest and a tall girl—were
looking not at the approaching king and his two guards
with their javelins, but at the slight figure of a girl wearing a combat jacket and grubby trousers who was leading

them. "Franny, look—it's Zerra!" whispered Louie.

"Shh," hissed Francina.

"Zerra has come to rescue us!" Louie whispered excitedly.

Francina said nothing. She was pretty sure that was the last thing her sister was planning.

The king's procession had reached the wide steps at the far end of the platform. "Stand aside, Spy," the king said. With the two gate guards by his side, he strode past Zerra and approached the group of prisoners. Zerra hung back and anxiously watched a cluster of sharp-looking lights flickering along the edge of the cliff. They gave her the creeps. She walked slowly up the steps and saw the king jabbing the Enchanter threateningly in the chest.

"So, RavenStarr," Belamus was saying. "Here are those pretty lights we have come to see. We'll let them get on with things, shall we?" The king waved his arm at the lights that had formed up into a net and were, Zerra was sure, dancing toward *her*. She glanced around to see if there was anywhere she could hide. There was nowhere at all.

"Jackal!" Belamus sounded somewhat overwrought, Zerra thought. "Unchain the Beguiler and his little friend." The king let out a high-pitched laugh. "We don't want you going over the edge with them, do we? Not my last Jackal in the whole world. Oh no!" He wheeled around to Louie and Francina's Jackal. "You! Unchain the

Beguiler brats. They can have their own little dance with the Xin." Belamus rubbed his hands together. "Oh, I am so looking forward to this. Goodbye to the last Beguilers in the kingdom!"

Suddenly Hagos understood. It was not only him and Deela who Belamus was planning to send plunging off the cliff—it was also two innocent children. Released from his chains, Hagos made a decision. He threw himself at the king and sent him flying off the platform and onto the track.

From her vantage point on the Puffer, Alex peered at the group of figures on Oracle Halt. "There's some kind of fight going on," she said. "Hey, they're on the track." She quickly made her way back to the driver's cab. "Danny, slow down!" she yelled, climbing onto the footplate. "There are people on the track!"

"People?" Danny looked shocked. "What kind of people?"

"*People* people!" Alex yelled.

And then, from the coal tender behind, a terrified yell came from Ratchet: "Skorpas!"

Alex and Danny wheeled around to see a huge pair of pale-yellow claws emerging from a mound on the desert side of the track. As the Puffer chuffed past, the Skorpas shot out from its lair. Ratchet stared at it in horror—the monstrous thing was nearly as big as the train. He saw it raise its huge, segmented tail over its head, and then a luminous yellow streak of venom came shooting out from the barb. "Get down!" Ratchet yelled, but his warning came too late. The venom hit Danny's Flyer jacket square in the back, the force throwing him to the floor. Ratchet scrambled from the tender and fell to his knees beside Danny. "Don't move," he told him. "Just a drop of this stuff will kill you. Stay completely still and let me take the jacket off."

"No," Danny protested. "We're going to crash into those people. Put the brakes on."

"Hey!" Ratchet yelled at Alex and Benn. "Get back here! Brakes, brakes!"

Alex heard the panic in Ratchet's voice. She scrambled back to the cab and stopped at the sight of Danny on the floor. "The brake lever!" Ratchet yelled. "There!" Alex grabbed the lever and pulled it down as hard as she could.

"Not so fast!" Ratchet yelled, but he was too late. The wheels locked and the heavy locomotive went skidding forward, heading straight for the knot of people brawling on the track.

The screaming of the brakes and the sight of the oncoming train broke up the fight at once. Everyone, except the king, jumped off the track. But Belamus stood his ground, watching the oncoming train with anger in his heart. "You don't fool me!" he yelled at Hagos. "It's a Beguilement!" He stood firm, waving his arms, yelling, "I'm not afraid of your cheap tricks, RavenStarr. I'm not!"

"Belamus, it's not a Beguilement!" Hagos yelled. "It's real!"

"Get out of the way!" Alex yelled at the figure with the winged crown and flowing silks that stood right in the path of the Puffer, waving its arms. Desperately she pulled on the brake lever again, but the mountain of iron, boiling water and steam continued to skid inexorably toward the king, its locked wheels screaming metal on metal. Alex closed her eyes. She was going to kill King Belamus. Palla's prophecy was about to come true.

Zerra could not believe that the king was still in the middle of the track waving his arms like a silly kid playing chicken. *He thinks it's not real*, she thought. *What an idiot*. As the squealing, smoke-belching locomotive headed straight for the king, Zerra could watch no longer. She hurled herself at him, grabbing at his silken cloak and pulling him— and herself—off-balance. The king fell sprawling to the ground just clear of the track. A second later, as he and Zerra lay winded on the gritty earth, a great rush of heat and noise came hurtling past. Zerra sat up and watched it continue screaming down the track, sending shards of light flying as it ran through the approaching Net of Xin. Some distance past the end of the platform, the engine at last came to halt, belching clouds of steam. Shaking her head in disbelief, Zerra slowly got to her feet—*where had that come from?* And then, totally dumbfounded, she saw Alex jump down from the driver's cab and throw herself to the ground. *Alex? What was Alex doing here?*

Alex was searching underneath the heavy iron wheels for the body of the king.

"Alex, it's okay," Benn's voice came from above. "The king's over there—look. Fighting your dad."

Alex scrambled to her feet and saw in the middle of a melee of Jackal the dusty red of her father's cloak and the tip of a winged crown. Suddenly the three Jackal broke free and, with Hagos held between them, began propelling him rapidly toward the edge of the cliff.

"No!" gasped Alex. "No. They can't do that. They can't!" She set off as fast as she could toward her father, but even as she ran, Alex knew she could not get there in time. She felt as though she were in a nightmare, her legs taking her nowhere, while three seven-foot-tall jackal-headed creatures pushed at her father with clawing hands. And now he was teetering on the very edge of the cliff and there was nothing she could do. Time slowed to an unbearable stillness as Alex headed toward something that she knew she could not stop.

It was Zerra who saved Hagos. As Belamus jumped up and down like an excited child, yelling, "Do it, do it! Push him off!" and Hagos was on hands and knees grabbing desperately at a last handhold of the dead scrub on the edge of the cliff, Zerra threw herself at the Jackals' spindly legs. She caught them unawares and they tumbled forward—oh so slowly, it seemed to Zerra—out toward the emptiness beyond the cliff edge. The evening breeze rose up from the ocean below and turned their flapping red coats into kites, sending the very last Jackal in the world tumbling slowly down toward the ocean far below.

Fingers scrabbling at the ground, with Zerra's help Hagos clawed his way back from the crumbling cliff edge and lay breathless, facedown in the dirt.

Belamus stared at his traitorous spy, who had just destroyed the last of his Jackal and was now helping the Beguiler, RavenStarr, to his feet. Joining her were two familiar figures—the Beguiler girl with the green sash and the boy who had escaped from Rekadom a few days back. Shocked, Belamus realized these were different brats from the two the Jackal had brought back. Belamus felt panic rising. How many Beguiler brats were there? He was hopelessly outnumbered. He wheeled around, looking desperately for help. "Guards!" he yelled. "Guards!"

But the gate guards were nowhere to be seen, and Belamus knew he was on his own. A surge of anger replaced the panic. He had been betrayed by everyone—and it was all the fault of the man he had once been so misguided as to call a friend—Hagos RavenStarr. Without warning, Belamus launched himself at Hagos with surprising force. Hagos went staggering back toward the cliff edge, but just in time, Alex and Benn grabbed him and pulled him back from the brink.

But Belamus was not to be stopped. He threw himself at Hagos once more and landed a punch. Hagos fell back toward the cliff edge yet again and Belamus went after him, but suddenly Zerra was there, pulling the king away, yelling, "Stop! Stop!"

Belamus wheeled around in fury and lunged at Zerra instead. "Traitor Spy!" he screamed. Zerra saw the king's piggy little eyes filled with hatred, his long nails, like Jackal talons, clawing at her, and with all her strength, she shoved the king away. His slippery-soled shoes skidded on the grit, he staggered backward, lost his balance and, with arms frantically windmilling, he tumbled over the cliff edge into thin air.

Alex, Benn, Zerra and Hagos stopped dead. They watched the king, his blue silks flapping like the useless wings of a flightless bird, seeming to hover for a moment and then drop from view, leaving only the briefest of shrieks hanging in the air behind him.

There was a shocked and horrified silence on the cliff top.

It was broken by a distant yell. "Skorpas! Skorpas!"

CHAPTER 40
Family Reunion

DEELA HAD MADE A TOUGH decision. As Hagos was being dragged toward the cliff edge, she had fought down her urge to help him. She could already see Alex hurtling toward him, and the rough-looking girl in the combat jacket looked like she was on his side too. But Deela knew that the two terrified children on the platform were in grave danger—why else would the king have brought them here?

Deela had caught the eye of the woman gate guard. "These children should not be seeing this," she said.

The gate guard nodded.

"I'm going to get them away from here," Deela said. "I'm taking them home with me."

The gate guard looked relieved. "Good," she said.

Suddenly the pimply young guard spoke, his voice squeaky with fear. "Can we come too?" he asked.

Determined not to look at what was happening on the cliff edge, Deela was already hurrying Francina and Louie away. "Yes. But be quick," she called to the guards over her shoulder. "Before anyone sees us."

Deela, Francina, Louie and the gate guards had run as fast as they could toward the Big Puffer. But now it seemed to Deela that she had brought everyone into even greater danger—for here, lumbering toward them, was a giant yellow scorpion, tail arched over its back, silver barb glinting and ready to fire.

"Get on the Puffer!" a stocky man covered in coal dust was yelling at her. "Hurry! Hurry!"

But Deela didn't want to get on anything, particularly when there was a giant scorpion heading toward it. She just wanted to go home and take two terrified children with her. So she headed to a patch of ground she remembered well and pulled up the trapdoor. "Down you go," she told Francina and Louie. "Don't be scared, I'm coming too."

Francina took hold of Louie's hand. "Come on, Louie," she said.

Louie looked at the darkness below. "No," he said.

Francina had no patience left. "Whyever not, you silly boy?" she snapped.

Louie stood his ground. "Wolves," he said. "Wolves down there. With white heads."

Behind Louie came the voice of the gate guard. "Don't you worry, young man," she told Louie. "I'll go first with my javelin and any wolf had better watch out. Okay?"

"Okay." Louie smiled. He followed the gate guard down into the darkness. Francina and the nephew hurried after them.

"Hey, you!" Deela yelled over to the two figures on the Puffer. "Get over here! There are steps down to the beach!"

Ratchet grabbed hold of Danny. "Come on," he said. "Let's do what the lady says."

Danny held back. "We can't leave the Puffer," he said.

"Yes we can," Ratchet told him, and he pushed Danny off the footplate, leaped after him and dragged him across to Deela. As they jumped down through the trapdoor, Deela saw Benn, Hagos, Alex and Zerra racing toward her. "Hurry!" she shouted. "Hurry!"

They needed no telling. They could all see the hulking shape of the giant yellow Skorpas rearing up behind the Puffer. Alex arrived first. She skidded to a halt and pushed first Benn, then Zerra through the trapdoor. Then she and Deela grabbed the exhausted Hagos and pulled him down into the darkness, slamming the trapdoor above them. As the door hit the surrounding rock with a *thud*, they heard the heavy *splat* of a glob of venom landing on it.

It was a long, stumbling climb down through the cliff, but no one minded. One by one, they emerged through the arch onto the beach to find the tide covering the causeway. Stunned by what had happened, they walked slowly down the sand to the water's edge. In the light of the rising moon, they watched the waves in silence. Only Zerra lingered awkwardly halfway up the beach, watching Alex sweep Louie up into a hug.

"Mind the pokkle," Louie told Alex. Then he laughed, let the pokkle go and hugged Alex so tight that she felt quite breathless.

Francina smiled shyly at Danny and Danny decided that Francina needed a hug too. "I knew you'd come and save us," she told him.

Danny laughed. "Me? I didn't do anything. I was flat on my face covered in venom."

"Venom?" Francina said anxiously.

Danny chuckled. "Yeah. But it takes more than a bit of venom to get rid of Danny Dark."

"You are *so* brave," Francina murmured.

"Foolish more like," Ratchet's growl came out of the darkness. "But at least I got the Flyer jacket back now."

"Ha!" said Danny. "I reckon you set that Skorpas up just to get your jacket back."

Zerra felt annoyed and a little ignored too—not one

of her siblings had even acknowledged her. She wandered down to the water's edge, where she sat a little ways away from Hagos and, just as he was doing, stared out to the darkness of the sea.

Hagos was thinking about the terrifying end his old friend Belamus had come to when Deela started jumping up and down, waving. "Palla!" she called out. "Palla! We're here!" Hagos looked across to Oracle Rock and saw a light moving down to the direction of the harbor. The light disappeared, but after some minutes it reappeared on the water, traveling steadily toward them. Soon the *creak-eek-clunk* of oars could be heard. Benn and the young guard ran to meet the rowboat and pulled it up onto the beach.

Palla leaped out and threw her arms around Deela, saying, "Deela, oh, Deela, you're safe!" She surveyed the motley collection of people somewhat less enthusiastically. "And you've brought friends too. How lovely. But you won't all fit in the boat."

It was decided that Louie and Francina, both trembling with delayed shock, should go back with Palla, along with Deela. Shyly, Francina asked if Danny could come with them. Palla looked doubtful. "Oh, go on, Palla, there's room," Deela said. "The poor kid's had a terrible time. Give her a break."

"He'll have to help row," Palla said somewhat ungraciously.

"It would be my pleasure," said Danny, and he stepped quickly into the boat before Palla could change her mind.

They were all ready to leave, but first there was something Palla wanted to say. She walked over to Alex and said, "Alex, I saw King Belamus fall. It is the end of the prophecy now. You must not feel bad about this. You could not help your actions. They were decided ten years ago in the Oracle Chamber."

It took Alex a few moments to figure out what Palla meant. And when she did, she felt as though she was going to explode with fury. "How dare you?" she yelled. "I did *not* push the king off the cliff. He did *not* die at my hand. No way. Your stupid Oracle was wrong. Wrong, wrong *wrong*!" Alex turned her back on Palla and stomped away up the beach, fighting back the urge to burst into tears.

Palla shrugged. "The Oracle is always right," she murmured. Unperturbed, Palla walked back to the boat and climbed in. As Hagos and the gate guards pushed the boat off the beach, Louie clutched the pokkle and watched Alex anxiously. "Frannie," he said, snuggling up to his second-favorite sister. "The pokkle wants to know why Alex is angry."

Francina hugged Louie. "Tell the pokkle that Alex is fed up with people blaming her for things she hasn't done," she told her little brother in a rare moment of insight.

With the *creak-eek-clunk, creak-eek-clunk* of the oars fading away, Hagos caught up with Alex at the top of the beach. Making sure to use her proper name, he said softly, "Alex, we all know you didn't push King Belamus off the cliff."

"He *fell*, Poppa."

Hagos sighed. "No, the Oracle was not wrong. He was pushed."

Alex looked up at her father, shocked. "*You* pushed him?"

Hagos shook his head. "No. Not me."

Alex frowned. "Then who?"

"Zerra."

"Zerra? So the Oracle *was* wrong."

"No," Hagos said quietly. "The Oracle was right."

Alex laughed. "But that would mean Zerra's an Enchanter's child. Which is ridiculous."

"What's ridiculous?" Zerra's voice came out of the darkness. "And why are you talking about me? And laughing? What's so funny?"

Hagos took a deep breath. He found Zerra hard work. "No one's laughing at you, Zerra," he told her. "But there is something you both need to know. Zerra. Alex. Zerra, you are my daughter. Alex, Zerra is your sister."

Alex and Zerra stared at one another, both equally dismayed. "No way!" they both said in unison. And then, "She can't be!"

Hagos sighed. "To be precise, you are half sisters. Zerra, I met your mother, Mirram, in Rekadom when I was the king's Enchanter. I ordered a cloak from her. She was a very good seamstress, you know. She used to make the king's waistcoats."

"I know," Zerra said, scowling.

"Well, things were difficult for me then. At home." Hagos glanced apologetically at Alex.

Alex scowled at Hagos too. He noted how similar the scowls were.

"Um," said Hagos. And then, "Oh dear." He looked at Zerra. "Your mother was lonely. And I . . . well, so was I."

"Is that why Ma left Rekadom?" Zerra asked. "Because you made her?"

"I did no such thing. I merely suggested it. To keep you safe, which it did."

Alex was looking at her father with an expression that reminded Hagos uncomfortably of her mother, Pearl. "Did Momma know?" she asked.

"No. Well, I thought not. But now I am not entirely sure. I do wonder if that is why she gave you to Mirram. So you would at least be with part of your family. I'm so sorry," Hagos said, falteringly. "So very sorry for all that I have done. And for all that has happened to you both."

Alex and Zerra looked at Hagos accusingly. "Huh!" they both said. And then they turned away from Hagos and walked together down to the water's edge. And there they stood, staring out to sea in silence.

Some minutes later they heard the welcome *creak-eek-clunk* of oars. This time it was Danny alone in the rowboat. He rowed fast up onto the beach and plowed into the wet sand. Then he jumped out and handed the oars to Alex with a grin. "The boat's all yours, Alex. I'm off."

"Off where?" Alex asked.

"Gotta get back to the Puffer. I'm taking him back so he's there for Jay in the morning."

"But what about the Skorpas?"

Danny laughed. "I'm no Beguiler, I'll be fine."

Hagos and Ratchet joined them. "You coming up to the Puffer, Ratchet?" Danny asked.

"Of course," Ratchet replied. He turned to the two gate guards and, fixing the aunt in particular with what he hoped was a winning smile, he said, "Would you care to come along with us, ma'am?"

The aunt blushed. "I'd love to," she said.

"Take care," Hagos told them anxiously. "I fear that the escape from the Iron Tower will have damaged any Enchantments it touched."

Alex felt terrible. Hagos had confirmed her fears—she really had let the spider and the Wraith mist out. "I'm so, so sorry," she said. "I thought I closed the door."

"What door?" asked Hagos.

"The Iron Tower door."

Hagos was puzzled. "The Iron Tower?"

Alex nodded. "I was so sure I closed the door. But I must not have. And now those Wraiths are out there, and I keep thinking of all the people I've put in danger, and—"

"Hey, hold on," Hagos interrupted her. "Why would you ever think that? It was me who let them out, not you."

"*You*, Poppa?"

"Yes, me. I am the careless one here, Alex, I am sad to say." He turned to Ratchet. "I believe the Wraith flow has damaged the Skorpas. I fear the Skorpas see us all as Beguilers now."

Ratchet looked uneasy. "Even a horse?" he asked.

"Even a horse," Hagos agreed.

"Well, we're not horses, so we'll be just fine," Danny said cheerily. He fished in his pocket and pulled out a shining brass washer threaded onto an intricately knotted string. The washer spun on the string; on one side of it, tapped out in tiny dots, was FRANCINA, and on the other side was DANNY. "Hey, Alex. Would you give this to Francina, please?" Danny asked. "She didn't understand why I had to come back to the Puffer. She got a bit upset and ran off before I could give her this. Tell her I made this especially for her. And that I promise I'll be back tomorrow. Okay?"

"Okay," Alex said, carefully placing the wristband in her sash next to the Tau.

Alex and Benn rowed the boat over to Oracle Rock. As

they came into the harbor, Hagos said, "Alex, were you really in the Iron Tower?"

Alex nodded.

"But why? *How?*"

Alex said nothing. She waited until the rowboat was safely tied up and she could let go of the oar, then she put her hand into the secret pocket inside her sash and drew out the shimmering T-shaped amulet.

Hagos gasped. "Oh! Boo-boo!"

A splutter of laughter came from the back of the boat where Zerra was sitting. "Boo-boo!" Zerra giggled. "*Boo-boo.*"

"Poppa," Alex said with a sigh. "My name is Alex now."

"Sorry. Yes. I was quite overcome. But you have the Tau. Where did you find it?"

"In the Iron Tower, of course."

Hagos shook his head. "But how did you get in there?"

"I found this at the back of the cupboard." Alex took out the little handkerchief, and Hagos gasped.

"The handkerchief I made for Pearl! Oh, poor Pearl . . . ," he said, his eyes filling with tears.

"I was thinking of the Tau, and it took me there. Like you said it would," Alex explained. She passed the handkerchief to Hagos. "Here, Poppa. You need it."

Hagos blew his nose noisily on the little handkerchief and hurriedly stuffed it in his pocket. The rowboat rocked,

Alex fell sideways, and the Tau tumbled to the floor.

"Please put the Tau back in your sash," Hagos begged. "Do you know how deep this harbor is?"

"Two hundred feet," Benn informed them cheerily. "Do you want a hand getting out, Mr. RavenStarr?"

Hagos suddenly felt very shaky. He took Benn's hand, staggered onto the steps and waited while the rest of the rowboat's passengers followed. Benn secured the boat, and then he and the young gate guard made their way up the long winding steps to Deela's cottage.

But the Enchanter and the Enchanter's two children took the narrow path around the rock to the Oracle Chamber. There was some serious Disenchanting to be done.

CHAPTER 41
The Power of Three

IT TOOK ALL THREE OF them—Danny, Ratchet and the gate guard, who had shyly told Ratchet that her name was Mavis—to coax the Big Puffer back into life. Ratchet was shoveling in yet more coal when Mavis called out anxiously, "Skorpas!"

"It's not after us," Danny said.

Ratchet was not so sure. "It was after you before, Danny."

"Mistake," Danny said cheerily. "I reckon it was after Alex. She's not here now."

Ratchet watched the creature high-stepping its way toward them. "We ready to go?" he asked anxiously.

His answer was a sudden hiss of steam from beneath the driving wheel and a pressure dial dropping back to zero. "No," Danny said. "We're not."

In the chill of the Oracle Chamber, Hagos RavenStarr took off his cloak, carefully laid it on the smooth rock floor and sat down cross-legged in front of it. "Come," he said to Alex and Zerra, "let us sit around the cloak. It is our fire."

Zerra made a snorting noise as though Hagos had made a bad joke. Alex sat down and frowned at her father. Why didn't he tell Zerra to be more respectful? But Hagos merely took his codex from his pocket and laid it on the cloak. Zerra fidgeted and uncrossed her legs so that her feet stuck out and dropped sand on the cloak.

Alex watched Zerra warily; she was sure she would do something to mess up the Disenchantment. In fact, Zerra was already spoiling things by not taking them seriously. Determined to push Zerra out of her thoughts, Alex turned her attention to the codex, which sat quietly on the threadbare red cloak. She thought how happy she was to see it again. Ever since Nella had given it to her, the heavy little book had felt like a friend. It had been a window into a world that Alex had been so excited to discover she was truly part of. And now it was about to allow her to be truly part of the real world too, just like anyone else, and to live anywhere she wanted without fear of the Twilight

Hauntings. Alex glanced at Zerra. It was the same for her too—not that Zerra seemed to understand that. Alex supposed it was because the only time Zerra had been outside Luma or Rekadom at night she had been protected by Flying the Hawke. Until her encounter with the Rocadile, Zerra had had no idea what it was like to face a Haunting. And clearly even that hadn't made much of an impression, as she was now busy picking her nose. Alex looked away in disgust.

Hagos was opening the front cover of the codex to show the little pocket in which Alex's set of seven Hex cards sat in their rightful place. "We have the codex, and we have the cards. 'One is One. Two is One,'" he quoted from the codex.

Zerra extracted her finger from her nose and rolled her eyes.

Steadfastly ignoring Zerra, Alex finished Hagos's quote. "And Tau is Three," she said. Alex felt butterflies in her stomach—this was the moment she had been longing for. From inside her sash she drew out the Tau and let it lie in the palm of her hand, its brilliant blue light illuminating their faces in an ethereal glow.

"'One to make it. Three to break it,'" Hagos quoted. "We can now break all Enchantment of the Twilight Hauntings; both the perfect and the imperfect, the complete and incomplete. Wherever they may be. Forever."

Zerra watched the Tau warily. This was all so weird.

Suspiciously, she watched Hagos open the codex to show a block of pages all stuck together with brilliant blue edges. On top of the block was an empty T-shaped pocket. Zerra made a face—even she could tell what needed to go in there. It was stupidly simple, like a baby's puzzle.

Now Hagos was speaking in a low voice. "Alex, you rescued the Tau, so it is right that you unlock the sealed pages."

Zerra scowled. As ever, it was Alex doing the important stuff, Alex getting the attention. No one had asked *her* to do anything. She had had enough. She stood up and said, "This is so *stupid*. I'm going." And she headed out of the chamber to the narrow path above the sea.

A flash of irritation crossed Hagos's face and he got to his feet.

"Let her go, Poppa," Alex said. "She'll just mess it up anyway."

"No," Hagos said. "The three of us began it and the three of us must end it."

Alex watched her father head off in pursuit of Zerra. In the blue light of the Oracle Chamber, she sat alone by the red cloak. Here together at last, she thought, were her Hex cards, the codex and the precious Tau. This was the moment she had longed for and fought so hard for. She'd braved all kinds of Hauntings—the Gray Walker, Xin, Stinger Eels, Skorpas, Rocadiles—for this precious moment when she and her father would use the power of

Three to rid the land of them all. Forever. This was the moment when at last she would be able to live her life free of fear and to live it with people who truly cared for her. *And what happens?* Alex thought angrily. *Zerra. Zerra happens.*

Alex could hear the low urgency of Hagos's voice outside the chamber as he talked with Zerra. She felt furious. She didn't want Zerra to be her sister. She didn't want to share her father with Zerra. And, most of all, she did not want Zerra to have anything to do with this precious Disenchantment, and most probably ruin it on purpose. And so, as the voices continued outside—Zerra was now arguing back—Alex cradled the Tau in her hands. The buzz of its Enchantment swept through her, followed by a sense of calm and purpose. *I am with you, you are with me. We are Two with the Power of Three*, she heard. It was the same voice that had guided her out from the horrors of the Iron Tower, the same voice that had come to her as she had fallen from the cliff, the same voice that had spoken when Merry was being swept out to sea.

Unaware that Hagos and Zerra had just walked back into the Oracle Chamber, Alex slipped the Tau into its pocket at the front of the sealed pages. There was a blinding flash of brilliant blue and somewhere in the distance, Alex heard Zerra scream.

Squinting through her fingers, Alex watched the iridescence of the sealed edges melt into a puddle of blue and the pages flutter as they drew apart. She became aware of a movement by her side and she looked up to see her father, his eyes shining with excitement.

"You did it," he said. "You did it!"

Alex looked at the codex. The sealed pages lay open, their liquid blue seal pooled upon Hagos's cloak. But now, she realized, came the part she did not know how to do—the actual Disenchantment.

"Sit!" Hagos told Zerra, as if she were a bad puppy.

To Alex's surprise, Zerra sat.

"There are three parts to the Disenchantment," Hagos said. "Each must be spoken by a different Enchanter. I shall go first, then Zerra—"

"I told you. I'm not an Enchanter," Zerra said sulkily.

"Tell that to the next Rocadile you meet."

Zerra rubbed the gash on her arm and sighed dramatically.

"Like it or not, Zerra," Hagos told her, "you are an Enchanter's child. You will speak now. And Alex will finish. Ready?"

"Ready?" Up on the cliff top, Ratchet was asking Danny urgently. "Because if not, we need to run for it *right now*."

Danny watched the approaching Skorpas warily. He didn't like the way it was arching its tail over its back. And he really did not like the way it was pointing the barb right at the driver's cab.

"We used to watch them from the gate lookout," Mavis said. "They never miss, you know."

"Okay, okay," said Danny. "I got this."

"Get down!" Ratchet yelled. "Get down!" Mavis threw herself to the ground. "Danny!" Ratchet yelled. "Get down now! Now!"

"Now the Disenchantment begins," Hagos was saying.

Hagos picked up the codex. He passed his hand across the pages, which fluttered open like butterfly wings in the breeze and settled on a page with a dense forest of writing in tiny, cramped letters. In a low voice, Hagos slowly spoke three words, and as he did so, the same three words on the page lit up in blue. He passed the codex to Zerra, his finger pointing out the next three words for her to speak.

Alex held her breath. *Please don't let Zerra destroy this. Please*, she thought.

In a surprisingly serious voice, Zerra spoke the words, watching the page intently as they too became a brilliant blue. Then she turned to Alex and handed her the codex.

Alex needed no prompting, for she saw the last three words of the Disenchantment already burning bright upon the page. With a sense of awe, she slowly spoke them: "Ita fiat esto."

There was a blinding flash of blue light and Alex felt the world around her shift. She felt the vicious Night Wraith, the Gray Walker—which was at that very moment curling out of the sink plughole and into Nella's kitchen—dissipate like smoke on a windy day. She felt the Netters Cove Xin—which were advancing on Kirrin as she worked late in the Harbor office—shatter into a million shards and fall harmlessly to the ground. And she felt Danny poke at a small, yellow desert scorpion that had fallen at his feet and laugh out loud.

Hagos picked up the codex, which Alex saw was a whole lot thinner, and handed it to her. She nearly dropped it in surprise. It felt so light. "The weight of the Hauntings has gone," Hagos said. He lifted his cloak off the ground and put it on, and Alex saw how it shimmered all over with the blue from the edges of the sealed pages.

Hagos, Alex and Zerra walked quietly out of the Oracle Chamber and stopped for a few moments to look out over the ocean, which was sprinkled with sparkles of phosphorescence. A great feeling of joy came over Alex as she watched the gentle swell of the sea. She was free. Free to live where she wanted, free to go where she wanted and free to be herself.

CHAPTER 42
The Midnight Train

ALEX, ZERRA AND HAGOS HEADED back up to the cottage, where they found Deela, Palla and the young guard warming themselves by the fire in the little sitting room. Hagos gave them the news that the Hauntings were gone and Benn let out a loud whoop. "You can come and live with us now," he said to Alex.

Alex smiled. "I'll just go and say good night to Louie," she said, and slipped out of the room. She found Louie already asleep on cushions beside Deela's bed with the pokkle curled at his feet. Francina lay sleeping peacefully in Deela's bed. Quietly, she laid the wristband from Danny on Francina's pillow, and then she kissed Louie good night and pulled his quilt up around him. She turned to find Zerra standing in the doorway, watching her.

"Oh," Alex said.

"Yeah," said Zerra.

There was an awkward silence and then Zerra said, "It's good that Frannie and Louie are okay. You know, after all that's happened."

"Yes," Alex agreed. "It's been horrible for them."

"Do you . . ." Zerra paused. "Do you know what happened to Ma?" she asked.

"Mirram?" said Alex. "You mean after you Named her, got her locked up in the Vaults and put on trial?"

Zerra looked down at the floor. "I mean after you rescued her. Where did she go?"

Alex wished Zerra would get out of the way. She was blocking the door. "She's in Santa Pesca at the moment. Excuse me please, I'm off to bed. Good night."

Zerra stood back for Alex to leave. As she went by, Zerra said, "Your—I mean our—dad's okay, isn't he? I mean, he's a nice guy."

Alex nodded. "Yes. He is. G'night, Zerra."

"G'night, Alex," said Zerra as she climbed into bed beside Francina.

Halfway out the door, Alex paused for a moment. "Sleep well, Zerra," she said.

Zerra looked up, surprised. Then she looked Alex in the eye. "You too," she replied.

Hagos and Benn were outside on the landing waiting for Alex. Each was holding a lantern. "I came to say good night," Hagos said. "I can't sleep until I know that Danny is safe. The causeway is clear and Benn has kindly offered to guide me up those hateful steps inside the cliff."

"I'll come too," Alex said.

"I thought you'd say that," Benn said, smiling.

The pale sand of the causeway shone in the light of the moon and as they walked across the wet sand, Hagos's Enchanter's cloak glowed with its new brilliance of blue sparkles. Benn led the way into the cliff and Alex followed Hagos, lighting the way for him up through the damp and dingy steps that reminded him way too much of the Rekadom dungeons. Two-thirds of the way up, they took the branch to the right that would take them out at Oracle Halt. As they neared the top, they all began to feel fearful of what they might find.

They pushed up the trapdoor and emerged into the moonlight to see the square shape of the Puffer dark against the starry sky, steam pouring from the funnel and hissing from the vents beneath the wheels, an orange glow coming from the driver's cab. "Danny?" Hagos called out. "Danny, are you there?"

There was no reply.

"Danny?" Hagos called out. "Danny?"

There was a sudden movement from inside the coal tender and a dark shape reared up. It was brandishing a shovel. "Ah, Enchanter," came Ratchet's rasping voice. He threw the shovel to Mavis, then he stepped down and shook Hagos by the hand. "I can call you Enchanter now. Ugly name, Beguiler, don't you think?"

"I do indeed," Hagos agreed. "But where is Danny?"

"Hey, Danny!" Ratchet yelled out.

"What?" yelled Danny from inside the driver's cab.

Hagos laughed with relief. He hurried through the belching steam and stopped at the footplate. "Danny," he said. "You're here."

Danny grinned. "So I am." He jumped down to join Hagos. "Got something to show you," he said, taking a small toolbox off the footplate and placing it on the ground. "Stand back, guys. The occupant is just a teeny bit angry." Danny flipped open the box with the tip of a screwdriver, and then he picked up a lantern and held it above the box. "Just don't get within spitting distance."

Gingerly they leaned forward and peered in. Lurking in the darkest corner was a tiny, iridescent yellow scorpion.

"Skorpas?" asked Alex.

Danny grinned. "Ex-Skorpas. It's the one that came gunning for us. It was about to shoot when there was an enormous blue flash and it vanished. Or I thought it had. Then Ratchet spotted it, looking not at all pleased, I can tell you. So I picked it up with the tongs." Danny closed the lid, picked up the box and handed it to Hagos. "It's for you. I thought you'd like some proof, Mr. RavenStarr."

Warily, Hagos took the toolbox. "Why, thank you, Danny. No one's ever given me a scorpion before. But I really do appreciate the kind thought."

"My pleasure. We're off now. Taking the Puffer up to the Rekadom loop, turning him around and heading right back. I want to be there by morning for when Jay arrives. Can we give you guys a ride?"

Benn looked at Alex. "I'd like to get back to see Jay too. And Gramma."

Alex felt wistful. She wanted to go with Benn to see Nella, but she also wanted to be with Hagos.

"Hey, don't look so sad," Danny told her. "We'll be back tomorrow. I promised Francina, remember?"

Ten minutes later, billowing steam and with much hissing of brakes—gently applied this time—the Big Puffer drew into Rekadom Station for the first time in ten long years. Ratchet and Mavis threw open the gates of Rekadom and began spreading the news about the ending of the Hauntings and the king's fall from the cliff. Slowly, lights came on all over the city and people ventured out into the streets. The king's Slicers were rapidly dispatched, and for the first time in ten long years the nighttime streets of Rekadom echoed with the sound of excited voices and laughter. As the hubbub of excitement spread, people came out of the city to see the Big Puffer and the few remaining guards threw down their javelins and came out to join them.

And so it was that once again Hagos and Alex found

themselves in the middle of a crowd on the Rekadom platform at midnight, with the Big Puffer belching steam, ready to go. And this time they held tightly on to each other's hands and did not once let go. The mews clock struck twelve and Hagos put his arm around Alex. "Boo-boo. Sorry. I mean, Alex . . ."

Alex smiled. She didn't mind being called Boo-boo at all, she realized. In fact, her baby name made her feel special. And it helped her understand that she had been fortunate. Unlike Zerra, she had at least spent time with her father when she was little. "You can call me Boo-boo if you like, Poppa," she said. "It's nice."

Hagos returned her smile. "Well, Boo-boo. When I last stood on this platform at midnight watching the Puffer, it was taking you away. And Zerra too, of course. I never dreamed that one day it would bring us both back to Rekadom together."

With a strangely happy-sad feeling, Alex watched the Puffer pull slowly away from the station, taking Benn and Danny back to Lemon Valley. She followed the progress of its solidly square, dark shape, illuminated by cascades of orange sparks flying out into the night, until she could see it no more. Then, arm in arm with her father, she walked through the open gates into the city where she had been born. They stopped for a moment under the Beguiler Bell and waited. It stayed silent.

And it never rang again.

Life after the Hauntings

THE BIG PUFFER

Danny, Francina, Jay, his girlfriend Bella and Ratchet set up and ran the new Lemon Valley Train Company. They built one, then two, then three new passenger carriages for the increasingly popular service that ran from Luma Station, via Reed Cutters Halt, Salt Oak Stop, Netters Halt and Oracle Halt to Rekadom City. They began to lay new track along Lemon Valley up to the old stations at High Plains Halt and Seven Snake Forest. They hoped one day to replace every inch of the track that King Belamus had torn up.

Ratchet took great pleasure in making sure the train always ran on time.

Alex RavenStarr

Alex decided to live with Hagos. It was a tough decision. She missed Benn and Nella at the roundhouse, but she felt she belonged in her old home with her father at the top of the Silver Tower.

Slowly, Rekadom woke from what became known as the Curse of the Oracle, and Alex began to discover the city where she was born. The old school was reopened and many families who had fled over the years returned so that very soon Alex met new friends, although they were never quite as special as Benn. Which is why every other Friday—and more often during school vacations—Alex would catch the four o'clock train to Reed Cutters Halt, on the riverbank across from the roundhouse. There, Benn would be waiting for her in Merry, just like the old times.

Louie D'Arbo

Louie stayed at the roundhouse with Nella. He loved picking lemons and helping out on the farm. He went with Benn to the little school in Santa Pesca, and sometimes after school he had to go with Benn to the scary house where Benn's father lived and where—for some reason Louie did not understand—his mother now lived too. Although it was nice to see Momma, Louie was always relieved when it was time to go back to the place he now called home with Benn and Gramma Nella. And the pokkle.

BENN MARKHAM

Benn went back to helping Nella on the farm—he realized it was what he enjoyed most. Sometimes he took the train to Rekadom to stay with Alex, but he much preferred it when Alex came to stay with him, Nella and Louie.

DEELA MING

Deela Ming left Oracle Rock and moved into the Silver Tower. Although her rooms were on the floor below Hagos, she spent much of her time on the top floor with him and Alex. She loved seeing Hagos's delight in being able to pass on his knowledge of Enchantment to his daughter. She taught Alex to knit and was almost as proud as Alex was of her first knitted lobster.

BARTLETT

Some three days into the celebrations that swept through Rekadom in the aftermath of King Belamus's demise, one of the guards remembered to let her out of the dungeons. Bartlett was horrified to discover the fate of the king and was appalled to see how happy people were. When the citizens of Rekadom gathered in Star Court and voted not to appoint another ruler but to govern themselves, Bartlett left in disgust. She took a horse and the best peregrine falcon and, after writing a very rude note to Ratchet, she rode away and was never seen again.

RATCHET AND MAVIS

After the departure of Bartlett, Ratchet and Mavis moved into the mews together. Mavis loved the birds as much as Ratchet did, and if he was away with the Puffer she happily ran the falconry. Hagos gave Mavis the partly Enchanted Hawke egg and she tended it with great care. After it hatched, Ratchet loved to see how the ungainly, gentle bird followed Mavis everywhere. Ratchet spent many days away on the railway with Merle, but he always loved returning to the mews and his Mavis.

ZERRA

Zerra had trouble settling. She stayed for a while with Hagos and Alex, and then, after a big argument with Hagos, she moved downstairs to Deela's new rooms. That did not go well either. She tried helping out on the train, but hated shoveling coal, and no one would let her drive. She stayed with Nella but decided that lemons were "the most boring fruit in the whole world." After a heated discussion with Nella one day about how she hadn't done the dishes *again*, Zerra stomped off to see her mother in Santa Pesca. And there she stayed. She particularly liked helping Benn's father in his new position as judge in the Santa Pesca courts of law, and she loved the smart uniform she got to wear, and the complicated regulations that became her job to enforce. But the best thing was when, to her amazement, Mirram told her she was proud of her.

PALLA LAU
Palla was pleased that she was now in charge of the Oracle, and even more pleased that hardly anyone came to hear the Oracle anymore—people now considered the Oracle to be bad luck. But Palla was not entirely alone on Oracle Rock; the young guard seemed to have forgotten to go home. He made himself useful by bringing the coal up the hundred steps from the harbor, and he was good at cooking fish too. Palla decided it was worth letting him stay.

SOL'S SPIDER
At the moment of the Disenchantment, Sol's spider suddenly found that everything around it had become enormous. But it didn't mind at all, because it realized that at last it was back home. It scurried up the drainpipe and took refuge in its old hiding place—inside the cannon under the bed in Sol's old room. And there it stayed. Except occasionally, when it ventured out to terrify Benn.

ENCHANTERS
With the Twilight Hauntings gone, many of the surviving Enchanters returned to their old homes. Hagos set up a

small Enchanters' Academy at the top of the Gold Tower; its motto was: Do Only Good. It took Hagos some time to work out why people referred to it as "Dog School." When he did figure it out, he didn't mind at all. Hagos had learned that when people can at last laugh about things, they are no longer Haunted.

Acknowledgments

Thank you.

It is true that books don't write themselves, but they also don't get themselves all sorted out with fabulous illustrations and glitch-free text, and then beautifully packaged and ready to sit on a bookshelf somewhere. They need, as Zerra would say, "a whole ton" of people to do that.

So I'd like to thank everyone who has made these two Enchanter's Child books happen. First, huge thanks to my publisher, editor and friend, Katherine Tegen. Thank you for your wisdom, your insight and your fun sense of humor. Since I've been with you at HarperCollins I have learned so much about writing from you. Thanks to Sara Schonfeld for your valuable insights, careful reading and great blurb skills—also for making things go so smoothly too. And to the amazing editors and proofreaders: Megan Gendell, Kathryn Silsand, Sonja West, Bethany Reis, Daniel Seidel and Jaime Herbeck—who all worked on these two books—I have no idea how you manage to hold a whole new world in your head and at the same time remember the exact words someone said about something obscure in the previous book. I can only imagine it's a bit like riding a unicycle (backward) while juggling cupcakes. And a banana. So thank you. You never even dropped the banana.

I also want to thank Amanda O'Dwyer, to whom I am very grateful indeed for her eagle-eyed ability to spot the smallest of glitches and for her particular talent in Jackal counting. Thank you so much for tracking me down and spending so much of your time on this.

One of the best bits of finishing a book is seeing the characters through other people's eyes. So huge thanks to the fabulous artist Justin Hernandez for making the amazing images that added so much magic and fun and made the characters sing. And especially to Amy Ryan and Joel Tippie at HarperCollins, who not only hunted down Justin to begin with but also put his amazing images into such a perfect package. Thank you so much.

Massive thanks too to the wonderful narrator, Fiona Hardingham, who made every single character come alive so evocatively on the audio. Wow. Thank you!

To my agent, Eunice, whose theme song surely is "Always Look on the Bright Side of Life," thank you for just being there at the end of the phone, always.

And last but never, ever, least—thank you to those who put up with the grouchy author every day, make great coffee and listen to all the awkward bits; you know who you are. Huge hugs.